Kitchen of My Heart

Stephanie Young

Paperback ISBN: 978-0-578-34914-5
eBook ISBN: 978-0-578-34915-2

Front Cover Illustration and Design: Allyson Lassiter
Book design and typesetting by Jess LaGreca, Mayfly Design

Library of Congress Catalog Number: 2021925634
First Printing: 2022
Printed in United States of America

Proceeds from *Kitchen of My Heart*
go to national food banks.

For my family
and our river town

Contents

Kitchen
of
My Heart

Chapter 1
Double Cheeseburger

J'AIME MCWILLIAMS'S ENTIRE LIFE FIT INTO A Whole Foods shopping bag. Twenty-three moves in sixteen years had a way of straining a person down, making them to-go size. Tugging a wandering canvas tote strap back onto her shoulder, J'aime stood in the dark doorway of rented kitchen number twenty-four. She brushed her hand against the wall until her fingers grazed the light switch, but she didn't turn it on, not yet.

J'aime was familiar with two types of apartment kitchens, Lean Cuisine and Kraft Mac & Cheese. A Lean Cuisine kitchen is meant for microwaving not cooking. The burned-out oven's only job is to store boxes of cereal. A Kraft Mac & Cheese kitchen requires semi-functioning appliances to cook quick industrial meals. Houses, though, have Nestle chocolate chip cookie kitchens. That was J'aime's theory, anyway, since she'd never lived in a house. This new place was a duplex, almost a house. Maybe she'd get an upgrade to a Crockpot kitchen, but she sincerely doubted it.

With a flip, the glare of overhead light revealed her new favorite room.

"Mac & cheese all the way, baby," she said.

Truth was, her dad could only afford a place with appliances that had witnessed 1970's fondue.

J'aime inspected the GE electric stove. Just like powdered cheese, it glowed harvest gold. The temperature dial for the largest burner had lost most of its markings. All that was left of

MEDIUM was a single U. Decades of warming canned soup had rubbed away the rest of the letters. J'aime cranked the dial hard to the right. The largest black burner stayed cold. It didn't even smoke. A dud.

Patiently, J'aime turned every dial to high until the kitchen smelled sour with burnt crumbs, and the stovetop glared with hot spiral eyes. Three out of four burners worked.

"Not bad," J'aime said, turning off the heat. Maybe she could finally put all those hours of cooking shows to the test and make something besides instant pancakes.

She set her stuffed grocery bag on the sticky linoleum floor. Inside was everything from rolled up underwear to her last great hope. Nestled in one of her V-neck T-shirts was a McDonald's burger box. J'aime picked it up. Through the paper shell, she felt the other half of her charbroiled double cheeseburger tip over with a soft meaty thud. Her stomach gurgled deeply as if the call of McDonald's had awakened the beast. Truth was, her stomach had been in hunger mode for a few hours already, but eating the rest of her one meal of the day wasn't an option.

The Frigidaire's rusted racks rattled when she pulled open the door. She closed her eyes and listened. Refrigerators have a secret language. It's a subtle dialect that's easy to ignore. Their electronic timbre blends in with the hissing vents and low buzz of kitchen lights. Once she picked up on fridge-speak, she couldn't tune it out. It's not like she was an appliance whisperer, or you know, crazy. When you spend a lot of time looking into empty fridges, wishing food would magically appear, you get to know their quirks. This breed of refrigerator tended to squeak like a mouse when the motor kicked on.

Around apartment fifteen, she started this private moving ritual. The first night in a new place, J'aime always made sure there was food in the refrigerator, even if it was just a couple of bites. Call it a kitchen superstition, but it was J'aime's way of hoping future meals would find their way into her fridge.

Looking into the chilled emptiness, she slid the burger box gently onto the shelf. Under her breath, she said her mantra, "My fridge will be full, just like my life."

With a predicted squeak, the cooling motor started—the sign to shut the door, end the ritual. Maybe it was the *whirr* of this particular model, or the cramped hours on the road stirring up her anxiety, but something caused a little voice inside her head to whisper, *Quit dreamin' girl. Life doesn't care about people like you.*

J'aime took a deep breath and one last look at her burger. "I won't be a starving nobody," she said and closed the fridge.

She needed to clear her head. Finding her tools would do the trick. Crouching down next to her Whole Foods bag, she dug until her hands struck a handle. She resurrected a red saucepan and a tiny seven-inch skillet from the depths of clean leggings. Flipping them upright, J'aime checked their nonstick coatings. No new scratches. Gently, she sat the pans on the counter and dived back into the bag. She pulled out an old-fashioned hand crank can opener and a rolled-up cardigan. Laying the bundle on the countertop, she carefully unrolled it. A yellowed plastic spatula with a slightly melted edge gleamed against the black sweater. Her cooking tools had survived the eight-hour drive even if her nerves hadn't.

"Hey." Her dad stood in the kitchen doorway, hands on his hips like a syrup bottle. "Did you get all your stuff from the car?"

The small-talk question didn't even warrant an answer. She had no other stuff except what was in the kitchen, unless he was counting the plastic bag of cheap makeup and tampons. That freebie Whole Foods tote was her suitcase, purse, and school backpack all-in-one. The funny thing was, for a wannabe chef, she'd never bought anything at Whole Foods. Without any cash, all she could do was just wander the aisles, dining on organic free samples.

Her dad surveyed the spillage of clothes. "What are you doing? You planning on sleeping in here?"

He was trying to joke, but her kitchen obsession got under his skin. Plopping a twin mattress between the cabinets and snuggling up next to the stove always crossed her mind, and he knew it.

"Maybe," J'aime said, imagining her socks in a drawer next to the sink.

Her dad shook his head. "Quit your kitchen inspection and come help me with the chair." He walked away, not waiting for a response. He didn't want one and she didn't have a choice. Her happy place would have to wait.

J'aime followed her dad. A bare front-porch bulb cast a mix of orange glow and midnight shadow into the living room. The partially furnished duplex was a big step up from their last place. Shockingly, Wi-Fi and a TV with basic cable were thrown in with the rent. J'aime smiled. Basic cable meant one thing—the Food Network. Sure, it was granny TV, but the Food Network chefs were always there, no matter where she lived. Plus, there was something hot-cocoa-comforting about watching butter melt on a big screen.

The one piece of furniture the McWilliamses owned sat on the bungalow's front porch. The hulking, pink Cozy Comfort recliner waited in a swirl of dive-bombing bugs. J'aime had already helped lift, shove, and drag the sherbet beast from the back of their beat-up Suburban.

Through the propped-open front door, her dad bent down and disappeared behind the worn upholstery. "I'll grab the feet and tip it."

J'aime flung her arms around the top of the recliner. Faint whiffs of coconut drifted up from the wads of stuffing. Tropical shampoo. Toward the end, when her mom was really sick, shampooing her hair right there in the chair was better for everyone, except the Cozy Comfort recliner. It got stuck with a permanent cheap vacation smell.

J'aime adjusted her grip and the scent hit her again. She breathed in the fading memory of her mom smiling up at her with wet sudsy hair.

"On the count of three," her dad instructed. "One, two, three…"

The top half of the recliner slammed against J'aime's bones as her flip-flops moonwalked backward across the threshold. Every last bit of her strength kept the massive burden above the floor.

"You know," she grunted, "a burger isn't exactly the fuel of champions."

Her dad's strained face was Hot Tamale red. "You're the one who ordered sweet tea instead of fries," he groaned back. "A dollar menu's a dollar menu. You gotta make the most of it."

J'aime's muscles ached as she inched the chair this way, then that. Part of her wanted so badly to snap at him, *Make the most of a dollar menu? You're the genius with four bucks to feed two people.*

But J'aime couldn't say that to him. The second smoky-flavored meat hit her taste buds, that four dollars seemed like a fortune.

The width of the recliner caught on the doorframe. She pulled, but the wide chair didn't budge. "It's stuck," she said.

Still holding his end of the chair, her dad re-evaluated from the front porch. His voice drifted over the pink monstrosity. "I think it's the armrests."

"It's always the armrests," she muttered.

"Get ready," her dad yelled.

The sherbet chair came flying at her, hard. Her flip-flops skidded, almost slip-sliding her balance right out from under her. Unjammed, the heavy recliner threatened to smush her into the floor.

"Jesus, J'aime," her dad yelled. Clinging to the bottom of the chair, he was almost through the doorway. "Keep moving."

"Crap recliner," she groaned.

Slowly, they shuffled across the hardwood floor. Raw upholstery burns trailed down J'aime's forearms. Hunger hollowed her out like a chocolate Easter bunny, stealing her strength by the second.

"Screw it," she said. With a fluffy thud, the top end of the recliner landed on the duplex floor. The spot was not ideal. When the chair went into recline mode, it would block the front door. J'aime waited for her dad to freak out and tell her to move it again.

Instead, he sighed. "Close enough."

Her dad waved at her to help him set her mother's chair upright. Reaching into the seat, her dad picked up a rolled-up quilt. Just like J'aime's cardigan, it protected something sacred.

Half shaking and half unrolling, her dad let a glass pickle jar fall onto the recliner cushion. Green showed through the glass, but nothing inside was pickled. Bumping against the armrest, cash flurried around like dollar bill moths. Her mother's diabetes had cost them everything. The day her dad paid the last medical bill was the same day he swore off banks and took up a deep distrust of the "Feds." If it didn't pay to keep a roof over their heads, then every buck, tip, and penny was saved in their new vinegar-scented bank.

Counting the cash through the glass, J'aime knew she could fill the fridge for months if he would let her spend a little of their money on food, or even put a dent in her school lunch debt. A trail of cafeteria bills followed her across state lines. Collection agencies hired by her old schools called her cellphone every single day. J'aime's diploma was the true price for her lunch. She pushed the thought away. That money was for urgent bills. She was just a junior. There was still time to repay her debts and get her future back, right?

She reached for the jar, but her dad beat her to it. He swooped up their bank, setting it on the floor next to him. In their family, only one person got to touch the money jar.

"I was just trying to get it out of the way," she explained.

His answer was to shake open the quilt, letting it clear the night air. Years of restaurant employee T-shirts flapped in the dim porch light. Rough yarn knots dotted the quilt squares, holding the McWilliamses' past together. Between J'aime and her parents, they'd worked at so many diners, dives, and buffets, her mom could've made quilts for all three of them, but she ran out of time for that.

Gingerly, her dad draped the handmade blanket over the stained recliner. This was his moving ritual, whether he realized it or not. "I'm going to get your mom's boxes," he said. "Go ahead and pick your room. Ladies' choice."

J'aime focused her attention on the two closed bedroom doors. They were identical in their beat-up-ness. Scuffs from previous renters' shoes still kicked the white paint and grubby hands forever pushed open the doors. She flipped on both ceiling lights. The rooms were identical, twin beds shoved in the corners, dressers with missing random knobs, and painted-shut windows.

At least she still had a roof over her head. The whole giving up food for paying bills strategy was a risky game. If you lost, you ended up sleeping on sidewalks. How close had her family come to that? Way too close.

J'aime gently pressed down on the door's push-button handle. One-too-many unpaid bills, she'd lose the safety of having a bedroom and a door she could lock.

"Check out that yard," her dad said, climbing the porch steps with a stack of boxes. "I can't believe I get to mow something." He stayed in motion, carrying his cardboard tower past J'aime.

She looked out the open screen door at the grassy patch. It was 12:15 a.m. The awe-inspiring yard was spiky lumps of black, softly chirping insects, and a single streetlamp shining for no one. J'aime longed for the honk of Chicago taxis, and the rumble of the L-train.

"Why would a casino want to open in Manureville?" she asked.

"Hannaville," her dad corrected. "All we care about is that I'm a freaking manager now." He shoved her mom's old boxes into the corner. "No more juggling waiter shifts."

Judging by his level of mild enthusiasm for this job, J'aime guessed she'd probably live in Hannaville for three months, tops. His new position was actually a huge deal. Being a manager meant a bigger paycheck, but she knew it wouldn't last. Per usual, he'd get fired, or as good as fired and be forced to quit.

She glanced at her father. In the lampless living room, the glow of his phone illuminated his balding head. He was on the verge of ignoring her completely and that was perfect. J'aime had a kitchen to clean.

"Why don't you eat the rest of that burger?" her dad said without looking up. "I don't know when my first paycheck is coming, but you might as well go for it."

The idea of her teeth sinking into that soft sesame seed bun hijacked J'aime's senses. Her stomach let out another insistent growl.

She gave her dad the answer he was looking for. The one that would give him permission to scroll away on his phone, making him feel like a good father, and keep her food karma safe in the fridge.

"Sure," J'aime lied.

Chapter 2
Ramen Noodles

AFTER COLLAPSING ONTO THE RICKETY TWIN bed, J'aime drifted off into one of her reoccurring pizza dreams, the one where she's in a random school cafeteria, piling every slice of cheese pizza onto her lunch tray. Whole Foods free samples may have expanded her taste palette, but that didn't stop her from craving hot plasticky cheese even in her sleep. The worst part was waking up with the intoxicating melt of warm, fake mozzarella stuck to her brain and a stomach running on fumes.

J'aime's alarm went off extra early, but she didn't snooze it. Today was her first day working at the casino buffet and getting written up by her dad for being late was a sucky situation she wanted to avoid.

Luckily, extra early also meant extra time.

Hannaville's only food pantry, St. Lawrence's, was open Saturday mornings. The idea of breakfast *and* a chance to cook a real dinner in the duplex kitchen was enough to hustle J'aime out of bed. The church was on the way to the casino. If she breezed in and out, she could squeeze a pantry trip in before work.

That was the plan anyway.

When she walked up to St. Lawrence's, the line for the pantry wrapped down the sidewalk and kept going for at least half a block. At 10:00 a.m. on a Saturday, J'aime wasn't the last person in line, but she was definitely at the butt end.

Kids chased each other in the parking lot while their parents or grandparents inched closer to the pantry door. Wadded-up plastic shopping bags peeked out of back pockets, a few canvas totes dangled from fingers, but most people depended on the church to give them a way to get their groceries home.

J'aime shifted her Whole Foods bag onto her other shoulder. Getting her food, signing out, then walking to the casino was going to have to happen at warp speed. As a plate dealer, her one responsibility at the Silver Dollar Casino was to make sure the buffets were always stacked with clean plates. When her dad got hired, he promised her a step up from busing tables. She'd been thinking line chef, but clean plates were technically better than gravy-smeared ones. At the thought of gravy, her stomach moaned.

J'aime turned around. A mom carrying a sleeping, pajama-wearing toddler crept along behind her. "Excuse me," J'aime asked. The toddler buried his face into his mother's neck. J'aime took her voice down a notch. "Have you been to this pantry before?"

The woman nodded, adjusting her hold on the boy.

"Do they care if you," J'aime hesitated, "snack while you shop?"

"I don't know," the mom whispered, rubbing her child's back as if to soothe the tumbling trains printed on his PJs, "ask Father Eric."

J'aime nodded. Pantry priests were all the same—uptight and expecting you to trade prayers for food. *Gratitude is so complicated*, she thought.

Judging by the crazy long line, the pantries J'aime typically went to were much smaller than this one. A food closet tucked into a community center couldn't support a crowd this big. It looked like most of Hannaville was rolling through the church doors this morning. If there were this many hungry people, where the heck did all the food come from for the pantry?

On the St. Lawrence's website, it said that Hannaville was classified as a "food desert." J'aime Googled and sure enough, the closest grocery store was forty minutes away in Churchill.

That's a long drive to buy Tuna Helper. How could a town not have a grocery store? Seems like there should be a law against that.

"You're new," a man's voice said.

J'aime spun around to find a thirty-something guy in a hoodie, smiling at her. He was carrying a half-empty basket of cookies. A sweet hint of cinnamon swirled around him. "Um," J'aime said nervously, "I just moved here."

"Welcome to Hannaville." The man smiled and unzipped his jacket an inch, flashing his priest collar. "I'm Father Eric. I run St. Lawrence's pantry."

"Oh," J'aime said. This guy wasn't musty at all. "You're the priest?"

Father Eric chuckled. "Sometimes I can't believe it either, and you are?"

"I'm J'aime McWilliams," she said, stiffly shaking hands.

Father Eric smiled. "Nice to meet you, J'aime." He held out the basket to her. "The Rioses brought cookies. Want one?"

I love you, Father Eric, she thought. Which wasn't really true. She loved his cookies. She loved his pantry. She loved the fact she finally got to eat something. J'aime reached into the basket. Sugar dusted her fingertips. Her stomach gurgled in breakfast anticipation.

"Take two," Father Eric said. "Or I'll end up eating all the leftovers."

"Thanks," J'aime said. She grabbed another cookie and shuffled forward with the rest of the patrons.

Father Eric turned his attention to the mother with the sleeping toddler. As J'aime scarfed down the baked goods, she heard him say in an exaggerated whisper, "Hi Bettie. Gabe's sure conked out. Is he feeling all right?"

J'aime tapped her grocery list against her sugary lips. She wasn't going into this pantry trip unprepared. She had goals.

Picking up lunch food for school was a no-brainer, but the thing that got her excited was cooking a from-scratch meal that night. Flipping "just add water" pancakes didn't make her a chef.

It barely even made her a cook. The duplex's Kraft kitchen had three working burners, which were way better than average. To take full advantage of them she needed real ingredients.

Her favorite Food Network show, *Get Fresh with Bentley*, had given her an idea for her first serious meal. She loved how Bentley put creative, healthy twists on standard recipes and his British accent didn't hurt anything either.

The episode "Easy Cajun Dinners" featured two pantry staples. If St. Lawrence's had any food left on their shelves, J'aime was ready to bet her only spatula, it would be beans and rice. It might not be the right kind of red beans and rice that the recipe called for, but that's where her creative chef-ing would have to come in. As for the rest of the ingredients, they were a total tossup. She might get pantry lucky and there'd be fresh peppers, but it was a long shot.

J'aime read her grocery list again. What if she cooked a real meal and it turned into a total red beans and rice fail? She'd never tried anything this complicated before. She bit her lip. How did TV chefs do it? Recipes seemed to just flow out of them. She'd already texted her dad that she was making them a feast tonight. Hopefully, a recipe could just flow out of her too.

A stretched rainbow of bungee cords held the pantry door open for the steady flow of patrons. Holding onto her list a little tighter, J'aime stepped inside St. Lawrence's finished basement. The cross-shaped clock was ticking. The large room was laid out so dry goods were first, then fresh foods, then the exit. That made her must-have ingredients the last things in line. With a hurried politeness, J'aime swam upstream against the crowd until she reached the fresh goods table. She peeked over adult shoulders.

What she needed was an onion, a green pepper, and celery. What the pantry had was bags of prepackaged shredded lettuce, baby carrots, and a huge pile of bananas.

J'aime grabbed the bananas then doubled back. "Excuse me," she said, slipping her hand through the crowd to snatch a bag of carrots.

Hurrying to the beginning of the line, J'aime scanned the steel, heavy-duty shelves along the walls. The dry goods section was pretty picked over. She glanced at the clock again. She had seven minutes to find chef-worthy supplies. Snuggling the bananas under her arm, J'aime got to shopping.

Two cans of red beans and a box of long-grain rice plopped into her bag. Amazingly the exact ingredients she needed. Next up, chicken broth. Nope. Gotta substitute chicken and rice soup instead. How about smoked chicken sausages? *Yeah, right. Try Vienna sausages.* But they kind of look like baby fingers, so she passed. That taco dinner kit has "zesty" seasonings. Couldn't those also be "Creole" seasonings? It's a stretch, but possibly close enough.

The clock chimed. She couldn't only shop for this one recipe. She needed groceries for the rest of the week too. "Food pantry Cinderella time," she said and started grabbing any of her pantry favorites still left on the shelf.

Soon her Whole Foods bag was filled with the standard fare of canned vegetables, cereal, peanut butter, crackers, tuna, beans, soup, and of course, instant pancakes. J'aime sat her heavy tote bag on the floor and contemplated the last jar of "100% natural" Prego.

"Need some pasta?"

J'aime jumped. She'd been so focused on speed shopping she hadn't noticed the man standing next her. Wait. Strike that. He was a boy, maybe around her age, possibly Latino, and definitely cradling a cardboard box filled with Top Ramen noodle packages. The pillowy plastic bags almost hid his St. Lawrence's T-shirt. He was teen worker bee, a volunteer scoring Good Samaritan points for his college application.

Crap, J'aime thought. *We probably go to school together.*

Google had also told her there was only one high school in Hannaville. Tomorrow, when she saw him in the hallway, she wouldn't just be the awkward new student, but the pity pantry girl too.

He shifted the box to get a hand free and a few ramen bags fell on the floor. "We're out of spaghetti," he said, picking them up. He held out a crinkly package to her. "Noodles are noodles, right?"

J'aime eyed the ramen. It was soy sauce flavored. What was this guy thinking? She didn't have time for this.

"You think I should mix Italian tomato sauce with instant Chinese noodles?" she asked.

The boy gave her a Dunkin' Donuts-hole stare. "Sure," he answered, totally not sure. He flipped over the noodle package and inspected the back. "I thought ramen was from Japan?"

Ramen is a Japanese dish with Chinese wheat noodles, J'aime desperately wanted to say. She'd watched every episode of *Wok Talk* . . . twice. But she wasn't going to waste her time educating a dude who probably believed Pizza Hut invented pizza.

J'aime shoved the Prego into her heavy bag and hauled it up into her arms. "No thanks," she said and hurried over to the line.

A gaggle of church ladies sat at a folding table, minding the sign-out sheet. The mom and toddler were up next. The now wide-awake child was in full grouch mode while his mom signed her name. The little boy wailed as the church ladies rounded up another cookie.

"Hurry up," J'aime said through tight lips. She shot a pleading look at Father Eric. He was right behind the chaos, chatting with a woman who was piling plastic bags of bread next to the sign-out sheet. The bread looked fresh, maybe even homemade. J'aime should've reached for a loaf, but she was way too worried about the clock.

The church ladies finally gave the whimpering toddler another cookie. As they sent him and his mom out the door, the busy-body ladies turned their focus on J'aime.

"You've got a full bag, Sugar," one of them said.

J'aime nodded and sat her bulging Whole Foods tote onto the folding table. Since she was new to this pantry, she had to fill out extra information. Thank God she saved their new address into her phone. J'aime bent over and started to write. With a whoosh, a plastic bag of bread landed right next to her scribbling hand. The bread slices shuffled inside like soldiers in ranks.

The church lady leaned down to read her name. "Hi there . . . , *Jay-mee*," she said with the uncertain pause that always came with people trying to pronounce her name.

J'aime didn't bother to look up. She nudged the bread out of her way and kept scrawling down her basic info. "It's pronounced *Jem*, not *Jay-mee*," she explained for the eighty-zillionth time. "The *a* is silent. It's French."

"Sure, Sweetie," the church lady rambled on. "We're open two days a week, but you can visit the pantry once a week. That's the rule. We'll get a new delivery of food next Tuesday from Kansas City, so come back then."

J'aime double-checked the form then stood up. There was the Ramen Noodles Guy. He was behind the table, helping the woman unload more baked goods. *How'd he get up here so fast?* she wondered.

He hadn't noticed her—yet. She needed to get her wilted-cabbage self out of this church before Ramen Noodles Guy started more charity chitchat.

"Thanks," J'aime said quietly. Scooping up her Whole Foods bag in both arms, she dashed toward the exit.

"Jamie! Don't you want some bread?" she heard the church lady yell after her, but J'aime was already down the steps.

Chapter 3
Red Beans and Rice

AFTER A LONG EVENING OF SILVER DOLLAR Buffet training videos and fussy casino customers, J'aime finally dropped her bag of pantry goods on the duplex kitchen counter. She didn't want to admit it, but binge-watching cooking shows sounded way better than actual cooking.

"Nope," she said, digging through the bag to find her recipe. "Tonight, you gotta out-chef the TV chefs." Before she dug too deep, J'aime noticed something extra in her tote. She pulled out a package of soy sauce Top Ramen.

The package crinkled in her hand. It must've somehow slipped into her bag when that Ramen Noodles Guy fumbled the pasta. *Weird*, J'aime thought.

The instant noodles were just destined to come home with her, but she set them aside. Cajun cooking was on the menu tonight, not Japanese fusion.

She felt past the groceries until her fingers hit paper at the bottom. Warning lights flashed when she read the recipe ingredient, *vegetable oil*. Why hadn't she noticed it when she was at St. Lawrence's? But then she remembered the salad dressing.

On her break at work, she'd been at the salad bar, filling her plate with her free shift meal when she had a *voilà!* moment. Right there on the buffet were the missing fresh ingredients she couldn't find at the food pantry that morning.

J'aime pulled a casino to-go box out of her Whole Foods bag. Cracking the lid, she eyed the chopped peppers, onions, and celery. The Silver Dollar didn't keep measuring cups next to the cooling bins, so she had no idea if she tonged out the right amounts. She did accidentally get olive oil and vinegar salad dressing on the vegetables. Maybe that drip of grease would make up for the fact she didn't have any real oil to sauté them in.

Testing her cooking flow was her goal tonight. J'aime tossed the recipe near the sink. She didn't want to be bound to it. Close-enough ingredients would keep her in the ballpark and let her natural talent do the rest. If she was going to be a chef, she needed to cook on her own terms, whatever those were. The oven clock flashed 7:00 p.m. Her dad might be home in two hours if he got off work on time.

She bent down, opened the cabinet, and surveyed her surviving kitchen tools. The seven-inch skillet wasn't big enough to hold all the ingredients. With her beloved, slightly melted pancake flipper in one hand, she passed by her tiny fry pan and grabbed the one-quart saucepan with the missing lid.

"I'll turn this recipe into a one-pot meal," she said. Food Network chefs were always promoting quick, all-in-one saucepan or sheet pan meals. This was supposed to be an easy Sunday-night dinner. She could totally make one pot work.

J'aime dialed the biggest burner to medium high. As the ring started to flare, so did her nerves. This wasn't just a chance to prove she could chef; several meals were riding on this experience too.

"I'm wired to cook," she self-talked. "I can do this."

She tossed her scavenged precut vegetables into the saucepan. Digging through the grocery sack, she pulled out the taco kit. The veggies started sizzling as J'aime tore into the box to find the zesty seasoning. She set the tacos aside and pulled out the shiny silver packet.

Opening the kitchen drawers, she muttered, "Of course we don't have scissors," and tore at the foil with her teeth.

With over-vigorous shakes, J'aime made every last sprinkle of taco seasoning fall on top of the vegetables. The quiet sizzle grew louder. A tangy smell of chili spice transformed the kitchen atmosphere from musty to fiesta.

J'aime squealed. Clapping her hands, she broke out into a kitchen dance. "I'm cooking. I'm cooking," she sang, waving her spatula in the air.

A whiff of burning interrupted her celebration. From the bottom of the saucepan, smoke drifted up from the chunky pieces of white onion and diced green peppers. Frantically, she tried to stir them with her spatula, but the blackening vegetables stuck to the bottom of the pan.

"You got this," she said. "Cool things down. Add the broth."

Pulling open the lid of the Healthy Choice soup can, she instinctively dumped the whole thing onto the burning ingredients. A single piece of celery floated up to the top and bobbed on the soupy surface. The can of liquid put an end to the smoke, but her nerves flared again.

"Maybe it wouldn't hurt to check the recipe." J'aime searched for the piece of paper, and finally found it in the sink. She pulled the mostly wet recipe away from the dripping faucet. According to the smeary directions, she was supposed to add two more cups of water to the pot.

She eyed the soup skeptically. There wasn't a lot of room left in the saucepan. If she added water, would it overflow? The recipe came from a celebrity chef. It had to be right. Filling her soup can up with water, she dumped it into the pot. The saucepan brimmed with liquid.

"Now I've got a soup swamp," she said, irritated. "How am I supposed to fit the rest of the ingredients in here?"

Running to the bathroom, J'aime grabbed a clean hand towel. Standing at the soup pot again, she wrapped the fuzzy green cotton around the hot handle. To get everything into the one pan, she was going to have to reduce the broth, aka pour liquid out. Using both hands she glided the full saucepan through the air, over to the kitchen sink. The heavy weight at the end of the thin, long handle tugged at her wrists, making her forearms shake. Resting the pan on the edge of the basin, she leveraged it against the counter, tipping it slightly. Soupy water slowly dribbled into the sink, but the unbalanced weight of the pan was too heavy. The dribble turned into gushing. Broth and vegetables splattered into the basin.

"Nooo!" J'aime yelled as the food poured down the drain. She straightened the saucepan back up. All it took was one accidental spill, and half of her ingredients were gone. "I can't waste food like this." She steadied the pan and herself. "Okay. Don't think about it. Just keep cooking."

It was time to add the rice. Due to the spillage, she had no idea how much liquid was left in the pot. The rice box had specific measurements for cooking.

"Why didn't I buy a measuring cup too?" she asked the cooking gods, but she already knew why. The day she bought her cooking tools, a measuring cup cost two more dollars than she had in her wallet. She'd have to half-ass measure, which meant no measuring.

Setting the saucepan back on the burner and crossing her fingers, she poured in most of the long grain rice and both cans of beans. Cooking was like breathing for celebrity chefs. Even YouTube chefs never broke a sweat. J'aime on the other hand was dripping buckets. She wiped her forehead and reluctantly picked the recipe back up. She scanned the instructions looking for a guarantee that she'd get a meal out of this mess, but the recipe only pointed out the truth—that her natural no-sweat cooking instincts were in serious question.

"Let simmer for one-and-a-half hours," she read to the hissing, resteaming pot.

Pancakes didn't require simmering, but the act of simmering seemed easy. It was only warming up water. Chef Dee, on *Deelicious*

Kitchen, said that simmering didn't mean boiling. J'aime had seen boiling and simmering. On the cooking shows, tiny bubbles sporadically broke the surface when sauces and soups *simmered*. If the water boiled, the pot looked more like a hot tub. She wasn't sure what heat to set the burner on to make the delicate bubbles steer clear of hot-tub mode. Real chefs occasionally stick their bare fingers in the water to test the heat. J'aime eyed the steaming water. Accidentally boiling her skin off seemed like a bad idea.

To be safe, she turned the burner temperature down a notch and took a step back to stare at her creation. Things weren't going according to her chef plan, but hopefully through the magic of cooking, the meal would turn out all right. Even if it was mediocre, she could still eat it. All it had to do was simmer.

"Come on rice and beans," she encouraged the steaming pot. "Don't make me serve Dad cold taco shells with peanut butter for dinner."

J'aime turned her back on the saucepan. Her feet were aching from standing at the buffet all day. Zoning out while her dinner cooked on the stove seemed like the best way to salvage this situation. She sank into the recliner. With a press of a remote button, the Food Network clicked on. Before watching an episode of *Snack Attack*, she set her phone alarm for one hour and laid the glowing screen on the chair's crooked armrest.

An hour and thirty minutes later, stretched out in full sleep-recline mode, a sour scent woke J'aime's nose. Dozily, she itched it. What was that smell? The air had a taste to it. On TV, the Food Network had switched to a sushi competition. *Snack Attack* was long over. The slicing sound of hurried knives made J'aime reach for her phone to check the time, but it wasn't on the armrest anymore. A faint quacking came from underneath the recliner. Duck sounds were her alarm setting. How long had it been going off?

J'aime bolted the recliner upright. "Beans and rice!"

By the time she reached the kitchen, she was beyond too late. Every drop of watery broth was gone from the pan. Her dinner had transformed into burning creole cement. The red beans and rice had cooked down into a dried-out brown sludge, frying itself into oblivion.

Reaching for the handle, she desperately wanted to save her meal and her last saucepan. Hot plastic seared her palm. "Ouch!" she cried. "Where's that stupid towel?"

That's when the flames started.

Red fire flicked up from inside the pot as if the Cajun dish was out for revenge. Giving up her search, she grabbed the hot handle, shoving the flaming concoction into the sink. With a spurt of water, the fire was out. In her sleep-wrinkled uniform, hand throbbing, stomach growling, J'aime looked into the smoking pot of disaster. She'd watched so many cooking shows. This should have been easy, but it was so hard.

"I can't suck at this," she panicked. "I can't."

Grabbing the cooling pot handle, she took the saucepan out of the sink. With the plastic pancake flipper, she tried to pry out the charred red beans and rice. The harder she poked at it, the less it crumbled. Her glorious meal was welded to the pan. It would taste awful, but maybe somehow she could still eat it? Jabbing the mostly melted spatula in between the side of the pot and the food, she gritted her teeth and pulled hard. The bean cement wouldn't give. Her dinner was 100 percent inedible.

With a plastic crack, the spatula snapped—and so did J'aime.

She jerked the scorched pot off the counter and what was left of the broken pancake flipper. In a burst, she ran past the judges eating dessert sushi on TV, and out the front door. Running down the porch steps, she screamed in food frustration, hurling her last pan into the dark front yard. It flashed silver like a tumbling satellite before disappearing into the dense cloud of bushes lining the driveway.

Raising her arm to chuck the broken spatula, she stopped. Clutching her favorite piece of cookware to her chest, she sank down on the porch steps.

"What am I going to do?" she cried. "I have to cook. I have to eat."

The promise of a homemade meal came back to her. Her hungry, tired dad would be expecting a feast when he got home. Without a saucepan or a freaking microwave, she couldn't even cook the bonus ramen noodles. All that was left for her to make was the dreaded peanut butter taco shells. Her stomach rumbled at her again. She needed dinner too. Wobbling a little, she stood up. With the spatula handle in one hand, J'aime made her way back to the kitchen.

Chapter 4
Lobster Tails

BEFORE WALKING TO WORK SUNDAY MORNING, J'aime stood on the sidewalk, staring at the dew-sprinkled leaves hiding her cooking disaster. Digging through wet bushes for a saucepan search-and-rescue seemed like a scratchy idea, and who knew what condition the burnt pot would be in once she found it. The last thing she wanted to do was leave it for cooking-dead, but the Cajun concrete disaster had already made that choice for her. This meant no more cooking until she had a new saucepan and some kind of cooking utensil.

It was the spatula that really broke her heart. The day she decided to teach herself to cook, she bought that spatula. Sure, it was flimsy and cheap, but still. That spatula had survived everything. Except Hannaville.

Damn.

Peeking inside her canvas bag, her black cardigan was rolled up like an ice cream cake. The sweater protected what was left of the sad cooking utensil. She just couldn't leave the broken spatula handle at home.

"I'm losing it," J'aime said, walking away from the duplex.

She crossed the road and followed the sidewalk toward Cliff Drive, a mini mountain posing as a street. Perched at the top was the Silver Dollar. She gazed up at the casino on the hill. If any of the cooks at work knew she was carrying around a broken pancake flipper like a blankie, they would think she was crazy too.

The cooks at work . . . they could cook, right?

Suddenly, J'aime pushed herself to hike up the hill a little faster. She had a new idea.

In the break room, she locked her Whole Foods bag into a casino locker and swiped in at the time clock. It was 10:45 a.m. The Sunday buffet didn't open until eleven. Plenty of time to find out the information she needed.

She hurried past the brunch crowd lined up and waiting to pay for their endless plates of omelets. Inside the restaurant, a few workers scurried around stocking stations. The thick smell of greasy bacon hovered over the empty tables and booths like a breakfast fog. Pushing open the casino kitchen's swinging door, she plucked a pair of mandatory disposable gloves from the box. Compared to the closed dining area, the kitchen had a spring break vibe to it. Cooks in their gold chef jackets dashed back and forth in random patterns, yelling, dumping, and squeezing giant plastic bags of food into huge warming vats. It was perfect.

This was where I should be, not out there being a pathetic plate dealer.

In the prep chaos, J'aime looked for her epiphany, the one man who had the info she needed to get her cooking again.

She spotted her dad. The zigzag lines of a brown hairnet covered what little hair he had left. His busy hands were hidden behind a meat slicer. Absorbed in his task, he didn't even notice her standing there.

"Uh, Dad?" she asked cautiously.

"What do you need?" he barked then looked up. "Oh. What are you doing back here? Are you out of poly gloves?"

J'aime waved a limp pair of plastic hands back at him. "No. I wasn't up when you came home last night and—"

"The tacos," he interrupted. "You want to know what I thought about the tacos."

Not at all, she thought. Leaving him three taco shells filled with creamy Peter Pan peanut butter was the last thing she wanted to talk about.

Her dad stepped out from behind the meat slicer. Instead of a tray of cold cuts, he was holding a clipboard. He cracked a smile and J'aime waited for him to make fun of her grand meal. "They were all right," he said. "Kind of like those pretzels filled with peanut butter."

J'aime stared at him, horrified. He actually thought those lame tacos *were* the feast she promised him. Was he just being nice? Or did he really like them? She didn't want to know.

"Hey," she said quickly. "I wanted to ask you something."

"Let's walk and talk," her dad said. "I've got other things I'd rather do than figure out the schedule." He hid the clipboard under a nearby sheet pan. "There are all these split shifts. Scheduling is way more complicated than I thought it would be." He waved at her to follow him then yelled, "Stan, I'll get the extra lobster. My daughter wants a tour. You get the chicken nuggets to the front."

I didn't ask for a tour, she thought. *Why did he say that?*

"You haven't gotten the lobsters yet?" an exasperated voice shouted back from deep within the blur of gold cooks.

Her dad ignored Stan. "This area's the main kitchen," he said nervously then gently grabbed J'aime's wrist and took off walking. "Hey, I've been meaning to tell you," he said, "you look really grown-up in your casino uniform. It suits you."

She raised her eyebrows. That compliment and this impromptu tour had nothing to do with her. Her dad was using her to run away from his work problems.

J'aime pulled back her hand. "I look less ridiculous than I did when we worked at the Tudor Table. No one should bus dishes in a peasant gown."

"You never look ridiculous. I always think you look very, you know, professional," he said as they weaved their way through his scrambling employees.

After her mom died, he started saying these nice things out of the blue. It was sweet, but totally awkward. How is she supposed to respond to something like that? It seemed weird to say thanks to your dad . . . who was also your boss.

Stay focused, J'aime reminded herself. *You're on a mission.*

"Sunday brunch is really intense for the chefs, huh?" she asked, peering around, trying to see what the kitchen was cooking up.

Her dad was in high-speed mode, walking her past kettles of steaming food and through another door. "My supervisor says Sunday is the busiest day for buffet," he said. "A lot of locals come in to chow down."

They stopped in an empty workstation. It was quiet compared to the main kitchen. Her dad pointed at the stoves and metal counters like a distracted realtor. "This is the back kitchen area," he explained. "It's a good place to hang out when you need a break from all that chaos." He paused as if realizing he shouldn't have maybe said that out loud. "Anyway, we store the extra seafood back here."

He pulled open a giant silver refrigerator door. A gleam of plastic shined out at them. The whole fridge was stuffed with bags of frosty lobster tails.

"*Whoa,*" J'aime said at the massive amount of fanned shells. "That's a lot of crustacean."

"The Silver Dollar's got a big budget," her dad said. "The amount of food we order each week puts everywhere else I've worked to shame." With a heave, her dad pulled out a torso-sized bag. "Luckily, these guys are already cooked. All we have to do is thaw them out and warm them up in the butter vats," he grunted, then dropped the bag of frozen sea creatures on a long metal table. "Man, these are fat lobsters. Stan was right. I should have gotten them out sooner. We're going to have to quick thaw them. Can you hand me those scissors on the wall?"

She tucked her gloves into her pocket and reached for the round blue handles dangling from a magnetic strip. "That's kind of what I wanted to ask you about," she said, trying to sound casual.

"Quick thawing?" Her father struggled to cut the thick plastic bag with the dull blades.

"No. At the casino, which chefs cook from scratch?"

Her dad set the scissors down. "Is that the question you wanted to ask me? I thought you wanted off early or something. What do you mean from scratch?"

"You know," she said, pointing at the lobsters, "like not pre-cooked stuff, unprocessed food. Professional chefs making up recipes."

Now her father laughed at her. "Hell, J'aime. All this food is processed. It's a twenty-four-hour buffet." He picked up his scissors again and tore at the plastic bag with a single blade. "Without a little extra help from science, how could this food look good under the heat lamp for hours?"

"Not everything comes precooked, right?" she pushed. "I mean, the whole kitchen staff wears chef jackets. Someone has to have the skills to match?"

Her father grabbed a stack of hotel trays. "I guess it depends on what you mean by skills?" He loaded the seafood. Frozen lobster clunked onto a tray. "We do a lot of frying. No one here is cooking from a real recipe. It's more like complicated reheating. Even our fried chicken is prebreaded. All the food comes from corporate."

J'aime dreaded what was coming, but she asked anyway. "So you mean no one at the casino does any real cooking?"

Her father tossed one mangled claw back into the bag. "Cut my staff some slack. Did any of them go to culinary school? No. Are they doing the kind of cooking chefs do at fancy restaurants? No. But our food still tastes good. You don't have to be certified to do a job right. Anyone can *learn* a job."

He was getting defensive. Talking more about himself than his employees. Her dad continued to sort frosty lobsters. "You wanted to work in the kitchen. Is that what this is about? I tried to get you a spot, but there weren't any positions left."

Lined up on the metal tray and crusted with ice, a dozen lobster tails pointed at her. They weren't bright red like you'd expect, but a dull orange. Those tails used to swim and flow in a wide ocean. Now they're frozen and stuck on a baking sheet. She couldn't explain to her dad that learning how to reheat food was never going to be good enough.

J'aime sighed. "It's kind of about the job, but it's more about cooking. I was just curious about who worked in the kitchen. What kind of culinary training they have?"

"If a position opens up, I'll try to get you in the kitchen," her dad said. Once again, he wasn't listening. "No guarantees though. I'm the newbie. There are three other managers and they are always on me about something. I'm barely getting through the day without really screwing up."

J'aime felt the firing clock start ticking. If he was telling her that, then he must have already "really screwed up." *I knew this manager job was way over his head.*

Her dad waved a lobster at her. "It's about time to open the brunch gates. You better get out there. I can't have my plate dealer being a no-show."

She left him to his shellfish. Walking deep into the quiet, empty stations, she found the last possible sink. She turned on the faucet and squeezed out some soap. Cooking shows made it seem like every chef went to culinary school. She'd expected her dad to tell her that there were at least five people with culinary training that worked here. Five seemed like a reasonable number for a hick town. But nope.

Clear lather bubbled up between J'aime's fingers. Her new idea was trashed. Finding a trained employee who could train her wasn't going to happen.

All those fancy appliances and the casino is still a Lean Cuisine kitchen.

She held her hands under the warm running water. It would be nice to stand here and wash her hands for the rest of the day or, you know, forever. Without a pot to cook with, she'd be eating a cold dinner when she got home tonight. To be honest, she'd be eating cold meals until she asked her dad for money to buy new pans.

God. That would be more awkward than his sweet talk.

Her dad never spent money on anything unless it was cigarettes or an emergency, and food was never an emergency to him.

He wouldn't understand that this wasn't about cash. It wasn't even about being hungry, not in the way that old buffet leftovers could solve. What if she just took ten bucks from the money jar? Her dad would be pissed, but it wasn't all his money. Her tips went in there too. Technically, it was the family savings, and she was family. Learning to cook with a new pan and spatula meant she'd share the meals with her dad. It could be one happy circle of food, couldn't it?

Nervous anxiety spread through her veins. Would he even notice that a few bucks were missing? Stupid question. He noticed every time their cellphones rang. He noticed every time he got a new voice mail. "Lunch money vultures," he'd say, never even listening to the debt collector's messages. He'd notice for certain if she lifted a nickel from a jar she wasn't supposed to touch. The red beans and rice dumped in the bushes was a perfect example of why she shouldn't even think about the cash. Wasting her dad's savings on something she couldn't cook wasn't an option.

J'aime turned off the faucet. Before she could convince herself to move away from the sink, she heard a hollow tapping sound; a steady beat that was familiar and out of place at the same time. The curious rhythm echoed off the steel cabinets, bringing her back to the casino kitchen and away from thoughts of stealing.

Waving her hands in front of the automatic paper towel dispenser, she peeked around the other side of the towering Hobart dishwasher. Half-expecting to see the red feathers of a lost woodpecker, she saw the black hair-netted head of a boy.

Ramen Noodles Guy.

Cold water dribbled down her arms. She needed to dry off so she could put on her sanitation gloves, but she couldn't stop looking at the guy.

What is he doing? Paper towel in hand, she leaned against the metal counter, sneaking a better look around the tall industrial dishwasher.

The first thing that caught J'aime's attention was the knife. It was a big one. Not a butcher knife for hacking whole animals, but still, the blade was scary long. A steady stream of chopping— that was the tapping sound. Ramen Noodles Guy was cutting up a whole red onion. Not slowly slicing or fumbling the blade, but chopping fast, like the chefs do on the Food Network.

In a swift movement, he quickly lifted the cutting board and scraped it with the dull knife edge. Evenly cut chunks slid into a bulging bag of precut red onions. Without noticing her, he laid the knife down as if his fancy chopping was totally normal. Picking up the bag of precut onions, he walked back into the rolling boil of the main kitchen.

J'aime pulled on her gloves as she went over to inspect the cutting board. A stain of purple water splashed across the white surface. The knife rested across the top of the plastic board, the sharp blade pointing down. Its handle was perfectly in line with the edge. The knife lay there, looking so professional. Not a stray piece of onion was left. J'aime glanced toward the kitchen, then back down at the knife.

Ramen Noodles Guy knew how to cook.

Chapter 5
Cheese Pizza and Tater Tots

J'AIME'S FIRST DAY AT HANNAVILLE HIGH started off bad, like incinerated burnt-toast bad. First, she missed the school's free breakfast because she was trapped in the office, filling out paperwork. No breakfast meant she was forced to eat her bringer pantry lunch in second period. By the time the noon bell rang, she was starving.

To keep her stomach's dull empty ache from completely taking over her brain, she had to eat lunch . . . again.

This is the worst day for this to happen, J'aime thought as she made her way to the school cafeteria. By the end of her Sunday shift, J'aime had decided to have a cooking talk with Ramen Noodles Guy. She'd kitchen-spied his name badge while he was prepping the salad line, but when she clocked out, *Robert Rios* was already gone. That meant she'd have to talk to him at school, which was way more nerve-wracking. A week ago, she wouldn't have dreamed of asking a stranger for cooking help. She was supposed to be a natural chef with a TV education. This new J'aime knew better.

Waiting in a stalled lunch line in the school cafeteria, J'aime eyed white bags of tater tots. Blotches of translucent grease stained the thin paper sacks. Next to the burgers, the tempting bags of potatoes snuggled close under a heat lamp. Her whole body begged her to sneak a warm tot from its cozy sack and pop it right into her mouth.

Instead, she focused her attention on her lunch tray. Right in the center was a single slice of her beloved cheese pizza. J'aime didn't have any cash, but sometimes lunch ladies let her slide by, giving her a freebie hot lunch. Other times they dragged her to the principal's office, calling her a dirty thief, even though they were the ones with grease smeared on their clothes. Getting fired for giving free food to hungry kids wasn't the spaghetti hill most lunch ladies wanted to die on, but sometimes there were wild cards. Today J'aime was hungry enough to gamble.

She snuck a peek at the register. A bored lunch lady, with tattoos sprawling down her arms, swiped ID badge after ID badge. She was a lot younger than most lunch ladies. Her vintage apron made her look like the hipster bakers on the extreme cupcake show, *Frosted*. The lunch lady wasn't much taller than some of the freshmen darting around the cafeteria, but she still scared the grape juice out of J'aime.

Keeping her eyes down, J'aime shuffled up to the register like everyone else. Finally, the lunch lady's palm reached out. Flying above the pizza slice, an inked bluebird glided across the translucent skin of the lunch lady's under wrist. Her open hand waited for J'aime's ID card.

Without looking up, J'aime rolled the dice. "I'm new to this school, like today new," she explained. "I don't have a lunch account . . . yet."

"Got any cash?" the lunch lady asked in a disembodied, bland voice.

Drops of moisture bubbled up on J'aime's pizza slice. The gooey cheddar was starting to cool. The right answer meant a meal. Her stomach growled, shaking the truth out of her. "I don't have any money," she admitted.

The lunch lady sighed. "You know what that means."

J'aime knew too well what that meant—the wrong answer. The bluebird tattoo flew forward. The lunch lady grabbed her tray. The instinct to hold on, tug back rushed through J'aime, but fighting with a lunch lady was a one-way ticket to detention. She let her meal slip from her fingers. The cafeteria worker held her lunch tray over a nearby trashcan. Suddenly, J'aime felt the line of students behind her go still.

Everyone was watching.

With a flick of her wrist the lunch lady triggered a pizza landslide and splatted her lunch on top of the garbage. She tried not to picture her dream meal oozing onto all kinds of grossness.

With a clatter, the woman tossed J'aime's empty tray onto a pile of dirty dishes.

"There's a substitute cold meal I can give you," the lunch lady explained as she returned to her register. "I still have to charge your account a dollar. If you take the cold meal, I'm required to tell you that if you don't pay your lunch debt, you don't graduate."

J'aime didn't need to be reminded.

The lunch lady reached under the register. She pulled out a browning, overripe banana and held it out to J'aime. "Here's the cold lunch."

Anger rose up from deep inside J'aime's hungry guts. "You call that a lunch?" she snapped, instantly regretting it. She waited for the lunch lady's wrath to begin.

Instead of scowling or calling over a security guard, the young woman lifted her eyebrows and smiled. "Dang, girl," the lunch lady chuckled. "You deserve an extra banana for that sass. I'll charge you a dollar for the first one and throw in a free one for later."

Later. Or the Food Free Zone, as J'aime thought of it. That dreaded gap between lunch and, quite possibly, lunch the next day. While the rest of the students behind her snapped back to life, shifting their trays impatiently, J'aime stared at the fruit. $1,999.97—that's how much she owed her previous schools for meals she couldn't afford. A dollar banana would make her lunch debt over $2,000.

"I'm not adding to my debt," J'aime said, sticking to a promise she'd made to herself—no matter what, no more lunch debt. Her stomach rumbled in protest. She needed to walk away right now, or she'd give in and grab the banana. J'aime turned her back on the lunch lady.

"Suit yourself," she heard the woman say.

J'aime pushed down her hunger. Instead of pushing her luck with more sass, she whisper-practiced what she was going to say to Ramen Noodles Guy.

"Hi. Your chopping's really impressive. What other chef skills do you know? I mean. Can you really cook?"

The more J'aime practiced the more she sounded like a drooling, food geek from Venus. What if Robert Rios could only chop onions? Then what? Professional knife skills were awesome, but not enough. She wanted to learn everything from recipe to plate.

Right now, her nerves needed to focus on walking up to his lunch table, then she'd worry about what came next and how she'd get through the rest of the day on an empty stomach.

J'aime focused on the tangle of students in the cafeteria. She spotted Ramen Noodles Guy eating with some cowboy types. Robert looked totally different without his chef's beanie. She hadn't noticed at the pantry that he wore his black hair high and tight; sides shaved close, with the top combed back into a smooth velvet wave.

He looks like a cast member from Grease. Which pretty much clashed with his lunch table of "farmie" friends. One of the country bros must have said something funny, because suddenly Robert laughed. His head kicked back with a smile that lit up the whole table.

Sunday afternoon, when she'd made trips into the main buffet kitchen to get fresh plates, she'd spied on him. Most cooks in the casino socialized while they reheated, but not Robert Rios. He didn't talk to anyone, and he definitely didn't smile; not like that.

It felt like she vibrated over to Robert's table.

What am I doing? You don't just walk up to people and weirdly start talking to them, especially not a guy who thinks I'm a charity case.

She tried to calm her doubt. Even if it was a pity hello, he was nice to her at St. Lawrence's.

Before J'aime even realized she was there, she saw her fingernail tap twice on the shoulder seam of his gray T-shirt.

Robert turned. His whole table stopped talking and stared at her.

"Yeah?" Robert asked, holding a hamburger in both hands. A tomato slice and a leaf of lettuce dangled past the bun line. A bag of French fries sat on his tray.

J'aime pulled her finger back. The guy she was counting on to teach her to cook chose to eat the most basic all-American lunch. Disappointment kept her lips as stiff as a dried linguine. She shifted her balance, so she was standing on one foot.

"Hi," she said, making her mouth work. "You might not remember me—"

Robert put his burger down. "You're being friendly now?" he asked. His face read, *NOT JOKING.* He totally remembered her.

J'aime panicked. She was a little snotty at the pantry, but not that bad. She chose to ignore the comment and stuttered ahead. "I'm J'aime, J'aime McWilliams. When we met at the . . ." His friends were listening. There was no way she was saying pantry.

"I mean. I work at the casino buffet too."

He picked up a French fry and gave it a twirl. "I heard you're the boss's daughter."

J'aime hadn't practiced for that answer. "I guess," she said. "Um, I was wondering if you know how to *really* cook?"

The rest of the table lost interest at her question, going back to their lunches and previous conversations. Robert kept watching her though. He raised a suspicious eyebrow. "Really cook? What do you mean? Like more than instant-noodle cook?"

J'aime grimaced. Maybe she was a lot snotty at the pantry.

"Well, yeah. I saw you chopping a whole onion. Your knife skills are amazing, like a professional chef. I thought you might know how to, you know, cook from scratch?"

Robert lowered his voice. "You saw me with that onion?"

"I was washing my hands in the back kitchen," J'aime explained nervously. He looked irritated. Why would anyone be irritated over vegetables?

"Forget the onion," she said quickly. "I was wondering what kind of culinary training you've had?" She grimaced at the word *culinary. Yes, I am a food nerd.*

Robert slowly chewed his fry. "I grew up in a restaurant. I better know how to chop."

J'aime squeezed her hands into fists to stop her courage from evaporating. She looked to his lunch for a clue on how to talk to him. His burger was completely average, probably smeared with ketchup. His French fries were plain and soggy, nothing special to hint at his personal quirks. Then she spotted it. Behind two wadded-up napkins, she saw a random packet of ranch salad dressing. It was open. What was he doing with that ranch dressing? He didn't have a salad. Why would he bother to take it from someone else's lunch? It had to be for his French fries. Ranch dressing was as Midwestern as you could get, but it had a lot more flavor than cafeteria ketchup. *Stop the kitchen sink psychology,* she thought. *He thinks you're a jerk. Show him you're not.*

J'aime smiled awkwardly. "Is your family's restaurant in Hannaville?

Robert puffed his chest out a little and pulled the edges of his T-shirt to smooth out the decal. It read, *RIOS RANCHEROS*. A cartoon green pepper character leaned against the last *S*. The pepper cartoon was happily tossing a small jalapeno into its mouth.

Even vegetable cannibalism is questionable, J'aime thought.

Robert bypassed the taco and pointed to the address below the taco's feet, 870 University Row, Churchill, Mo.

"Churchill. Right," J'aime said. "We drove through that town on our way here. They have everything, McDonald's, Chipotle, Panera."

Robert stared at her like a carrot was sprouting out of her head. "AND Rios Rancheros, plus like 30,000 college students."

He raised his serious eyebrow again. "Why did a Silver Dollar buffet manager send his daughter to question me about cooking?"

"Question you?"

"Yeah. Does he want to learn about the local competition, or something? Rios Rancheros is the best Mexican restaurant in the whole county. Silver Dollar's taquitos don't even come close to Rancheros." His voice got even quieter. "Or are you supposed to make sure all his employees follow the rules?"

"What?" J'aime asked. "I don't know what you're—"

"Tell your boss dad that I know what the casino policy says," Robert whispered, "but it's stupid to waste an onion when I can chop it."

She could barely hear him. Were there casino policies about onions or did she miss what he'd said? She shook her head. "Listen. I don't know what you're talking about." She swallowed her pride. "I was wondering if you could teach me how to cook?"

"Cook?" Robert smirked. "You mean, really cook, that's what you said a minute ago."

"Yes. Really cook," she said. "That's exactly what I mean."

Robert paused. He plucked a BBQ potato chip off his neighbor's tray and ate it. "Why?"

She didn't want to tell him that she'd scarfed down a can of uncooked green beans last night for dinner, or when she sincerely believed her life wouldn't change, she fought the urge to curl up in the recliner and never leave the house again.

"No matter how much *Chef Academy* I watch," J'aime said, "I can't simmer or sauté on my own. I just figured out, like yesterday, that my brain needs someone to stand at the stove with me and walk me through the steps. TV lessons aren't going to cut it. So can you really cook or what?"

Robert picked pale seeds from his burger bun. "I never should have admitted to that onion," he sighed, more to the hamburger than J'aime. He stared up at her. "Boss's daughter, when you report back to your dad about this conversation, tell him that I should be promoted to the fryer. Honestly, I'm shocked that half those casino cooks haven't deep-fried themselves to death. They're crappy fry cooks at best."

Robert turned his back to her. He swiped a few more BBQ chips from his neighbor, who apparently didn't mind sharing. His hands lifted the top hamburger bun then shoved the chips on top of the lettuce. Giving the bun a slight squeeze, it crunched loudly. As he lifted the burger to his mouth, his fingers kept the trapped toppings in place.

J'aime could almost feel the weight of the sandwich in her hands. She knew what he was doing. Adding those BBQ chips seasoned the patty with an outdoor grill taste. Not to mention, the texture of the soft beef combined with a crisp chip would be like a breaded burger. That squeeze held it together, creating a perfect first bite. His teeth sank deep into the bun and a drip of ranch splatted onto his lunch tray.

Of course. BBQ chips and the tangy ranch: a classic combo, and way more flavorful than government-issued ground chuck.

Ramen Noodles Guy knows exactly where pizza was invented, J'aime thought.

Robert took a second bite. The conversation was over. He was eating like she wasn't even standing there.

J'aime's cheeks blazed like her oven burner. She turned on her flip-flops and left the Ramen Noodles Guy to his lunch. The boy was paranoid, but also kind of right. She did spy on him at the casino. If Robert's family owned their own restaurant, then why did he work at the buffet? It would be so amazing to have a family restaurant. You'd always have a place to work and do any job you wanted. The Rioses were lucky. If her dad wasn't such a mess maybe they'd own their own place, and every day would be filled with full happy plates.

"Like that's ever going to happen," she muttered.

Staring into the lunchroom anarchy, she searched for an out-skirt table. She wanted to get through the rest of this depressing non-lunch lunch hour without having to talk to anyone else. The hard fact was Hannaville was a small school with an even smaller cafeteria. There were no empty tables. Frustrated, she forced her feet to move. *Just sit somewhere. Anywhere.*

On the edge of the crowd, she spotted a small, thin girl with sunflower-blonde hair, eating by herself. The girl casually took a bite from a sandwich and turned a magazine page. In Chicago, L-train riders read on the subway as a signal that they didn't want to chat. If J'aime had to sit with someone, then a chick that didn't want to socialize was the next best thing to an empty table.

The girl looked sporty with her thin thermal zip-up and the way her hair was pulled back in a tight ponytail with a hot-pink headband. J'aime walked around the rest of the chaotic lunch-room to the vacant end of the girl's lunch table.

The girl flicked her eyes up from her crumpled magazine for a half-a-second of acknowledgment. "Hey," she said then returned to *Runners Weekly* and her meal: peanut butter and grape jelly on whole wheat with a bag of pretzels.

J'aime didn't acknowledge the mandatory, "Hey." All she could do was stare at the girl's food. *Salty and sweet, one of the most perfect food pairings ever*, she thought.

J'aime wanted to stuff that sandwich in her face but studied it instead. The crusts were neatly trimmed off. Picky eaters are weird, but you kind of have to admire their hyper attention to ingredients. J'aime dropped her Whole Foods bag on the floor. It hit the flimsy metal table leg, rattling the girl's pretzels in their disposable bag, but she kept on reading.

No-Crusts Girl wasn't going to give her any trouble.

Pulling out a chair, J'aime sat down and dug into her tote. She pulled out an old Aguatista water bottle. The thin plastic crinkled and popped as she unscrewed the cap. Luckily, she'd remembered to stop by the water fountain before lunch. It wasn't the smooth bliss of melted mozzarella, but it would have to do.

With a slight tremble to her hand, J'aime lifted the bottle of bland, lukewarm water to her lips and took a sip of her lunch.

Chapter 6

Happy Onions

AN APPLE SLICE HURTLED PAST THE ROW OF hanging whisks. Arcing high, it flew toward the ceiling of the casino's deserted back kitchen. J'aime yelped every time her knife thwacked against the cutting board and sent a slice flying. The third time an apple missile launched into the kitchen stratosphere, she started to believe that the fruit was messing with her.

"Come on," she begged the dwindling pile of pre-cut salad bar slices. "Are you going to cooperate, or what?"

Wasting food wasn't a habit she could afford to start. She nibbled on an apple wedge and tried to picture Robert chopping. If she remembered right, his blade barely skimmed the cutting board, leaving a trail of perfect chunks. It was like watching a magician work.

J'aime set a half-eaten slice on the white surface, gripped her knife, and lifted the cutting edge high above the apple. With a loud thud, the apple slice shot from the counter, ricocheting off a cold oven. That definitely didn't happen on cooking shows. Grabbing another slice, she raised her knife again.

"I wouldn't do that if I were you," a voice came from behind her.

She looked over her shoulder to find Robert scooping up her most recent fruit projectile. He tossed it into a trash barrel. "Why are you torturing apples?"

He was dressed for work in his casino issued chef's jacket, beanie, and pants. Before she'd even clocked in, J'aime had checked the schedule. Robert Rios wasn't working until 6:00 p.m. She'd figured she had plenty of time to practice chopping before sneaking out to the front of house, avoiding him completely. Yet, at 5:30 p.m., he was standing right in her personal chopping space.

J'aime turned her back on him. "I'm not torturing fruit," she mumbled, laying out a whole row of slices. "I'm chopping—"

"Your fingers off," Robert interrupted.

He wasn't going to teach her, but he was going to make fun of her. Before she could turn on her *LEAVE ME ALONE!* body signals, Robert was suddenly standing next to her at the makeshift chopping station. He held out his hand, giving her a, *c'mon, hand-it-over* wave.

Cautiously, she laid the knife down on the cutting board.

"You're chopping scared," he said. "Don't hold it way back here."

He gestured toward the end of the handle, furthest from the knifepoint. "Hold the knife here." Robert's fingers moved up to where the plastic grip met steel.

"You want to control the blade," he continued, "so you have to be close to it. Squeeze the handle like you mean business." His loose fingers wrapped firmly underneath the grip. The back of his hand covered the whole handle, practically making it disappear.

"Getting comfortable with your knife is like having a pet shark. You've got to respect it. If you're afraid of it, it'll bite you. Giving a newbie a sharp knife is the fastest way to weed out the fake cooks."

"I'm not a fake cook," J'aime snapped.

"Okay, but judging from the apple slices on the floor back there," Robert said, "you're not a good cook either."

He raised his left hand up and curled his fingers into a tiger paw. "The trick to chopping is the claw technique."

Robert pulled a yellow onion out of his pocket. Round and whole, dirt still coated the layers of papery skin. That onion didn't come from the casino. Commercial kitchen vegetables are power-washed to oblivion. He quickly rinsed and peeled the onion then sliced off the dangling roots with a close knife cut.

"See how I left some of the root?" Robert pointed to a porous moon at one end of the onion. "Roots keep us together. It's pretty true for people, and 100 percent true for onions."

J'aime leaned in to take a better look at the onion. She kept her mouth shut. Even if he was rude, he was about to explain how to chop. She hoped no employees would wander in here and interrupt the random lesson.

Slicing through the thin, centered root, Robert's knife cut the onion in half. He picked up one side and showed her the end again. "There's part of the root on both halves of the onion. When we chop, it'll keep the onion layers from flying all over the place."

J'aime tried to pay attention, but the word "we" distracted her. Did this mean he'd changed his mind about teaching her to cook? He brought his own onion into work and was chopping it right in front of her; that should probably be answer enough.

Robert shaped his hand into a claw again. He rested the tops of his fingers on the rounded curve of an onion half. "See how the claw makes the knuckle on my middle finger stick out? It turns that knuckle into a guide, a shield, so you don't hack off your fingertips."

He lost the claw shape and laid his fingers flat on the onion, the way J'aime had been holding her apple slices earlier. "Like this, there's nothing to protect your hand. Your fingers need to stand up in the claw shape. You've got to chop with your claws out."

Robert lifted his fingers, flashing the claw shape again at J'aime.

Was she supposed to laugh at that? Was he teasing her about her lack of skills? She tried to push the prickle of defensiveness aside and cleared her throat. "I guess I was chopping more jazz-hands style than claws."

He answered by slowly letting his right hand chop while his left hand scooted backward, down the back of the onion. His claw always kept its reverse dance a few steps ahead of the moving blade. A hollow chopping sound mingled with the soft crunch of vegetable.

The deep, sharp odor of earth and juices tainted the air. Automatically, her whole face squeezed shut against the bitter sting. When she relaxed again, the kitchen was bleary, and Robert was picking up a thin piece of onion from the trail he'd just cut.

"This isn't technically chopping, I'm making slices. Abbi calls them 'happy onions.'"

Onion tears ran down her face. "Happy onions?" J'aime questioned, wiping her cheeks. "

Using both hands, he flipped the onion slice over and held it near his mouth. A silly, white, translucent grin danced near his smiling lips. "You know, it's good with the bad, glass-half-full kind of thing. She's a pretty positive person."

There was that real smile, the one that lit up the whole lunch table. J'aime looked down at the cutting board and rubbed her eyes. Whoever this Abbi girl was, she made Robert happier than J'aime had felt in a long time. She didn't know what to say. Was she supposed to ask about his corny girlfriend?

"Anyway," Robert said, disappointment flavoring his voice. "There's a cool way to dice and chop at the same time, but you have to know the whole claw move to do that."

J'aime hesitated, looking at the slices scattered across the cutting board. "So," she asked, "are you going to teach me?"

Robert popped a raw onion slice into his mouth and shrugged his shoulders. "Why do you want to *really* cook?"

"I already told you why."

"You told me why you need a teacher. You didn't tell me why you want to cook. I want the *really* reason."

J'aime gently tipped over a remaining apple chunk. The creamy porous fruit glistened under the fluorescent lights. "It's complicated, but food is all I think about. It's everything to me. Plus, I want to learn how to cook better, you know, with fresh ingredients. No more processed stuff."

Robert raised his eyebrows again. "Are you one of those food people who want to farm fish in your basement?"

For a second, J'aime imaged herself in overalls with a pitchfork standing over a tank of swimming tilapia. She wasn't against it, but she wasn't going to tell him that either. "Yeah, sure. I'm a Farmer Fish Head all the way," she said sarcastically.

Robert didn't laugh. He wanted an answer just like she did.

Could she tell him that she was afraid of ending up like her mom—hungry, diabetic, and dead at thirty-six. J'aime had to take control of her food situation before it consumed her too.

Her voice lost its edge. "I told you it's complicated."

Robert shook his head. "I've got two jobs, school, and other stuff going on." He pushed the cutting board at her, then backed away toward the main kitchen. "If you were serious about becoming a chef, I might help you, but I can't donate my time to food drama."

Donate? J'aime thought. Robert hadn't mentioned the pantry at all, but that's exactly what he meant. J'aime's cheeks burned. He was already helping *the needy*.

The *really* reason hovered behind her lips. It was raw. It was her true self, her true reason for being. *Becoming a chef will save my life.* But she'd never told this truth to anyone, why would she suddenly reveal it to him? She didn't want a random guy who happened to know his way around a cutting board making fun of her, and she definitely didn't need his pity. The only problem was, this was the right guy, the right teacher. She could feel it down to her taste buds.

But the right guy was leaving. Walking through the empty workstation, deciding not to help her, and she was letting him go. A whiff of desperate onion stung her nose. The scent was overwhelming; J'aime furiously rubbed her burning eyes. The uncut half of the yellow vegetable disappeared in a blur of tears.

A few quick blinks, and the glossy glare of the kitchen returned. The knife handle was pointed right at J'aime. Her right hand grabbed the plastic grip. She curled her left fingers into a fast claw.

The wild slicing sound stopped Robert from pushing the swinging door open all the way. J'aime felt him turn around. He was watching her. Savagely chopping the onion, she knew the frenzied slices were awkward and dangerous, but every time her knife hit the cutting board, her eyes were less blurry. The sound of the blade tapped out one clear message—she wasn't a fake cook. She was serious.

Behind her, Robert said, "First lesson's tomorrow. Don't buy your lunch."

Chapter 7

Pineapple Salsa

THE CAFETERIA CLOCK TICKED AWAY. STANDING next to the pizza lunch line at Hannaville High, J'aime waited for Robert. Despite his instructions, she'd brought "sandwiches" made out of peanut butter and crackers. The pantry didn't stock lunch bags, so her PB and Saltines meal was tucked safely in a small to-go box from the casino. The Styrofoam shell kept her lunch in one piece better than flimsy plastic ever could. If Robert didn't show, at least she wouldn't miss lunch. J'aime's hunger wasn't taking any chances.

Where the heck was Robert? Farmie cowboys swarmed around his normal table. No one sat still for long before they were up and talking to someone else. She looked for his pompadour hair among the cowboy hats. Her stomach growled. She glanced nervously at the clock again. The lunch hour was well underway. *He probably thinks I invented this whole chef-in-training situation because I think he's cute.*

J'aime usually liked guys in the fan-geek crowd. Robert didn't seem like a farmie cowboy type, but he hung out with them. It didn't really matter. Farmie or fan-geek, guys never liked her anyway. All she wanted from Robert was for him to teach her how to cook.

"Hey," Robert said from out of nowhere. He was standing next to her, still wearing his backpack like he'd come straight from class. He pointed at the to-go box in J'aime's hands. "I told you not to buy a lunch."

She didn't want to tell him how hungry she was. Instead, she held the container up. Crackers rattled against the cushy Styrofoam. "I didn't buy this. I made it. And honestly, I thought you might ditch me."

"Ditching the boss's daughter isn't a wise career move." He held up a bright crayon-blue lunch bag. It was the kind of insulated tote that little kids used after they graduated from character lunch boxes. "I had to go back to my locker for the food."

He nodded his head at a rare empty table near the line. "Come on. We'll have to cook fast since we've only got fifteen minutes."

Cooking fast sounded great to J'aime. The perfect solution for getting her meal in and learning a thing or two. She sat her to-go box down as Robert slung his backpack onto a chair. Standing next to her, he pulled out two big Ziploc bags. One was stuffed with two child-size, orange cutting boards and a jumble of plastic silverware, the other with smaller sandwich bags of ingredients.

"Wait," she said. "We're gonna do it right here? In front of the lunch ladies?"

"I don't think they're going to care. Plus, where else would we cook?"

"I don't know, I just—"

"Help me get all this stuff out," he said, pushing the blue lunch bag at her. His eyes flicked over to his friends.

J'aime looked too. It was still just a bunch of cowboys eating lunch. They hadn't even noticed Robert, not yet. She tugged on the bag's Velcro lid.

Maybe he's embarrassed to be with me? Well, then he shouldn't have brought that dirty onion to work and been all show-off tiger claw about it.

She ripped open the fuzzy black seal. Fresh fruit and vegetables shined inside the puffy, cool lunch bag, a mini garden springing up in the middle of her boring day. She pulled out a dark bumpy alien egg, or at least that's what she thought avocados looked like. Giving it a squeeze, the dry, rough skin cracked immediately. Her fingers smashed into its surprisingly soft insides.

"Hey, don't do that," Robert said, carefully grabbing the alien egg. "Sorry. Chefs always squeeze avocados on TV."

Robert inspected the damage. "You *gently* squeeze it to see if it's ripe, not smash it like Godzilla. Haven't you ever seen an avocado before?"

He put the fruit by him and laid a child's cutting board in front of her.

J'aime wanted to fade into the vanilla paint of the brick wall behind her. Nothing like being called an atomic monster to start your lunch off right. And then there was the fact that they weren't sitting down. Who stands up during lunch hour to eat? Absolutely no one. She glanced around, but the students didn't seem to notice the two of them with their cutting boards. It wouldn't be long before everyone was watching her fumble her way through a recipe.

"I've seen avocados," she whispered. "Just only in guacamole form. At the Tudor Table, we served guac on the side when you ordered a Sorcerer's Flame Turkey Leg."

Robert stopped prepping. For a moment there was nothing but cafeteria chatter floating between them. "Did you say a Sorcerer's Flame Turkey Leg?"

"Yes," J'aime said, taking a lime out of the lunch bag. "It was a medieval restaurant with knights and stuff."

He raised those eyebrows again. "And mystical guacamole?"

"What else would we serve?" she said back, imitating his eyebrow disbelief.

The cafeteria clock ticked above their heads. Robert let questions about jousting and avocado dips go. "We gotta cook."

He plopped a travel-sized bottle of anti-bacterial gel down in front of J'aime. "We can't leave to wash our hands." He pointed his plastic knife at her. "And we're stuck with fake knives because I'll get expelled if I bring anything sharper."

J'aime squirted the cold cleanser and rubbed. "What are we making?"

"I thought I'd teach you some of our basic Rios Rancheros recipes. I've taught them to new cooks at the restaurant. The recipes are pretty easy," he said, sanitizing between his fingers. "First up is salsa. I didn't have time to run to the store. I snagged ingredients from home. We had some fresh pineapple chunks at the house, so I thought we could make pineapple salsa."

The avocado rolled back and forth on the table. J'aime steadied it. She hadn't thought this whole cooking teacher thing through. She couldn't expect him to pay for ingredients like he was her Foody Warbucks. What if his family was planning on eating this stuff?

"I don't want to take food from your family," she said. "What do I owe you for these ingredients?"

"Don't worry about it," Robert said. "It's not a big deal. I want to help."

The word *help* lingered in the air. His conversations were peppered with Good Samaritan words. It was pointless to pretend like she could realistically pay him back, but she'd have to do something. "I saw that Hannaville doesn't have a grocery store," she said, pointing to a Ziploc full of golden fruit. "Where did you find a fresh pineapple?"

"My family gets food in Churchill because of the restaurant, and we grow a lot of our own, like this red onion." Robert held up a bag of precut chunks of purple and white, then glanced over at his old table again. A few eyes under cowboy hats glanced back. "You know, I'm going to stand facing you so you can see what I'm doing." He slid his tiny cutting board to the other side of the table then turned his back toward his friends.

She looked over at No-Crusts Girl. She was reading, not wondering where J'aime was at all. *I don't have any friends to hide from.*

The avocado was on the move again, wobbling in between them like a fruit compass. Robert reorganized himself at his new makeshift station. Over his hunched shoulder, J'aime watched his friends talk, eat, and try not to stare at Robert.

She stopped the wandering avocado. "If you don't want to do this—"

Robert set a plastic cereal bowl on the table. Inside was a tiny green pepper. "Cooking's easier if your tools are at your workspace," he talked over her, "and if you have all the ingredients measured out at the beginning."

He grabbed a measuring cup and set it in front of J'aime. "Chefs call that good *mise en place*. I call it making a home for your recipe, but the French does sound a lot cooler."

"*Mise en place*, huh?" She felt her belly tingle. He did know more than just chopping. She leaned in to see better and the lunchroom faded around them.

"To start with," he said, "we'll need one-and-a-half cups of pineapple. You can use other fruits too, like mangoes. Do you like mangoes?"

She nodded. "I like McDonald's mango smoothie."

Robert rolled his eyes. "Fake mango isn't the same thing."

He dumped the pineapple onto his cutting board. "I'll dice the pineapple, you mince the cilantro." He handed her a sandwich baggie of green plant stems topped with delicate fan leaves. "This should measure out to a fourth of a cup."

J'aime pulled open the bag. The smell hit her first, a slight sourness followed by a whiff of sweetness. She lifted out the slender cilantro bunch. Its earthy scent masked the cafeteria's *eau de* chicken fingers. The cilantro looked like a weed that should grow through the cracks in the duplex porch, but J'aime loved each fanned leaf. She'd never cooked with a real herb before.

"You said mince, right?" Not that she really knew what that meant.

"Mincing means to finely cut," Robert instructed. "Think small, like a grain of rice. Get the pieces as little as you can. Start at the top of the leaves and mince until you reach nothing but stem, then add it to the bowl.

"It's okay to mince the stem too?"

"You can eat the stem," he answered. "It tastes just like the leaves."

Silently, their plastic knives went to work—his roughly slicing through thick yellow fruit, hers through flimsy herbs. The cilantro smell grew stronger as the plant released its juices. Her stomach moaned, reminding her it was past time to eat. She focused on the way the serrated plastic edge cut the thin wet plant.

Fruit juice puddled under Robert's hand. "Not using a real knife jacks up the pineapple," he sighed, sliding all of his jagged diced pieces into the measuring cup, then dumping them into the cereal bowl.

Cilantro slivers clung to J'aime's skin, covering her hand like stickers. "*Ack*, they're attacking me," she said, peeling a random leaf from her wrist. "I'm getting cilantro fingers."

"You look like you're sprouting," Robert said. "How'd you do that? There isn't even that much cilantro." He reached for the tiny green pepper. "I'll go ahead and seed the jalapeno. Just keep cutting, or tearing, or whatever you're doing."

"I'm mincing," J'aime corrected him this time.

"Sure," Robert said doubtfully. "Try to get some of it into the bowl."

He twirled the pepper by its bent stubby stem. "Abbi always says you can tell how hot a jalapeno is by how much its stem curls."

Putting down her knife, J'aime tried to shake cilantro from her hands. Where was this Abbi person? Obviously, she didn't share their lunch hour, or else Robert would be hanging out with this all-knowing, all-cooking girl.

Robert kept talking. "You know how at some restaurants, they ask you how spicy you want your food?"

"Yeah. I bused dishes at Thai Fifty-Five for a month."

Robert forgot about his jalapeno. "How many restaurants have you worked at?"

J'aime eyed him and decided to answer the truth. "Six. You?"

He looked down. Before he even answered, she could tell she'd beat him at some private competition in his head. "Two," he said, slicing off the jalapeno's stem. "How spicy do you like your Thai food?"

"Mild," she answered.

"If you take the seeds out, then basically a jalapeno is mild on the spicy scale. If you leave the seeds in, it's hotter." The plastic knife stabbed through the pepper. "It's kind of gross to think about it this way, but taking the seeds out of a jalapeno is a lot like dissecting in biology class. You slice open the skin and remove the seeds by scraping them with your knife."

Splayed frogs danced through J'aime's mind. "Yep," she said. "I'm thinking about amphibian intestines in my salsa. Thanks for that."

He smeared jalapeno seeds on the edge of his cutting board. "You're welcome." He smiled cheerfully, cutting quick tiny chunks. "Dicing is better for a jalapeno. The smaller the pieces, the less bite for mild eaters." He scattered the jalapeno into the bowl of pineapple and dumped in the prechopped onion. "That's about a fourth cup of onion." Robert elbowed the bowl closer to J'aime. "Time to add the cilantro."

J'aime stared helplessly at her hands. Peeling every leaf off her cilantroed skin meant she'd be stuck in this lunchroom for the rest of high school. Accidentally, she brushed her index finger against her thumb. A sliver of herb fell onto the tabletop, and suddenly, she knew what to do. Holding her hands over the bowl, she rubbed them together as if she was trying to keep warm. The minced cilantro fell like garden confetti on top of the salsa.

Robert paused. "Wow. I've never seen cilantro added like that before."

She rubbed a little more confidently. "I'm patenting it."

"You'd be the first," he said, giving the salsa a quick stir.

The thud of trays hitting trash bins made J'aime look up from their mixing bowl. Miraculously, she'd almost forgotten they were in the middle of a high school cafeteria.

People were crumpling chip bags and screeching in chairs. The room was shifting from chewing to trashing. Lunchtime was almost over. They needed to move this thing along or there wouldn't be actual eating time.

Lost in the Zen of cooking, Robert's plastic knife carefully sliced through the avocado. "Peeling an avocado is kind of crazy," he instructed, picking up half of the fruit. "It takes practice, maybe I should do it for you? After the WWE grip you put on this guy, it's smooshed at a bad angle."

"*Um*," J'aime warned, "I think the bell's going to ring soon."

Robert's head shot up. "Grab that lime, cut it in half and squeeze it on the salsa."

J'aime fumbled her plastic knife. She sawed hard and the edge finally broke through the rind. Robert's thumb slipped behind the avocado skin, then he whipped it off in one swipe. Wicked fast, he peeled and chopped both avocado sides before she could squeeze the other half of her lime into the bowl.

"We add the tablespoon of canola oil," he said, drizzling yellow liquid from a snack-sized baggie over the salsa. He unzipped another bag and sprinkled a burnt-orange spice. "Add a teaspoon of ground cumin, then stir it up to spread around the flavor." He quickly swirled a plastic spoon around the bowl again, mixing everything as the lunch bell rang.

A catchphrase from a cooking show popped into J'aime's head. "Hands up," she shouted.

Robert's hands shot up into the air. "Spoons down," he shouted back, dropping his utensil.

"You know it's usually knives down, right?" she asked. "Which cooking shows do you watch?"

"No time," he said quickly, handing J'aime a sandwich bag of tortilla chips. "Eat up."

The lunchroom echoed with sounds of lunch ladies clanking empty steam bins. The warning bell rang. J'aime's instinct was to inhale this salsa on the spot, but she stopped herself. She'd minced, diced, shook, and stirred this food—she wanted to enjoy every tiny millisecond of that first bite.

She dipped a chip into a glob of bright-yellow salsa. Her teeth snapped the tortilla chip in half. Instantly her tongue tasted irresistible saltiness mixed with luscious pineapple. A tang of lime came next, followed by the rich heat of jalapeno and snap of onion. The flavors were bursting as they called out from all over her mouth. With another chew, the minty cilantro cooled the sharp sting of pepper—a perfect finish.

This was a real meal. She smiled. "It's so good."

"And once again," Robert said, shoving supplies into his lunch bag. "A Rios Rancheros recipe makes the world a happier place."

The third, and final bell sounded. J'aime and Robert were officially late to class. The lunch ladies stared at their cafeteria stowaways as J'aime's only bite of bliss dissolved into her need to feed. Hunger rang throughout her whole body louder than any school bell.

J'aime reached for the salsa bowl. "Screw class. I'm gonna eat this whole thing right now."

Robert jerked the bowl away from her. "Hey, I've got to eat too. How about I trade you your homemade lunch for our cafeteria cooking?

She picked up her Styrofoam container and handed it to him. "It's not a fair trade."

"I'll be the judge of that," Robert said as he cracked open the lid.

J'aime waited for a flicker of disappointment to flash across his face. He was giving up juicy pineapple for stale pantry crackers. Robert lifted a peanut butter cracker sandwich from the to-go box. Instead of demanding the salsa and chips back, he took a bite.

"Perfect," he said with a smack of his lips. "Just the right amount of peanut butter."

Chapter 8

On-the-Go
Huevos Rancheros

FRIDAY. J'AIME AND ROBERT HAD THEIR FOURTH
cooking date.

No. Not date. Cooking lesson.

Not date.

Robert already had their ingredients spread out on the prep
table by the time J'aime got there. After the first pineapple salsa
lesson, J'aime had kind of figured that was it. She couldn't really
expect him to cook with her *every* lunch. But then Robert showed
up with cooking supplies on Wednesday. And then again on
Thursday. They didn't discuss a schedule or anything, but spending every lunch hour this week, teaching her how to peel an avocado seemed to be his plan, and that was totally fine with her.

Luckily, they'd kept the table in the back of the cafeteria to
themselves all week. Then again, it might not have been luck.
Guerilla cooking in the cafeteria was definitely not normal
Hannaville High behavior. Everyone had to notice that they were
slicing food rather than just putting it into their mouths and probably wanted to steer clear of the cooking freaks.

"I made the salsa last night," Robert said, pointing at a repur-
posed cottage cheese container and talking to her like they were
already mid-lesson. "It's a classic pico de gallo. It's good to practice

new recipes over and over again, but I figured learning two salsas in less than a week might be salsa overload."

"Hi to you too," J'aime said, slipping her Whole Foods bag into a chair. She liked his way of talking. When Robert was in cooking mode, he spoke "recipe" only. "So what are we making?"

"On-the-Go Huevos Rancheros. It's on-the-go because we don't have a stove. I modified the recipe to work with our lunch table situation." Robert looked up from his pile of ingredients stuffed in plastic baggies. "Wait. Have you ever had huevos rancheros?"

"No." J'aime dug in her tote bag for a moment and pulled out a can. "But will black beans go with it?"

Robert cocked his head to one side. "Are you suggesting an ingredient?"

After Wednesday's lesson, J'aime broke down and decided to sacrifice one of her food pantry finds. She didn't want to be a moocher, especially not with him. "I wanna, you know, contribute. I had a can of black beans, so I thought I'd bring them."

She waited to see if he was offended, but he actually looked impressed. "Black beans are perfect," Robert said. "I hope you brought a can opener."

J'aime reached back into her bag and pulled out her hand crank model. "Never go to school without it."

"Really?" he asked.

"Uh, no." She smiled.

"Don't wave that thing around too much. You'll make the security guard nervous," Robert picked up an egg. It was peeled and naked in the fluorescent lights. "Do you know how to hard boil eggs?"

J'aime wrinkled her nose at the glistening white oval. "I don't eat eggs."

"Eggs are the best. How can you not eat eggs?" he asked then switched into a Yoda-like voice. "There is no 'do not eat.' There is only 'eat.'"

J'aime tried not to grin. "No thanks, Jedi Chef. Buffet eggs always taste like Styrofoam. I don't like them."

"On buffets they use frozen egg yolks. Farm fresh eggs are amazing."

Robert sat the hard-boiled egg on her cutting board and added a second one. "These beauties are from my cousin's chickens. You're going to love eggs after this meal."

One of the spongy eggs rocked onto its side, moving an inch closer to J'aime. She Purelled her hands then started to crank open the black bean can. "I'm not making any promises." *And I'm definitely not eating those eggs*, she thought.

"I thought you wouldn't be picky about anything?" Robert asked.

She froze, mid-crank. *What's wrong with this guy?* Just because she got food for free didn't mean she liked *every*thing. Her stomach might not be choosy, but her taste buds had the right to be. She considered turning on her heel right then—but didn't do it. This is what she'd wanted, cooking lessons, right? If he wanted to be an ass, fine, then she'd put up with that. For now. She resumed cranking the can opener and didn't answer his question.

Robert laid a slice of pepper jack cheese on top of each tortilla. "If you want to be a chef, you have to try everything. There's no room for pickiness in a professional kitchen. You've got to try foods to know what 'cooked right' tastes like."

She hadn't told Robert she wanted to be a professional chef, not directly. She'd only asked him to teach her to cook. *How'd he know?*

She pulled the can's lid off. "Fine. I'll try a tiny bite of egg."

"Okay," he said back. "Down to business. For this recipe, we each have a couple whole wheat tortillas, topped with slices of pepper jack."

He opened the faded IGA cottage cheese container. "Go ahead and add one tablespoon of pico to the cheese."

A hot, peppery salsa scent floated up from the recycled container. "That's too spicy for me," J'aime said.

Robert handed her a stained white tablespoon. "Stop being such a baby and scoop. Make sure it's a big, spicy scoop too. I didn't make all this salsa for nothing."

J'aime took the measuring spoon from him and spread the chunky pico de gallo on top of each piece of cheese.

"Let's add your black beans next." Robert dug around in his backpack and produced a fork. "Use this to strain them or the liquid will make everything soggy. Technically, we should wash the beans to get the salt off; but hey, we're cooking in a school cafeteria, so anything goes."

J'aime scooped into the can, trying to balance beans on flat fork tines. She was in the middle of carefully sprinkling when Robert decided to make conversation.

"Are you going to try cooking at home this weekend?" he asked.

A bean slipped from her fork and landed on the table. Due to her lack of cookware, odds were, this weekend would be a feast of employee shift meals and casino kitchen "leftovers" her dad rescued before they hit the trash.

She finished distributing the beans. "I won't cook this weekend. We're busy, you know, working and stuff."

"What?" Robert asked. "You should cook. That's what this is all about." He popped a black bean into his mouth. "Why wouldn't you? You've got supplies."

J'aime's spine straightened. Even if she still had her saucepan, she'd eaten through most of her donation food. This can of black beans was about it, except for a jar of peanut butter and a few remaining crackers. Her dad had brought home some stray desserts. A couple of boxes of deep-fried cheesecake that was too old to sell at the casino. Last night she tried to pretend like the soggy desserts were invisible, but they kept losing their cloaking devices. Especially after she ate that last can of corn.

"Are you going to tell me what to do with these disgusting eggs, or what?" she asked, trying to change the subject.

"Fine," Robert sighed, pointing a plastic knife at the two hard-boiled eggs on J'aime's cutting board. "I've already peeled the hard-boiled eggs to make this go faster. I felt kind of bad about it because they are fun to peel." His finger traced the wide bottom part of the egg. "There's a hollow spot here under the shell, so you hit it there, but not too hard or your egg will explode all over the place."

"Talking about exploding eggs isn't helping," J'aime warned.

"Whatever. It's time to slice." He made a claw with his left hand and gently rested his fingertips on top of one of the eggs.

J'aime imitated him. The surface of her egg was just how she expected it to feel: squishy and clammy, like one of those blow-up bouncy rooms left out in the rain.

Has anyone ever thrown up from just touching an egg? J'aime did not want to be the first. They started slowly cutting off the narrow tip of their eggs. A pure white circle toppled from her knife. She cut the egg slices too thin at first. By the time she started the second egg, she had a few solid yellow yolk bullseyes almost a half-inch thick.

"Nice," Robert said. "Now lay the slices right down the middle of the salsa and beans."

The yolk crumbled as she removed the egg from her cutting board. Parts of her body that didn't even have to taste the damn thing were freaking out. Goosebumps crawled up her arms as if they were scrambling away from the egg.

Robert lifted the corner of a tortilla. "It's already cold. The tortilla might tear when you fold it."

J'aime pinched the edge of one of the flat wheat circles. "Already cold? Do you have a microwave in your locker?"

"Mrs. Maupin let me use the one in the biology lab," he said.

J'aime dropped her tortilla. "I don't even want to think about that."

Robert tapped her cutting board with his knife, instructor like. "Take the edge of your tortilla and wrap it around your filling, then tuck it under like you're making a bed."

J'aime pulled the right-side edge of her tortilla over the thickest part of her filling. As predicted, it tore. The white curve of an egg slice peeked through the rough tear.

"It'll be alright," Robert said. "Now take the other end and pull it over the top. All you have to do now is fold the tortilla up from the bottom then flip it over."

J'aime took a deep breath, folded, and flipped. Salsa dripped out of the open end of the pudgy tortilla, and she tried to scoot the chunks back inside with her fingers.

"Don't worry. Salsa always falls out." Robert picked up his portable huevos rancheros and took a massive bite. "Try it," he said.

There was nothing else for her to do but eat a dreaded hard-boiled egg. She lifted a soft, bundled tortilla from her plate. Spicy jalapeno caught her nose again. She inched her teeth out and nibbled on the bland wheat folds.

"Ah, come on," Robert protested. "Take a big bite or cooking lessons are over."

Gross. Gross. Gross, she thought. Why did it have to be eggs?

She forced her lips open. Her teeth parted. She took a huge chomp. Tomato oozed with each chew, mixing with the simple richness of black beans. A smoldering heat came from the pepper jack cheese and salsa. It was hot like a hot summer sidewalk, scorching but bearable.

Then her taste buds found the egg. It was moist, smooth, and very un-Styrofoam. Blending with the whole-wheat grains, the hard-boiled egg gave off a salted, honey-butter flavor.

"Well?" Robert asked, watching her eat.

Bliss, it's freaking bliss, she wanted to yell, but she wiped a yolk crumb off her lip instead. "Not bad."

"Not bad?" Robert laughed. A short curl on the front of his forehead bounced back and forth. He took another bite himself.

The cafeteria chattered while they chewed. Now that the cooking was over, J'aime felt like it was her turn to make chitchat. God. This was not her specialty. Her folded huevos rancheros called to her, telling her to forget about making friend talk and focus on eating. She looked over at Robert's old table. The farmie cowboys were joking around, completely forgetting about this side of the cafeteria. Perhaps people were getting used to the cooking freaks in the back. She calmed her hunger, resting her tortilla near the crinkled edge of her paper plate, and whipped up her courage.

Clearing her throat, she said, "So, are you working this weekend?"

Robert swallowed a huge bite. "Not at the casino. My family's restaurant is selling street tacos at the Wagon Wheel Festival."

"Street tacos are cool."

He eyed her, trying to figure out where this was going. "I guess so."

J'aime squeezed her tortilla, and pico de gallo spilled out. "Working at your own restaurant must be pretty awesome."

"My mom's restaurant," Robert corrected. "Big difference."

"I know you don't own it," J'aime added quickly. "I meant cooking in your family's place has got to be better than—"

"I don't cook at Rios Rancheros anymore," he said, cutting off the conversation then filling his mouth with egg and cheese. His eyes were entirely focused on the paper plate in front of him. His body was hunched. Gone was the cheerful cooking Robert. Clearly, he didn't want to talk about this topic.

But why wasn't he chef-ing at Rios Rancheros?

J'aime couldn't help herself. "Is it because you cook at the casino now?"

A drip of salsa slid out of Robert's mouth. He caught the tomato chunk with his tongue. "The casino's not serious cooking. You know that. I don't cook at Rios Rancheros because I'm not allowed to."

"You're banned from your own kitchen?" she asked in disbelief. "Where did you prep all this?"

Robert pushed his plate away and crossed his arms. "I didn't say I was banned. I cook in Abbi's kitchen mostly." With an irritated swipe, he grabbed his lunch bag. "Listen, we better pick this stuff up."

J'aime glanced at her mostly uneaten huevos rancheros and the cafeteria clock. "No way. We've got like five minutes."

A hasty rip of black Velcro cut off her protest.

"I was late to English on Wednesday," Robert said, snapping the lid onto the salsa container and shoving it into the blue lunch bag. "Mr. Smith won't like two tardies in a row."

She watched him scoop supplies into his backpack. She might be a lame cook, but she was becoming an observant one. The hurried, careless way he was stashing his cooking tools had nothing to do with too many tardies and everything to do with Rios Rancheros.

Interesting. J'aime crammed in another bite of her lunch. *Even families with full fridges have things they want to hide.*

Chapter 9
Lunch Lady Surprise

THE FIRST LUNCH BELL RANG. HALF OF HER On-the-Go Huevos Rancheros waited for her. It would be another dine and dash to geometry. Once they were through the cafeteria doors, she and Robert would go their separate ways, dripping pico de gallo behind them.

If they walked to class together, even for a little bit, he might tell her what was up with his mom and their restaurant. From what she could taste, he was an amazing cook. So why wasn't he cooking there? Not that it was any of her business. Not that she wanted him asking around about her mom either.

J'aime tossed a paper towel onto the lunch tray they used to collect cooking trash.

"Hey," a woman's voice commanded.

J'aime looked up. Hands on her hips, the tattooed lunch lady stood next to their cooking table. A chill of authority passed over their tidied space. If huevos rancheros could quiver, J'aime knew the hard-boiled eggs would be shaking in their crumbly yolks.

The lunch lady waved her plastic-gloved finger at their cleaned-up cooking station. "What are you guys doing?" she asked.

Robert stood up a little straighter and picked up the trash tray. "Bussing our lunch table."

"Right," the lunch lady said, flicking her eyes over at the thermal lunch bag. "From the line over there it looked to me like you're doing food prep. Do you have knives in that bag?"

J'aime picked up the rest of her lunch. If she was going to get into trouble she was at least going to eat. She took a huge bite from her tortilla. After one successful week, cooking lessons were already over—a failed soft opening. If the casino had policies about chopping onions, did schools have them about student's cooking their own lunches? She chewed fast. *Please, don't let her drag us to the office and make my on-the-go huevos rancheros live up to their name.*

A metal serving spoon clattered in the background. The lunch lady ignored it. Waiting for Robert's answer. He rummaged around on the trash tray and produced a plastic knife.

The young woman gave him a nod of approval. "You know," she said to Robert, "You're a pretty good cook."

He dropped the plastic ware back into the trash heap. "I grew up in a restaurant," he answered, then flashed that smirk of his. "I better know how to chop."

J'aime groaned. That was the same line he'd used on her. The principal's office was up two flights of stairs. Climbing and gorging eggs at the same time would be like doing a Minute-to-Win-It challenge. She took another huge bite.

"Your family owns Rios Rancheros, right?" the lunch lady asked.

Robert causally nodded his head like it was nothing to have a restaurant with your last name on it.

"The Rancheros taught you right," the lunch lady said. "Even from way over there I can tell you've got good skills." She waved her arm at the cafeteria, giving her tattooed birds a chance to fly. "Why are you cooking in here?"

Robert pointed his thumb at J'aime. "We both work after school. Lunch hour was the easiest time to get together."

With her mouth full, J'aime mumbled the only explanation a school might not punish. "He's teaching me to cook." She swallowed. "It's educational."

The lunch lady stared at J'aime as if chunks of salsa were spraying out of her mouth. The warning bell rang, rattling through the emptying cafeteria.

"Meet me here right after school, at 3:30." the lunch lady said. "I might have something that'll help you out."

"We've got work," Robert repeated, but the young woman was already walking away, headed in the direction of the leftover tater tots.

"You'll want to squeeze it in," she yelled over her shoulder.

J'aime snarfed down her last bite. "Let's get out of here."

Robert watched the lunch lady disappear into the cafeteria kitchen. "What do you think she's got for us?"

"I don't care. I just don't want her to come back here." J'aime pushed his lunch bag at him. "Come on, you don't want to be late to English remember."

Robert noticed her empty plate. "Whoa. You ate your whole lunch while we were talking?

"Lunch ladies are trouble." She crammed her extra salad into her Whole Foods bag and slipped it onto her shoulder.

The final bell rang. They were late again. They ran out of the cafeteria. As he hurried, Robert's leftover huevos rancheros bounced in a shallow pool of salsa on his paper plate.

"I gotta know," he said. "She can't say something like that and walk away."

"Oh, yes she can."

With his free hand, Robert slammed the trash tray against the can. "What's wrong with you? Did a lunch lady spit in your pizza or something?"

J'aime ignored him. How could she explain that this was just lunch lady bait? Whatever the tattooed woman was offering would only get them in trouble. She slowed her pace as Robert speeded ahead. Watching his tennis shoes jog away, she came up with an excuse to get out of their doomed after school meet-up.

"I ride the bus," she shouted. "I can't miss it."

Robert waved at her from down the locker-lined hallway. He yelled back, "See you at 3:30."

•

Hannaville school bus number seventy-six departed the circle parking lot at 4:00 p.m. If J'aime wasn't on it, she'd be late to work again. A habit she wasn't too excited to continue.

"Five minutes," she promised herself. "Ten minutes max." That was all she could give this doomed lunch lady meet-up.

The basement hallway was eerily still. Schools were never this quiet. The students had scattered to buses, cars, and after school activities—sanctioned or otherwise. J'aime sneaked a peek into the round window cut into the cafeteria door. Through the fog of cleaner spots, she saw the tattooed lunch lady standing in the middle of the room. A janitor in a navy-blue zip-up uniform mopped the floor beside her. The lunch lady looked at her phone and then said something to the janitor. They both laughed.

Fast footsteps drumrolled down the hallway. *Robert*, J'aime thought.

After almost a week of cooking together, she was getting used to him—the way he moved, his general Robert-ness. That was a scary thought. J'aime didn't like getting used to people. There wasn't any point. He rounded the same corner he had disappeared around earlier. *I hope he waves at me.*

Halfway to her, he threw her the casual wave she was hoping for. Instead of waving back, she gave her notebook an undetectable hug.

"Is she here?" he asked between breaths.

J'aime peeked in again, watching the woman scroll. "She's in there."

The bright phone screen cast a spotlight on the woman's hairnet. "This isn't a good idea. I've had bad run-ins with lunch ladies."

"At least she didn't tell us to quit cooking in the cafeteria."

Not yet, J'aime thought.

"How can you have a bad run-in with a lunch lady?" Robert asked. "They aren't gang members. They're grandmas." He looked in the window too. "Okay, she's probably not a grandma. How old do you think she is?"

J'aime shrugged impatiently. "Like twenty-five? I don't know. If we're going to do this, can we just get it over with?"

Robert pulled open the door. "Don't worry. She's nice."

"Sure," J'aime said back. *I'll believe it never.*

They walked carefully across the mopped gleam of cafeteria tile. The janitor gave them a squeaky nod. "See ya tomorrow," he said to the lunch lady as he wheeled his water bucket over to another section of the room.

"See ya," the lunch lady answered. She slid her phone into the thin front pocket of her flowered apron and turned her attention to Robert and J'aime. "Hey, glad you two could make it."

"Of course!" Robert said.

"We can't stay long," J'aime added.

"Right. Lives to live. I get it," the lunch lady answered. "This will be quick, I promise," she said, waving for them to follow her.

When J'aime walked through the door to the school kitchen, she held her breath. No matter which school she went to, students rarely got to go beyond the food service window. The cafeteria kitchen was a forbidden place and there they were, Robert and J'aime walking through the shiny silver world of giant cooking kettles and scrubbed griddles.

They followed the tattooed lunch lady past a hand-washing sink and through a backdoor into a cramped, narrow hallway. Taking a metallic purple key clip from her apron pocket, she clicked open a door marked 4B.

In a flip, the buzz of fluorescent lights filled the room. Huddled in a corner was a group of objects draped in cream-colored sheets. There were so many lumps and bumps, J'aime couldn't tell what was hiding under the covers. The whole room had a strong storage-unit vibe to it.

Robert walked over to the other side of the room. "There are at least three cooking ranges in here."

A tall two-door refrigerator caught J'aime's eye. It was stainless steel from top to bottom—professional grade. J'aime moved closer to it. Reaching up, she ran her finger over the brand name. It was called True. Restaurant kitchens were loud, and this classroom was so quiet. J'aime tilted her head, brushing her ear against the cool steel exterior. She didn't care if she looked weird. She wanted to hear the motor of a professional appliance with such a worthy name, but all she heard was silence.

"That fridge isn't plugged in," the lunch lady said. "There's a forty-three cubic foot freezer too. They came from a restaurant auction."

"Which restaurant?" Robert asked

"The Pig and Pickle in Blackwater," she answered. "You can't have two barbeque joints in a small town like that. One of them had to go. The Pig and Pickle was too big for its britches."

J'aime stopped her appliance awe. "Why do you know so much about this fridge?"

Taking a rag out of another apron pocket, the lunch lady gave the metal counter a proud wipe. "This used to be my classroom."

"You're a teacher?" Robert asked.

"I graduated from college three years ago," she said, leaning against a cool stove. "Moved back to Hannaville to be the new Family and Consumer Sciences teacher when Mrs. Price retired."

J'aime glanced over at the lumpy covered objects. Sewing machines. They had to be sewing machines.

"I taught for a year, then the state cut my funding," the lunch lady explained. "It was either me or art class, and art won." She turned a dial on a stove and a blue flame perked up under a burner. "Now all the equipment sits here getting dusty." The thin smell of gas tainted the room. "The kitchen staff gets to school around 5:30 in the morning. I'll unlock the door first thing when I get here."

"Are you saying," J'aime said, "you're going to let us cook in here?"

The lunch lady turned a dial, and the spurt of stove flame flickered out. "Heck yeah, I'm gonna let you cook in here. Why not? This room is waiting for chefs-in-training."

Robert opened an oven and stuck his head inside. "They aren't restaurant grade, but close." He shut the door again. "

"Everything is basically new." The lunch lady sighed. "The sinks, and prep stations we got at discount from a restaurant supply store. Like I said, the students only used them for a year. The crazy school district spent grant dollars to update this whole classroom then shut it down." She paused. "Are you in?"

No matter what this fridge's name was, this situation was too good to be true. In the middle of Hannaville High, she and Robert had stumbled into a gingerbread house in the woods. J'aime glanced at Robert. The shine of commercial steel sparkled in his eyes.

"Won't people notice us?" he asked.

The lunch lady crossed her arms. "We'll be cooking in the main kitchen at the same time. Your food smells should mix right in with ours. Plus, the other lunch ladies will love having you around. All you have to do is promise me that you'll make it look this clean when you leave, and you won't burn the school down."

Robert nudged J'aime out of the way and pulled open one of the refrigerator doors. "Are you sure it still works?"

"It'll be cold by dawn," the lunch lady said firmly, trying to hurry up the kicking of the tires.

Robert closed the heavy insulated door. "We're in," he said, without looking at J'aime. He didn't even ask her opinion.

"I don't know," J'aime said. Her lunch lady apprehension reared its ugly head. "We'll get in trouble."

"C'mon. You have to be in," Robert pleaded. "How are we supposed to sauté? That's not happening in the cafeteria."

The lunch lady laughed. "Don't sweat it. I've got your back."

"That's what I'm worried about," J'aime mumbled.

"The school system isn't going to fire me. I'm the only lunch lady under fifty in the entire county." She lifted her arm and flexed her bird-painted muscle. "Someone's gotta lift boxes without straining her back."

The lunch lady gave them a serious look over the bridge of her nose. "In the morning, you have to be out of here fifteen minutes before the first bell rings. Agreed?"

"Agreed," Robert said.

"Good," the lunch lady answered, flipping off the lights.

"Shouldn't we talk about this some more?" J'aime whispered to Robert as they left the discarded classroom.

"Don't be crazy," he whispered back.

But J'aime knew she wasn't being irrational. All the fairy tales teach you that gingerbread houses cannot be trusted. She also knew that learning how to really cook required heat. They couldn't cook at the duplex. J'aime didn't want Robert to see her mac-and-cheese kitchen, and his place seemed to be off limits. Cooking in the abandoned kitchen was the only answer. When the principal finally caught them sautéing vegetables before school, she'd remember this moment.

There was also the transportation reality check. She couldn't drive, and school buses didn't run on J'aime's personal cooking schedule. In order to cook at 5:30 in the morning, she was going to have to walk through Hannaville in the creepy predawn darkness. Safety First was not the motto of this situation.

Back in the hallway, the lunch lady pushed open a nearby back door. Suddenly the narrow space was filled with parking-lot glare. "I'll leave this open for you. The room will be unlocked on Monday morning. If you have any questions, stick your head in the kitchen and yell for me. You can get to your buses from here. My name's Lyn, by the way. Are you both seniors? What are your names?"

They walked through the doorway. From the parking lot, Robert stuck his hand back through the door, and Lyn shook it. "Yeah, I'm a senior and I'm Robert."

J'aime kept her hands to herself. "J'aime McWilliams. I'm a junior," she answered.

Lyn smiled. "*Bien, ma chère*," she said with a funny French accent. "You're a lucky gal to have a French name. The best food comes from France, you know."

"Ah! *La belle France*." Robert said with a bad French accent. "See ya tomorrow, Lyn."

The back door closed, but J'aime's mouth was hanging wide open. "No one ever gets my name," she said in shocked disbelief.

"I told you," Robert grinned. "Lunch ladies aren't evil."

Chapter 10
Simple Tortilla Soup

THE SOUR BURN OF CIGARETTE SMOKE CURLED through the layers of her mother's T-shirt quilt. Sleeping on her side, she squeezed her head under the edge of the blanket, trying to keep Saturday morning from waking the rest of her body. Cigarette smoke meant one thing: Dad was home.

J'aime blinked her eyes open. Cotton sun filtered through the thin stuffing of the quilt. The sleeves of her polo shirt pinched her armpits; her uniform was twisted from tossing and turning. The stitched steamboat logo that should have been above her heart had drifted across her chest. Not only did she fall asleep in her uniform, she fell asleep in the recliner.

With a cushioned thump, J'aime pushed the recliner upright and took a few steps away from the chair. She tugged the quilt back up and wrapped it around her body burrito-style. Even though they hadn't made burritos yet, Robert liked to talk about the pros and cons of Chipotle "rolling." Actually, what he did was rant about the chain's excessive tortilla stuffing and how it affected the way you wrapped a burrito. J'aime honestly didn't care—a stuffed burrito was a good burrito.

A spring breeze blew through the screen door, sending more cigarette burn into the room. Through the honeycomb grate of the metal door, J'aime saw her dad. The back of his shirt was creased with restless sleep, and his shoulders were hunched. Facing the empty street, he took another tired drag then tapped his cigarette on the front stoop. He looked rough like he'd worked all night, and he probably had. At least he didn't fall asleep in his uniform.

Shuffling her blanket burrito-self over to the screen door, J'aime reached for the handle, but her dad knew she was already there.

"Morning," he said as gray smoke swirled up from his left hand.

She creaked the door open and stepped outside. Flaking red paint coated the porch floor, with the occasional clammy patches of gray cement dotting the surface. Jagged little paint flakes jabbed her bare feet as she stepped toward her dad.

"You've got a bed, you know," her dad said then took a drag.

J'aime pulled the quilt a little tighter around her polo shirt. Before she could say anything, a steady slap of shoes hitting pavement echoed off the trees. The McWilliamses turned their heads to peer around the front porch pole and look down the street. No-Crusts Girl bobbed into view, jogging her way up Fifth Street.

J'aime pulled back, trying to make herself impossibly blend in with the brick front porch. Luckily, camouflage wasn't necessary. No-Crusts Girl was in the zone. Her eyes focused on the slow incline of the road, keeping her on her path. She was all business even down to her water bottles, tiny plastic canteens perched on a band secured to her hips. J'aime swore she could almost hear them sloshing. The girl's green sneakers clipped by oblivious to her audience. No-Crusts Girl was a lone runner and a lone eater.

We both know what it is like to be alone most of the time, J'aime thought.

If she were braver, she'd ask the girl to eat lunch with her and Robert. *It would be nice to have more friends.* The thought surprised J'aime. For so many years she'd avoided sitting with anyone at lunch, and now she enjoyed having a friend to eat with.

But Robert wasn't technically her friend, right? He was teaching her. Now that they had access to a secret kitchen, Robert had no reason to sit with her at lunch. Why wouldn't he ditch her for his farmie friends? After all, she'd only asked him to cook with her, not eat.

Maybe cultivating another friendship isn't such a bad idea, J'aime thought.

"That girl's already jogged by here twice," her father whispered as if No-Crusts Girl could hear him from the porch. "She's like a goldfish swimming laps in a bowl."

"Twice?" J'aime whispered back as No-Crusts Girl passed their neighbor's duplex. "What time is it?"

"Ten o'clock in the a.m.," her dad answered.

J'aime moaned. "The pantry. I forgot to set my alarm."

"Forget it," her dad said, taking one last drag. "I brought you chicken fingers from the buffet. Seth overcooked them. They're chewy, but all right."

Scorched, rubbery chicken fingers weren't J'aime's idea of an ideal breakfast. Later in the day, when she was running on empty, they'd be a lot more tempting.

Her dad snuffed out the butt end of his cigarette. "I've got to go in early today. A few cooks are out. There's some race out at the county fairgrounds, a mud run. I said they could go only because I have no idea what a mud run is?"

J'aime poked at the flaking porch paint with her toe. The casino buffet had been open for over a while now. Her dad's schedule should have leveled out. Instead, he basically came home and slept for a few hours, showered, then went back to work. He blamed it on being a salaried employee, saying his bosses can take advantage of him and not pay overtime, but J'aime knew a convenient excuse when she heard it. If he had time off and was awake, he'd have to finally go through her mother's boxes.

The single tower of boxes waited for him in the living room next to the recliner: an unintentional shrine. For five years, J'aime watched the cardboard slowly cave like a science fair project. Honestly, neither one of them had the heart to weed through the past.

Her dad glanced over his shoulder. "I almost forgot. That Rios kid from work sent you something. He made sure to tell me to put it in the fridge. Like I don't know anything about time and temperature control."

A light kicked on inside J'aime's body. "Robert gave me something?" she asked.

Her dad turned around to study her. "How do you know this guy?"

J'aime nervously played with the edge of the quilt. "We have the same lunch hour at school. It's no big deal."

But it was. Robert probably sent her home-cooked food. She wanted whatever was in the fridge to be a present from him, not a charity gift. The only way she could stop being his personal volunteer project was to help pay for ingredients or bring her own. She'd missed her chance to go to the pantry today. Since bringing food to cooking lessons wasn't an option this week, she'd have to take a more desperate step.

"Hey, Dad? I was wondering, could I keep some money from my paycheck?"

Her dad turned back around and longingly looked at his snuffed-out cigarette. "No way. All the money goes to the jar. You know that."

J'aime twisted the corner of the blanket. "You're a manager now. I thought maybe we could afford it. I just need like ten dollars."

The second she said the amount she regretted it.

"Have you lost your mind?" her dad sighed. He shook his head and was on the desperate verge of dusting off the cigarette stub. "How many phone calls did you get from those bloodsucking collectors yesterday?"

J'aime looked down at the way the blocks of the T-shirt quilt rumpled around her bare feet. The answer was eight. Her dad had a firm, but insane belief that if he blocked the creditors calls on either of their phones then the money leeches would know how to track their movements and read their text messages. According to him, it was all part of a global financial conspiracy theory he'd read about online.

In reality, this meant that J'aime's inherited phone buzzed constantly. It felt like the creditors called about her lunch debt all day. She had collector's area codes memorized and ignored every single buzz just like she was supposed to. It boggled her mind that school systems would spend so much effort to track down less than $2,000 from one student.

"I've got a new plan to get them off our backs, but we gotta keep saving cash," her dad said. "What do you need money for, anyway? You never ask for money."

"I was going to buy some food," J'aime said tentatively.

"Food? I brought you chicken fingers. What more could you want?" Her dad waved a hand at the porch ceiling, "I've got my own priorities to deal with like paying rent."

J'aime took a step back. This was pointless. Her dad was getting all puffed up. Next he'd start in on her ungrateful attitude toward deep-fried cheesecake. The last thing he'd understand was cooking ingredients. "Forget it," she said.

"It's because of that Rios kid," he muttered. "He better watch himself. I can fire his—"

J'aime went into the house and quietly shut the door on him. A slam would feel good, but only give him what he wanted. She knew where this conversation was going, and she had to defuse it, turn it off. The pattern of her parents' fighting was imprinted on her heart. Shouting was her mom and dad's favorite way of communicating. First she'd get him frustrated, then he'd get irrational, then she'd call him names, then he'd yell louder. J'aime didn't want to reenact that.

Dragging the quilt behind her, J'aime hurried into the kitchen. Homemade food was waiting for her. With a tug, the refrigerator door popped open. In the yellow glow was the expected to-go box. Next to it was a round blue storage container filled to the top with liquid. The contents were a hazy shade of purple. J'aime paused. What food was purple besides eggplant?

Did it really matter?

Reaching in, she grabbed the container. A folded note was stuck to the top. The sticky edge of the tape kept the paper in place, concealing the message at the same time. At least her dad hadn't read it. Unscrewing the lid, she caught the deep scent of tomatoes and sautéed onions. She smiled. Corn kernels and bits of cilantro floated on top of bright red broth. The blueness of the container made the soup look purple.

Careful not to spill a drop, she set it down on the counter next to the fridge. Peeling the note off, J'aime discovered the paper was really an envelope with the Rios Rancheros logo proudly printed on the pointed flap. Nothing was inside. She flipped it over and found Robert's message in the address space.

Be ready at 5:30 a.m. Monday. I'll pick you up.

P.S. This is tortilla soup. Heat it up. Obviously.

P.P.S. It's better with sour cream on top. No regrets. Do it.

Chapter 11
Dixie Fried

THE STREETLIGHT NEAR THE SIDEWALK SPUT-
tered with a tired 5:00 a.m. flicker. Stretched shadows on the street
twitched as J'aime waited for the towering streetlight to blink out.
The lamp glowed on; Hannaville was still too dark for the sensor
to turn the light completely off. Cold cement cut through the back
of her leggings.

Twenty minutes of sitting on the porch steps in the predawn
darkness was starting to get to her. J'aime watched the glowing
streetlight again. She'd never seen one shut off before. Suddenly
the idea of catching the city light blinking out at dawn had a
shooting-star quality to it.

A loose wreath of her dad's used cigarette butts was scattered
around her legs, their snuffed white stubs reflecting any hint
of light that hit the porch steps. He was never up when she left
for school; but this morning she had a feeling that if she didn't
leave a note, he'd wake up the moment she got in Robert's car.
Their genetic parent-child radar had been on alert all weekend
due to Robert's soup. Hopefully, the excuse about a before-school
activity she'd tucked into his cigarette box would keep him from
storming after her. Not that he'd ever done that either, but right
now, his *dad-ness* seemed to be set on high.

J'aime cradled the empty blue plastic container in her lap. Trac-
ing the clean lid with her finger, she felt every crevice and cranny
in the brand name stamped into the plastic. She'd scrubbed those

letters for at least fifteen minutes to get out all the dried soup. Licking the tricky spots clean didn't pop into her mind until the leftover droplets were already swirling regretfully down the drain. She'd gotten two meals out of Robert's soup. Using a coffee mug instead of a bowl helped stretch it out. For once, her family's lack of tableware paid off.

That simple tortilla soup had stirred things up. J'aime couldn't believe how irritated her dad had been about Robert, or how the soup warmed her whole body straight to her toes. This idea alone made J'aime change her shirt three times that morning. She flipped the clean container over like a Magic 8-Ball. The only floating answer she got was the clear stamp of the manufacturer's copyright.

The soup was a sad hungry-girl donation, nothing more, nothing less. J'aime stuffed the plastic storage container into her Whole Foods bag. Her nerves should really be focused on the fact she was about to break school rules to cook in an abandoned kitchen. Heat. Stove. Flame. Fire. She was going to master all those elements, and preferably not burn Hannaville High to the ground. She was minutes away from igniting a pilot light and chopping something tasty in an almost professional-grade kitchen. She couldn't let her fantasies about soup send her off into holding hands la-la land.

Robert is just my chef, my teacher, that's it.

The whirr of a car accelerating broke the sleeping silence. Standing up, J'aime peered down the street. Headlights bounced back at her as they cruised up the short incline toward her curb. A white Toyota truck, miniature compared to the diesel-fueled Chevys that usually roared by, rolled to a stop in front of her duplex. Dim gauges highlighted a shadow person behind the wheel. J'aime sucked in her breath. It had to be him.

Walking through the damp grass, she made her way to the truck. Before she reached the crumbling sidewalk, the passenger-side door swung open by itself. Inside the Toyota, the soft dome light shined a spotlight on Robert's outstretched arm as it followed his body back over to the driver's seat.

J'aime stopped in the yard, dew sprinkling her black leggings. *He opened the door for me. No boy has ever opened a door for me.*

"Morning," Robert yawned, but it looked fake, like he was trying to be funny.

"Hi," J'aime said. She set her tote on the floorboard and slid onto a Duct Tape-patched passenger seat. "Thanks for picking me up."

"No worries." He was wearing a T-shirt and jeans, like usual. His hair still looked a little damp from the shower, or maybe his gel was just very fresh. "It's way early. Hope you weren't waiting outside too long?"

J'aime shut her door. The slam caused a rubber key chain dangling from the rearview mirror to swing back and forth. A grinning skull with the flaming words "Live Free or Die" swayed above J'aime's head. The whole fiery skeleton mantra seemed very un-Robert—but then, she didn't know him that well. Maybe his whole bedroom was decked out in flaming skull wallpaper?

"No, I didn't wait long," she answered. "And thanks for the soup too. It was really good."

He shifted the truck into drive. "Tortilla soup. Abbi makes a big batch of it every weekend. I thought you'd like it."

The truck turned around in a neighbor's driveway, and J'aime's stomach flipped around with it. "Every weekend?" she heard herself asking.

Robert drove down the street and came to a complete stop at the stop sign. There was zero traffic, but he didn't roll through. "Soup's kind of her thing. Did you get enough? I mean, was it enough for a whole meal?"

She looked out the passenger window. An orange tabby dashed across the street. J'aime wished he wouldn't ask things like that. *Enough? There's never enough.* She'd gotten so hungry at work this weekend she'd nibbled off of bused plates in back. It was a habit she'd picked up from other waiters at other buffets. When half a steak is left on the table and there isn't enough food or work breaks in your life, why wouldn't you take a bite? Would Robert understand that? J'aime didn't want to find out at 5:45 in the morning. Yes, she gets her food from a food pantry. That doesn't mean she wants to talk about it.

"The flavor was really good," she said. "The cilantro stood out."

Robert grinned at her, completely clueless that he crossed a line. His white T-shirt glowed in the dashboard lights. "Says the Cilantro Queen. Have you patented that hand rubbing move yet?" he teased and pulled the truck out onto Ashley Road.

J'aime hid her smile. Cilantro Queen had a nice ring to it. Reaching up, she twisted the rubber skull, making it spin and sway at the same time. "You're big on living free?" she asked.

Robert stopped the swinging skull and put his hands back at ten and two on the steering wheel. "Isn't everyone?" he asked. "That's Chuck. He's my copilot."

"Chuck?"

"Ground Chuck." Robert took his eyes off the road for a second, checking for a laugh or a grin, but she gave him an eye roll instead. "He came with the truck. We used to sell produce at the farmers market. When the city closed it, my uncle loaned me this baby."

"Do you have to give the truck back?"

"It's sort of like a permanent loan, right, Chuck?" he said, pointing at the skull. It bobbed up and down as Robert drove over a speed bump.

"See, Chuck nodded. We're totally on the same page."

J'aime couldn't help but laugh. "You're super weird, you know that?"

"Super weird translates into creative culinary genius," he said. He turned the car left onto Main Street then fiddled with an iPod laying on the bench seat they shared. The screen faded as a golden oldie strummed from the tiny truck speakers.

"Hey, do you like rockabilly songs?"

"We're gonna talk music now?" J'aime asked uncomfortably. "I'm not big into music, generally speaking."

"Rockabilly isn't general, it's a genre." He turned the volume up.

A twangy, fast guitar plucked away in the background while the rest of the band thumped out a rock beat. A man's voice sang something about being "Dixie Fried."

J'aime had no idea what that meant. Was it a beer batter or something?

"I'm picturing a fried fish basket," she said. "Bar food and guys on motorcycles in really old movies."

"I don't know about the fish basket, but the bikers are right."

He was quiet for a second, listening to the end of the song. "It's vintage rock. You know, like Carl Perkins, young Elvis." His thumb turned the iPod back down. "Anyway, I like it. My uncle is in a rockabilly band called The Red Hot Mo's. He played Chicago last year. I thought maybe you'd heard of them," he added, "or saw their poster around town?"

Clearly Robert had never been to Chicago. Spotting a random band poster in a city that size was like trying to find a grain of rice in a gallon of sprinkles. "Was it the same uncle who gave you this truck?" she asked.

Robert shrugged. "I have a lot of uncles."

"How many people are in your family?"

"In the whole entire family? I don't know, a lot," he said, then clarified. "In my family-family, I've got my parents and my four sisters. They're all older than me. I was kind of a late baby. What about you?"

Through the windshield, passing yellow lines divided the street in front of them. J'aime looked down at her seatbelt buckle. The truck was less dark than when she got in, and she could feel Robert watching her for an answer. A nervous, tell-all floaty feeling tempted her lips. She wanted to say truths her dad wouldn't want her discussing with one of his employees.

"There used to be three of us," she explained.

"Used to be?"

"My mom died five years ago. Now there's just my dad and me."

Robert quickly looked out at Main Street. "Oh," he said, his forehead wrinkled, and his voice was softer. "Sorry."

J'aime tugged on her T-shirt, smoothing the wrinkles. "My dad doesn't like to talk about it." She shrugged. "I guess sometimes I need to say it out loud. Make it real."

Robert's hands loosened on the steering wheel, and J'aime could tell he was only half listening and mostly imagining a world without his mother.

"My mom's in charge of everything," he said. "I mean literally everything. Our restaurant, our family, every idea for a better Rios Rancheros future comes from her. My dad is a more laid back, very go-with-the-flow. I guess that's how they balance each other out."

Outside J'aime's passenger window, the low, square skyline of Hannaville barely stood out against the orange sky. Hanging in front of vacant buildings and shops, dark tubes of busted neon signs caught the glow of the city streetlights. Hannaville's downtown was so empty it didn't feel like a town, just nothingness. J'aime shuddered. Abandoned buildings gave her the creeps. In Chicago, she'd avoided them. She'd seen families from food pantries hiding out in the safe shadows of those hollow rooms. Ready for demolition, the half-open doors felt like they were waiting to welcome her when her dad's employment luck finally ran out.

Robert pressed on the gas, barely creeping above twenty-five. J'aime watched the dusty storefront windows go by. Then all at once, like candles on birthday cake, every streetlamp magically blinked out at the same time.

J'aime gasped.

"What?" Robert asked, braking in the middle of the road.

"Nothing," she flustered. "I, I just saw something."

"There's no one out here but us." Robert craned his head out the driver's side window. "Did I almost hit a squirrel?"

"No. The streetlights just . . ." She wanted to bury her head in the glove box. "Never mind. Keep driving. I don't want us to be late."

"We're like five seconds away from school." Robert drove over another speed bump. "First you think trusting Lyn is a bad idea, and now you don't want us to be late to meet her? I can't keep up with you, J'aime McWilliams."

Chapter 12

Spinach and Cheese Quesadillas

A DOZEN CARS HUDDLED TOGETHER ON THE blacktop parking lot behind Hannaville High. Dew beaded the parked cars' windshields, giving them a fresh coat of water before the sun spent the day heating up the glass. Robert pulled in next to them. He put the truck in park and flicked the clean soup container in J'aime's lap. "Bring that with you. We might need it."

As he unbuckled his seatbelt, J'aime dug into her cardigan pocket and pulled out a neatly folded five-dollar bill. "Hey, listen," she said, trying to steady her voice. "I want to pay you. I know it's not enough." She held out the money to Robert. The five bucks was a random tip she'd gotten on Saturday night. A sweet old man went back to the buffet five times and insisted on paying for her plate-dealing services. J'aime's dad had been on the other side of the sneeze guard when the tip happened. They both knew where that money was supposed to go, but J'aime hadn't handed it over to the jar yet.

Robert ignored the cash. "I'm not taking that." He opened his truck door and slid out.

J'aime waved the money at him while he grabbed his backpack. "You have to take it. I need to pay you back for the ingredients."

She leaned across the bench after him until her seatbelt snagged. Robert slammed the driver's door shut.

"Fine," J'aime muttered, sticking the folded money in between the dangling skull and the rubber, flaming motto.

Outside the windshield, Robert shook his head. "I'm just going to give it back to you," he said as she got out of the car.

She ignored him. Picking up her Whole Foods bag, she shut the car door on the cash. *I hope nobody breaks into the car and steals it. That would be my luck.* Or would it be karma, since she was practically stealing from her dad's savings in the first place? There were hundreds of dollars inside that pickle jar, why couldn't she just keep five of it? Her dad would ask her about the tip—guaranteed. The question was, how long would it take?

Walking toward the rear entrance of the school, Robert jogged ahead of her, glancing over his shoulder twice to see if she was chasing him.

"Boys, boys, boys," she chanted quietly, forcing herself to hang back. Visions of the mysterious Abbi filled her mind. She had no idea what this girl looked like, but she imagined the worst-case scenario. Adorable. Thin. In cute vintage clothes with a wooden mixing spoon in her hand and a miraculous bowl of tortilla soup in the other, a dream girlfriend for a chef like Robert.

When J'aime reached the back door, the birds were finally chirping, and Robert was tugging hard on the locked handle.

She hurried down the basement steps. "Is it locked? Did Lyn forget?"

Robert gave the door another helpless pull.

"I guess you were right," he sighed, taking a step back. "At least we won't get into trouble now."

J'aime pictured the gas burner flaring. The stove was right there on the other side of that door. They were so close to real cooking. She was afraid the situation would turn into a big old lunch lady trap, but at this moment, she was more excited to cook then she was worried about being sent to the principal's office.

"Typical lunch lady crap," she muttered, reaching for the door handle. Using all her disappointment, she pulled it hard. She waited to feel the jerk of the lock, but instead her hand easily yanked the door open. It flew back, clanking against the metal railing lining the short steps.

"Whoa," Robert said. "You're stronger than you look."

"It wasn't locked. You said it was locked."

"I pretended it was locked."

She shoved him lightly. Her hands hit his backpack.

Robert recoiled. "Hold your wrath!" he whisper-shouted. "You'll bruise the tortillas." He held the door open for her like a *maître d'* at a Michelin-starred restaurant, and her irritation deflated into a smile.

At the end of the basement hallway a drum-sized stockpot propped open the cafeteria kitchen door. In the wedge of fluorescent light, flashes of lunch ladies passed by, their black tennis shoes walking back and forth as they prepped for cooking. Clattering pans echoed down the hallway.

Robert and J'aime hesitated by the backdoor then ran for the home ec room.

With a swift shutting of the door and a flick of the lights, the gleaming classroom was all theirs. The oven clocks even glowed the right time, 6:01 a.m.

Robert pulled open a refrigerator door and stuck his head inside. "It's cold. Lyn kept her promise."

J'aime hurried over to check out the fridge. Robert wandered away, but she held the door open, listening to the gentle hum of a True appliance voice. Underneath the generic, steady fan was a low, barely audible *Om*. The sound vibrated like a hidden yogi was chanting in the gears. Of course, anything named True, even a hulking chill refrigerator, would have to be a little Zen.

Robert lifted two navy-blue aprons off the counter. Hannaville High's pirate mascot was printed on the front. "They must be for classroom use," he said.

J'aime closed the fridge door. She grabbed the aprons and inspected them. "I wish they had spatulas between their teeth instead of swords," she said, then noticed a note pinned to one of the pirate's hats. "Have fun," she read aloud, "and don't forget to clean up."

"Lyn's such a teacher," Robert said, digging in a cabinet and pulling out two skillets. "We should save her some food to thank her for all this."

J'aime dumped her stuff on a table. "What are we making today?"

"Since it's our first time using a stove together, I thought we'd start with something simple. You've had quesadillas, right?"

"I live on Earth," she answered. "Taco Bells are everywhere."

Robert paused, processing. "I'm going to pretend I didn't hear that. These are spinach and cheese quesadillas, which is way better than folded cardboard." He turned on a faucet and let it run for a second. "It's nice to have sinks. I prewashed everything just in case this kitchen didn't work out."

"You said you completely trusted Lyn."

"And you said you completely didn't trust her."

For a second, J'aime swore he was going to flick water at her, but this time, he was the one holding back. "Did you bring any surprise ingredients with you?" he asked.

She let him dig through cabinets for a minute before answering. "Not this time."

He threw two cutting boards onto the counter. "Dang. I kind of liked the random challenge idea. Go ahead and get out the stuff I brought. We'll do the straight-up recipe."

Inside Robert's backpack were bags of spinach, cheese, whole onion, and garlic mixed in with books and some kind of magazine photo collage of baked, grilled, and fried chicken parts.

"Hey," she asked. "What the heck is this? You've got poultry art in here."

Robert dropped the measuring cups and took his backpack from her.

She was about to apologize when he pulled out the decoupaged piece of cardboard and held it up proudly. "It's awesome isn't it? Mom thinks I'm in an art club. Every once in a while, I've got to make something."

He propped the poultry art up on the counter as if he were moving in. "I'm thinking about doing a macaroni portrait of Colonel Sanders next."

J'aime crossed her arms in front of her chest. "Wait. You made this willingly?"

"Yep." He pushed a chef's knife toward her. "I have to tell Mom something when I work at the casino, so I say it's art club."

One question swirled in J'aime's head, but she was worried about asking it. He'd closed down last time they talked about work and his mom. She didn't want to bring it up seconds before they started cooking. Luckily, Robert changed the conversation for her.

"You get to really chop an onion today," he said with a bit of awe in his voice. "God, and sauté for the first time. You're so lucky."

"I've chopped an onion before," she argued. "In the casino kitchen, that first time we really talked."

"You mean the third time we really talked, and to be clear, that was blind, wild slicing you were doing. This is going to be serious chopping. What time does the bell ring?"

"7:55, I think."

"Right," Robert said. They tied on aprons. "Remember what I told you about your fingers, and don't be afraid of how sharp the knife is. Its job is to cut things away. Respect that, and the knife will respect you."

J'aime made a claw hand at him, and this time she growled.

Robert laughed. It echoed around the secret kitchen, and for a moment they both forgot that they were cooking refugees.

"Okay, early morning, J'aime. Now you're the one who's being super weird." He slid a cutting board toward her.

"You're the one who made a chicken collage for a fake club," she teased.

"I'm a creative culinary genius, remember?" He retightened his apron strings. "Let's do this quesadilla thing. Set up your cooking space so the middle of the cutting board is always clear. Put quesadilla filling ingredients in each corner."

J'aime spread her ingredients out: dumping a quarter cup of spinach here, laying two cloves of garlic there, and adding a quarter cup of shredded *queso blanco* last.

Robert held up a yellow onion. "We only need a quarter cup each. I'll slice off the hairy root end, but then you have to do the rest."

J'aime nodded as Robert trimmed and peeled the yellow orb. She could joke around about the claw, but to seriously chop an onion on her own meant no more plastic knives. This was TV cooking. The yellow onion rested on her cutting board like a giant zombie eyeball staring her down. She didn't want to touch it. What if she messed it up?

Robert reminded her, "Make the claw and put it on one side of the onion, then cut it in half." He nudged her with his elbow. "Kitchen to J'aime. Come on. Cut into it. No guts, no guacamole."

She gave him a nervous smile and picked up the knife. It was heavy, but not as heavy as the knives at the buffet.

"Remember what I told you about gripping the handle," he reminded. "Low and tight. You have to control the blade from the top."

She adjusted her hold. The dull edge of the knife pressed coolly against her index finger. Making the claw with her left hand, she safely placed her fingers on the onion. Her knife blade was dead center.

She took a deep breath and calmly pressed down. There was a crunch, then the hollow tap of metal to plastic. The onion split into two halves, gently rocking open onto the cutting board. She grinned so big, she thought maybe onions were actually sprouting out of her cheeks.

"Now it really gets fun," Robert said, picking up an onion half. "Lay the flat side of the onion down on the cutting board. The part I just trimmed, the root end, should point left. Turn your knife on its side, so the blade is flat too, like you're done using it."

J'aime turned her knife on its side. It felt wrong and familiar at the same time. Which Food Network chef had she seen holding a knife like this?

"Now slowly slice through the onion, cutting toward the root," Robert said. "But stop before you get to the root. It holds the onion slices together during chopping."

J'aime's first mistake was that she took another deep breath. This time, the onion's defenses were up. Tears clouded her eyes.

"Stupid onion," she muttered, slicing her sideways knife into the wide middle and slowly wiggling her blade through the layers.

"Happy onion," Robert corrected her.

J'aime ignored him. She stopped her knife about a quarter inch from the root and pulled it out.

"Good job. You're going to draw lines across the onion with your knife point, like this." Robert put his hand on top of hers and started to move the knife with her. Electricity shot through her skin. She couldn't concentrate. All she could think about was the fact that he was kind of holding her hand.

"Stop," she said, pulling her hand away so he'd let go. "Just tell me what to do."

"Oh, sorry. I just thought it would be easier if . . ." From a safe distance, he pointed his index finger at her knife tip. "Near the root, poke the tip of the knife in, but this time cut across the onion, from left to right, making evenly spaced lines until the whole onion surface looks like notebook paper."

She followed his directions slowly. She needed to know how to do this, and that wouldn't happen if he got into her space so much.

Robert was talking quickly, as if the speed of his words could move this process along faster. "Onions have built in lines already. You can follow them too if it's easier."

The stinging in her nose and eyes grew worse. Heavy teardrops fell on her onion, dripping in between the freshly cut slices. She hated crying, even if it was vegetable induced.

"This is the last step," Robert said. "All you have to do is cut it normal. So hold your knife blade up and down, like regular, and start slicing at the non-root side. Stop when you get to the root."

J'aime wiped her eyes on her sleeve, then sliced. As her knife slowly cut through the onion, a trail of small onion squares followed her blade.

She squealed. "Look what's happening. I'm chopping like you."

"More like the snail version of me," Robert said, scooting his onion bits into a cutting board corner. "But after you do it a few times, you'll get faster."

He pulled two garlic cloves over and sliced each one down the middle, then cut them the other direction three times.

"I'll mince the garlic for us today. We need to keep moving." He picked up J'aime's cloves and did the same. "Why don't you turn the burner on and grab the canola oil. It's in the yogurt tub. Measure out one tablespoon and add it to the pan."

J'aime found the dial for the medium-sized burner. Before turning it, she rested her fingers on the small smooth stove handle. This was the moment she'd been waiting for, turning this dial, flaring up her life in the direction she wanted it to go.

"Light that fuse," she said under her breath.

Robert looked up from his cutting board. "Did you say something?"

J'aime's fingers turned; the dial clicked. There was the hush of escaping gas then the blue flame perked up underneath the cast iron burner.

J'aime smiled. "It's quesadilla time."

Her tablespoon of oil hit the pan surface. J'aime sighed then waited for a sizzle. She stirred the oil with a spoon. "Nothing's happening."

Robert stopped mincing. "Why are you stirring?"

She stopped moving the spoon through the canola. "I don't know," she admitted. "To see if it's alive?"

"Throw a piece of chopped onion in." He turned up her heat to medium high.

A single, thin onion sank into the shallow, thick pool. "Doesn't look like onions can swim." J'aime fought the urge to stir the drowning vegetable.

"It'll dance. That's how you'll know the oil is ready."

"Onions are happy. Onions dance. What else can onions do?"

A soft pop sound answered her question. The tiny chopped onion floated to the surface of the oil and started to jerk.

"Pan's ready," Robert said. "Add all the onion. Stir them around to coat them in oil then let them sit there until they turn clear."

"That's more like body spasms than dancing," J'aime said, poking her onions with her spoon.

"Hey, don't knock the food's moves." He scooped his onions into the pan. In a couple of minutes, the white chunks turned soft and translucent. He added the garlic and spinach to the onions. As the spinach began to shrink, J'aime stirred the mixture together.

After about five minutes, and a few more stirs, the wilted leaves started to stick to the pan. This was the crucial moment when her ingredients usually turned from sautéed to cinders. Panic bubbled up inside J'aime. She gripped the skillet's handle, stirring the vegetables fast with a wooden spoon. She'd do anything to keep them from burning.

Robert eyed her frantic turbo cooking. Without saying anything, his hand hovered above hers again. She could tell he wanted to reach in, direct her hand. It killed him that he wasn't the one doing the cooking. She shooed him off.

"What do I do?"

"Stop stirring," Robert instructed. "Lift the skillet onto another burner, a cool one."

J'aime did exactly what he said.

"See how it was starting to stick like that?" He poked a paper-thin leaf with his knife. "The spinach wants to be done," he said simply, turning off the other burner, "Let it be done. Let it cool off."

The sweet, hypnotic smell of garlic hung in the air. It wasn't sour and burnt, but just right. J'aime stirred the cooling spinach mixture with her wooden spoon. It was shockingly easy to not burn her meal. All she had to do was pay attention to what the food was telling her.

Her stomach growled. It was telling her something too. She had a spoon in her hand and could easily scoop up a little pre-dilla snack.

"Step away from the stove, McWilliams," Robert said. "You've got a quesadilla to put together before we eat it."

Chapter 13

Mess Magnifico

J'AIME WAITED BY THEIR CAFETERIA COOKING table for melty goodness to appear. That morning, it had taken only three or four minutes for the cheese to ooze, making their quesadillas flip-able. Not one tortilla ended up on the floor. By the time it was quarter till, she and Robert had washed dishes and wrapped their lunch up for later. Since Robert's class was closer to the home ec kitchen, as soon as their lunch bell rang, he was going to swing by, reheat, then bring the food to their regular spot. All that worry this weekend about him ditching her at lunch was for nothing.

The idea of eating a meal she cooked on a real stove made J'aime giddy. She danced like that tiny twitching onion in the pan. Her water bottle slipped from her Whole Foods bag and rolled on to the floor, right to the pedied feet of a preppy girl.

"Sorry," she said to the pink glitter toes before they turned and walked away.

"What are you doing?" Robert said, holding a tray of steaming paper plates.

J'aime stood up, tucking her Aguatista bottle into her bag. "I dropped my water."

Now that she was eye level with the quesadillas, she caught a scent of onion and melted cheddar. "Those smell amazing." Nodding her head at the two plates on his tray, she said, "You look like a Hannaville High waiter."

"Lunch is served," he said with a bit of proper snobbery.

Even though they weren't cooking, they sat in their usual cooking spots with Robert's back to his friends. J'aime watched No-Crusts Girl flip a page in her magazine.

"We've got the whole lunch hour to eat," Robert said. "I was thinking maybe we should take our first bite at the same time, to you know, really taste it."

"Like a wine tasting?" Her only reference for "tasting" was the annual *Food and Wine* highlights show from Colorado.

"Yeah, but," he said awkwardly, "with quesadillas."

J'aime opened her water and sipped. Even though she was out of pantry food, her need to feed was shockingly on low. She ended up nibbling ingredients during prep that morning and ate the hearty breakfast sandwich the lunch ladies delivered to every homeroom.

"I could handle a tasting," she said. "I think we should close our eyes, since you can't really swish tortillas."

"Awesome," he said, picking up a slice of quesadilla with his free hand. J'aime swore there was a slight blush to his cheeks. "Here we go."

As she picked up her piece, white cheese strings stuck to her plate like dairy tentacles.

Robert raised his hand and started a countdown. "One . . ."

"Wait, these cheese thingies aren't letting go." J'aime swiped her finger through the queso blanco fringe, freeing the quesadilla from the plate.

"Okay," she confirmed. "Two . . ."

"Three. Bite!" Robert said, almost shouting.

J'aime closed her eyes. The first taste to come through the blackness was wheat, or maybe it was only the texture of wheat. Warm salty cheese and the slight grease of onions mingled with the tart spinach and savory garlic. It was like pizza, but different. Real home-cooked, warm food tasted so much more amazing than anything off the buffet. For a second, J'aime imagined herself snuggled in between the two toasty tortillas.

"What do you think?" Robert asked, interrupting her cozy foodie dream.

She swallowed and blinked the cafeteria back into view. "Way better than Taco Bell."

Robert scowled. "I think the filling is a little bland. The recipe needs more onion and lime."

"No, you're crazy," she said, taking another full bite. "It's perfect." She paused. "Did you close your eyes too? Or did you watch me eat with my eyes closed?"

Robert got a sly look on his face. "Only the quesadilla knows."

"Okay, Mister Food Fetish."

They both tore into their food and an awkward silence settled on their table. J'aime didn't want to drift into another music conversation; and after this morning's chicken collage revelation, she really only had one question to ask him.

"So," she said as casually as possible. "Tell me more about this pretend art club you're in."

Robert bit off a pointy quarter and for a moment a piece of sautéed spinach dangled from the end of his lips. He caught the loose leaf with his tongue. "You want to join?"

"I'm kind of in it. I work at the casino too," she said. "Why doesn't your mom know about your job?"

He shrugged and kept eating. J'aime wasn't sure if she should keep asking or not. She didn't want to rock the quesadilla boat. With a whole lunch hour ahead of her, the last thing she wanted to do was dine and dash out of the cafeteria again just because Robert didn't want to talk about his family. She was about to switch topics, focus on cooking shows instead, when Robert piped up.

"It's because of the Mess Magnifico," he said.

J'aime swallowed. "That sounds like a breakfast special."

Robert cracked a smile. "It is special, but not in the fried egg kind of way. My sister came up with the name." He picked up his tortilla and tore a bit off the edge. The cheese was getting cold, so there was less oozing. "The Mess Magnifico is a family joke,

I guess. It's more like a family problem with a nickname. I told you I'm the youngest, right? I'm also the first kid my parents can afford to send to college. My sisters had to help out at the restaurant after high school. Rios Rancheros wasn't booming back then."

J'aime stuffed her mouth. If she kept it full, he'd keep talking.

Robert slouched in his chair. "The thing is, I don't want to go."

College wasn't even a blip on J'aime's radar. Culinary school, now that was a different matter. She'd give anything to go to culinary school. But until she paid off her school lunch debt, that wouldn't happen.

"Why don't you want to go?" she asked. "It's like a free future."

He eyed his old lunch table then picked at the tortilla in front of him. "Nothing about it is free. Mom is paying for me to be a business major. She says I have to go to business school, so I can manage a Rios Rancheros. She's got plans for a second location and a bakery opening soon. She wants me to run one of the restaurants."

"A manager?" J'aime asked, thinking of how her dad hid his business duties under kitchen pans. "That's a lot of responsibility. You've got to be good at schedules and budgets, right?"

He sighed. "Exactly. That's what started this problem. I won a district math contest when I was a freshman, one of those Math Olympics; and ever since then, Mom's made me do payroll. My whole family practically cooks or serves. She doesn't need another Rios in the kitchen."

She put down her lunch. "But she's tasted your food. She knows you're an amazing chef."

He spun his paper plate around. "Doesn't matter. My sister Mia would love to crank through numbers all day. She's the one who really wants to run the business side of the restaurant, but she's also good at managing the bar. Mom crowned her head bartender instead. Once Mom decides something, you don't mess with her plan."

"Mom made Rio Rancheros the most popular restaurant in Churchill," Robert explained. "We've won best Mexican restaurant for the last five years. My cousin Mateo used to pick fights with her about the business, and she straight up fired him. Mateo is practically banished from the family. No one crosses Mom about business." He fiddled with a torn spinach leaf. "That's why I've got art club. I can do what I love, and she doesn't need to know about it." Robert looked up at J'aime. "Cooking is everything to me too."

J'aime's stomach flipped. He remembered what she said. How she felt. In their own way, they understood each other. Heat flushed her cheeks. *Be cool*, she thought. *He's in the middle of trusting you right now.*

She took a sip of water. "Aren't you afraid she'll find out?" she asked.

He picked at his food and dismissed her question with another shrug. A half-eaten lunch on his plate told her he was worried about being discovered. She glanced at his old lunch table. *Maybe some of his friends work at Rios Rancheros too? Maybe that's why he acted all nervous cooking in front of them.*

She scraped a white pool of hard melted cheese from her paper plate. "I want to own my own restaurant," she said cautiously. "I want to go to cooking school first, though. Like a real cooking school." She had never said that out loud to anyone. "I can't afford any of it, but I still want it."

Robert stopped picking up crumbs with his greasy finger and glanced up at her.

"I don't know if I could stay in one place though," J'aime added. "I've never lived in one place for very long. Owning a restaurant seems so permanent."

"You could get a food truck," he suggested. "I've thought about that. Traveling around to small towns without a restaurant or a grocery store. Hannaville didn't have a real restaurant again until the casino showed up. The last diner closed up a year ago. Mom says it's hard to make money in such a small market. But I think if you put a lot of small towns together, you've got one big market."

"You already sound like a business major," J'aime said. "I hadn't thought of that, the food truck thing," she added quickly. "You should totally do that. You could be the chef and the owner."

Robert shook his head and leaned back in his chair, lifting the front legs off the floor. "I graduate in a few months. I've got to ride out this casino gig for as long as I can. It's not real cooking, but it's not front of house either. If Mom finds out I'm at the Silver Dollar, she'll be pissed. I'll have to quit. I should be doing her inventory, or food orders, or anything else besides cooking at her new competition. The Mess Magnifico isn't about what makes me happy. It's about what supports my family."

He slammed his chair back down on the floor with a thud. J'aime watched in horror as he crumpled his plate in half, crushing the rest of his fantastic lunch. That quesadilla was a cafeteria masterpiece, how could he throw it away like that? How could he waste his lunch?

Robert stood, about to walk over to the trashcan, but stopped when he noticed her shocked face. Carefully, Robert smoothed out the crumpled paper plate, revealing a ball of quesadilla. He plopped back down into his chair and screeched closer to the table. Without looking at her, Robert pulled melted cheese from the tortilla, eating it slowly.

As he chewed, J'aime stared at him. Here was a person with so much food in his fridge that he could cook something and throw it away without a second thought. What made her feel even worse was knowing that she's the kind of person who'd totally rescue his lunch from the trashcan and eat it later.

She pushed that image out of her mind. Robert wasn't the enemy. His chef soul was as hungry as hers. Money was such a trap, and the people we love can cause so many wrong decisions.

The first bell rang. Normally, they'd be scrambling, cleaning, and eating at the same time, but not today. Tardies or not, they were going to finish their lunch.

"Hey," J'aime said. "I thought of something else onions can do."

"What?" Robert asked, eating another piece of smashed quesadilla.

"Onions can change your life."

Chapter 14
Burrito Babies

SITTING ON HER FRONT PORCH SATURDAY morning, J'aime scrolled through her phone. Flashing back on her screen was a whole week's worth of cooking: spinach and cheese quesadilla, black bean sliders, rancheros salsa, enchiladas cilantro, and lime and pepper burritos. She didn't have a lot of space on her mom's data plan, but she couldn't help taking food pics of her creations. They were her proud little food babies, which was weird because she ate them. Wasn't there a Greek myth about that?

Snug inside the duplex fridge, two real burritos waited for her. Robert brought extra ingredients on Friday so they could roll some for her weekend meals. He didn't even ask her if she needed any take-home food. He just did it, and she didn't fight him about it.

After their serious lunch talk on Monday, J'aime also didn't bring up Robert's family again. The rest of the week, she told him funny stories about working at the Tudor Table: the ridiculous peasant outfit she had to wear to bus dishes, the knights who jousted during the meal, and anything else she could remember about the huge banquet-sized "medieval" kitchen.

A new dandelion bud peeked its stem through a crack in the stoop steps. J'aime reached down and touched the tightly closed bud. Inside the green leaves, hundreds of delicate white strands waited to sprout and be set free with a little gust of hope. Burnt-out Chicago J'aime, the one who lugged dragon dishes covered in mushroom gravy, would have pinched it, pulled it, and tossed the weed onto the sidewalk. But Hannaville J'aime was different. *Even weeds deserve a chance to bloom*, she thought.

Tapping her screen, she noted the time: 10:35 a.m. When she got home from the pantry at 10:15, she crossed paths with No-Crusts Girl, who was out for her usual Saturday jog. They said hi, but kept moving in their opposite directions. Odds were good she would jog by again. Since J'aime's shift at the casino didn't start until later, she made up her mind to wait for No-Crusts Girl.

A tiny gray compact car with a huge blue armchair tied to the top drove by the duplex. Ropes dragged behind the exhaust pipe like forgotten honeymoon decorations.

That looks like a disaster waiting to happen, J'aime thought, gathering her hair back into a ponytail.

All morning, trucks crammed with boxes and furniture had cruised down her street. They all came from the same direction, south of Hannaville.

Through the open screen door, the TV blared. "Can you guess the mystery recipe?"

The Food Network was running a marathon of the series *Mystery Meals*. J'aime didn't care much for that show; but the TV was company, and this morning she didn't feel like being alone.

A blonde head crested the hill. Without stopping, No-Crusts Girl took a swig from a water bottle as she passed the McWilliams's place. J'aime's instincts told her to shrink back, but she made herself stand up instead.

"Blindfolds on. Forks ready," the TV host instructed as J'aime pulled the front door shut and turned the key.

Keeping to the sidewalks, J'aime walked quickly in her flip-flops. No-Crusts Girl was already four houses ahead. At Water Street, J'aime had to jog to catch up. The sidewalk beneath her feet was cracked and rippled from tree roots fighting the cement surface. Her right big toe scuffed a jagged section of sidewalk. A stabbing pain shot up from her ankle to her leg bone, and she tripped.

In a matter of minutes and a few more hills, No-Crusts Girl was out of sight, and J'aime was out of breath. Plus, she had a throbbing shin splint. Why didn't she put on her work tennis shoes?

The sidewalk vanished as the city-street cement transitioned to country-road gravel. J'aime took a break and bent over to rest her elbows on her knees. Her body swayed. She took a few deep, slow breaths then carefully stood up. She'd eaten a banana on the way home from St. Lawrence's, but apparently that wasn't enough this morning. Her blood sugar was low. The last thing she wanted to do was faint on the side of the road.

"No more jogging," she warned herself. "Just walk."

A yellow truck whooshed by, cruising up the rolling wave of gravel road stretching out in front of her. Tall shoulder high grass rippled in the dusty truck breeze. She'd have to keep climbing hills if she wanted to catch up with No-Crusts Girl. Sweat trickled down her back. She pulled up her sagging shorts and continued to flip-flop up the gravel road.

After thirty minutes of nothing but fields and fences, J'aime thought she was hallucinating when she saw a driveway. It was connected to a farmhouse as old as the prairie it was built on. Two black metal horses guarded either side of the driveway's entrance. The horses were life-sized, but flat and cut out of black steel. The sprawling front yard was decorated with more of these strange metal shadows: a silhouette of a boy fishing, a leaning cowboy with his hat propped down over his eyes, and the dark profile of a dog standing on the words *Welcome Home*.

The folksy art reminded her of shadow puppets she'd seen in elementary school, but these were giants without a stage. She took a cue from the silhouetted cowboy and leaned on a metal horse. Her feet were killing her. Kicking off her right flip-flop, she inspected her foot. Specks of gravel coated the bottom of her heel and toes.

She glanced up at the farmhouse. Did No-Crusts Girl live here? Is this where she was coming from every Saturday? She tried to imagine the girl's peanut butter sandwiches being smeared together in this country kitchen. Instead, all she pictured was a one-dimensional shadow mom carefully trimming crusts off wheat bread.

At 11:10 a.m., her phone glared at her. She had to get home. J'aime pointed her feet toward town as another vehicle whooshed past her.

A pyramid of lawn furniture was stacked precariously in the truck bed. A green weed whacker was jammed into the knot of rubber-coated legs and waffle backs. The weed whacker's electrical cord lassoed the air high above the truck cab. As J'aime watched the waving yard trimmer disappear over the next hill, something gently brushed her elbow.

A blonde ponytail jogged by. The back of No-Crusts Girl's neon pink tank top popped against the blue sky as she lapped J'aime. Suddenly, the running girl turned around and jogged backward.

"What's your shoe size?" No-Crusts Girl asked as she inched down the road.

"Shoe size?" J'aime asked, surprised.

No-Crusts Girl kept trotting backward, waiting for an answer.

"Seven," J'aime said. Before she could ask why, the girl turned away and jogged down the sunshine drenched gravel road.

Chapter 15
Leftover Nachos

DIGGING THROUGH HER LOCKER FOR HER Thursday textbooks, the taste of nibbled nacho salad lingered on J'aime's taste buds. She was looking forward to eating the entire salad at lunchtime. Well, *mostly* looking forward to it. The tortilla chip base would be soggy by then. Not that Robert believed that. In the home ec kitchen, over the sounds of rockabilly guitars plucking from his iPod, he'd insisted that the chips would hold up until lunch.

"Who cleaned tables at Johnny's Macho Nacho Bar?" J'aime had asked then pointed at herself. "Trust the leftover expert. Fridge nachos are soggy."

"BUT," Robert said. "How many times have you made nachos?" He'd lifted a "shut-it" finger. "My nachos will not get soggy in the refrigerator." Then he'd mumbled something about Macho Nachos that she didn't quite catch. The words *toxic waste* might have been thrown in there.

Now in the school hallway, J'aime shook her head at him. Robert was the "chef" in their kitchen, so he considered himself right by default. "Not this time," she said, switching out her French II book for her *Language Arts Poetry Collection*.

"He's so wrong."

"Who's so wrong?" a girl's voice answered.

J'aime jumped and nearly knocked her lock onto the floor.

No-Crusts Girl stood next to her with a brown paper sack in her arms.

"Oh, Hi," J'aime said, trying to collect herself.

"Hi," the girl said, thrusting the brown grocery bag into J'aime's hands. "Running in flip-flops isn't a good idea."

Flustered, J'aime fumbled her French book under her arm. "I wasn't really running," she started to explain as she looked inside the bag. Nestled in the stiff brown paper was a pair of gray New Balance sneakers with a hot pink *N* logo on the side of each shoe. They looked new but dated. Sticky Band-Aids rubbed the soles of her bare feet. She'd almost used up the casino's whole box of bandages. No-Crusts Girl was absolutely right. Country roads and flip-flops don't go together.

"These New Balances were stuck in a box with a leopard lamp my mom wanted for our store," No-Crusts Girl explained. "They've never been worn. Nobody comes to the store for running shoes. She said you could have them."

J'aime didn't know what to say. No one had ever given her free shoes. Her face heated up. How needy did she look?

"I have sneakers," she said, thinking of her work shoes.

No-Crust Girl rolled her eyes. "Everybody has sneakers. These were top-rated running shoes like two years ago."

The sporty chick wasn't going to give up. J'aime quickly dropped her French text into her tote and dug for her wallet. "I should pay you for them."

"Forget it," No-Crusts Girl dismissed, pulling on the strap of her messenger bag.

"No," J'aime said, "I can pay." As she said the words, she knew the shoes were worth more than the five-dollar tip Robert had slipped back inside her bag.

The jarring sound of slamming lockers filled the hallway.

"I've got to get to class," No-Crusts Girl said. "You can have them for free, but whatever. If it makes you feel better, pay me a dollar."

J'aime flashed the bill. "I only have a five."

"Oh my God, just take the shoes," No Crusts Girl insisted. "If you want to run sometime, let me know. You're on my route." She gave J'aime an awkward wave and was gone.

J'aime opened the brown paper bag. The gray shoelaces were tied together in a neat, tidy bow. These sneakers weren't a donation, she realized. They were a present.

•

Robert scooped up nacho mush with his plastic spoon. "Just the way I like 'em," he grinned.

Admitting that J'aime was the leftover nacho expert was not on his agenda, but the nachos told a different story. *Fine*, J'aime thought, *as long as he's having a good time eating in denial.*

She nibbled on a rare crispy corn chip that had escaped their dollops of low-fat sour cream. Crunching the edge with her front teeth, she glanced over at No-Crusts Girl's lunch table.

"What's her name?" she asked Robert, and subtly pointed her spoon in the general direction of the girl.

Robert swallowed. "You don't know? You ate lunch with her."

"I'm not Mr. Personality like you," J'aime said, and paused. "How did you know I sat with her at lunch?"

"New girl. Small school." He scooped another spoonful from the nacho puddle. "That's Sarah Pruitt."

J'aime tapped her chip against her lips. "Why does she always sit by herself? She's nice enough."

"You don't want to ask her about that," he said, eyeing J'aime's corn chip. "How did you end up with dry chips? I'm counting like six on your plate."

J'aime held up another crispy corn chip and waved it in front of his face. "Tell me about Sarah, and this can be yours," she bartered.

"Challenge accepted," he said. "Sarah's mom is the epicenter for Hannaville gossip. People say that she and the mayor have had a thing going on forever, even though the mayor's been married to someone else for like twenty years. Also, Sarah's mom owns the last big store on Main Street. Her family goes way back here; pioneers who parked their wagon by the river and practically founded the town. People think that Sarah's mom is flaunting her founder status and affair with the mayor by having such a showy business on Main Street. Anyway, all of this is to say, Sarah doesn't really hang out with anyone."

The corn chip flicked across the table at him. Robert carefully caught it. "Thanks. I can't eat any more of these soggy nachos. It's embarrassing."

J'aime chewed on her spoon until the plastic gave slightly. "She gave me running shoes this morning. I think she felt sorry for me because she thought I was jogging in flip-flops."

Robert nibbled his solo chip with his front teeth to make it last longer. "You went jogging?"

She scooped up lettuce, pinto beans, and a glob of salsa. "It was more like walking with occasional faster walking. Honestly, I was trying to catch up to her to say 'Hi.'"

"You were running. She was running. What else is there to say?"

"We already established, I was walking," J'aime argued between chews. "That's not even the point." She pulled her wallet out of her backpack. "Can you break a five for me?"

"Seriously?"

J'aime rolled her eyes at him. "It's not for you. I owe her for the shoes."

With a dollar bill in hand, J'aime walked over to No-Crust Girl's lunch table. Homework was spread out across three place settings.

"Hey," J'aime said nervously.

"Oh, hey," Sarah said, flipping her history book shut.

J'aime held out the money. "Here's a dollar for those shoes." To her shock, Sarah took it without a fuss. J'aime smiled. "I don't know if you know Robert?"

At the same time, both girls looked over at Robert, who was casually stealing more crisp chips off of J'aime's plate. "That's him," she explained, "eating my lunch."

"I know of Robert," Sarah said, following with a guarded, "Why?"

J'aime cleared her throat. It was time to be brave. "I was wondering if you'd like to eat lunch at our table? You let me eat lunch with you, then I started eating with him, and I don't know, it feels wrong when you could be eating with us." She kind of marveled at herself, standing here, taking a friend risk, and being the welcome wagon to someone who'd lived in Hannaville all her life. "You don't even have to talk to us. I'm just saying if you want to eat with us, you might get free samples of what we're cooking. I'm learning how to cook. Did I mention that?"

Sarah barely shook her head. The girl had thrust a gift into J'aime's hand this morning and now she seemed like the one with nice-shock.

"Okay. I'm going to go back now," J'aime said uncomfortably. "And thanks again for the shoes," she added then hurried back over to Robert and her half-eaten plate of nachos.

"Did you introduce yourself?" he asked.

"I totally forgot!" She plopped down in her chair, exhausted from being overly friendly.

"Is she going to start eating with us?"

"No idea." J'aime snatched one of her chips back from his plate. "But I did see you stealing my nachos."

He pushed his whole plate toward her. "They're all yours, Miss Personality."

Chapter 16
Hot Dog

J'AIME STOOD IN HER LIVING ROOM, HANDS ON her hips. It was Saturday morning and she'd turned the duplex's TV on to the Food Network, but she wasn't paying attention to it. Staring at the stack of boxes next to her mother's chair, her eyes were fixed on one word, *JUNK*. It was scrawled in bold orange marker, barely visible against the tan cardboard. The light from the cooking show caught the fluorescent glare of the marker in just the right way, and J'aime finally noticed it.

She hadn't seen that box for at least three or four moves. Her dad must've been keeping it in his room. The timing was right. J'aime remembered buying her saucepan set at a garage sale about four moves ago. She'd paid $1.50 for the one-quart pot that was currently in the front yard bushes. The woman had thrown in the half-quart mini pot for free. The smaller saucepan had seemed useless at the time. Now that the junk box had reappeared, that small pan could get her cooking at home again. The bad news was the junk box was acting as a base for her mother's boxes. To get to it, she'd have to disturb her dad's shrine.

When her mom died, there'd been no choice but to cremate her. In the dawn light of that September morning, J'aime and her dad had been the only people standing in the cemetery. According to the family plot, they were her mother's only living relatives left. The tombstones told J'aime about a family she'd never met: Beloved Grandmother, and Veteran Grandfather, even Brother,

Deeply Missed. It was cheaper, easier to sprinkle the ashes on those graves rather than dig a new one or find a more poetic place to scatter her.

"They'd want to be together," her dad had explained, tapping into an emotional history J'aime knew nothing about.

Her dad had taken her straight to school after the funeral. No stopping for breakfast, no talking. J'aime was a zombie most of the day, she didn't even remember eating lunch. That afternoon when she walked into their apartment, the only evidence that her mom existed was the recliner, the quilt, and a stack of three boxes. Her dad had packed up her mom's things while J'aime was at school. Without really talking about it, her dad had claimed the boxes as his own. She hadn't seen her mother's belongings since.

Lifting the first box, the bottom sagged from the weight of her mother's memories stored inside. She set it down by her feet. If her dad came home right now, he'd go ballistic. Keeping these boxes sealed and stacked was his way of honoring her mom's memory. J'aime took a deep breath. *They're just cardboard boxes.* Sliding the other two boxes to the ground, she pulled the junk box toward her and hefted it up into her arms.

She carried the junk box into the kitchen and set it on the linoleum. Mentally, she crossed her fingers. What she was hoping for was the impossible. There might be randomly mis-packed kitchen tools in here. It was a super long shot, but J'aime's cooking desperation was strong enough to make her hope and dig. With a rip, she peeled back what was left of the packing tape.

Junk was the right word for what she found inside. Sifting through the random crap, J'aime wanted to chuck it all in the trashcan. Her mother must've packed this box a million years ago. Judging by the dismembered Happy Meal toys, they'd been hauling some of this useless stuff around since elementary school.

Near the bottom of the box, an object was wrapped in an old candy cane Christmas towel. J'aime pulled a cotton corner, letting the mystery thing rattle against the linoleum. Unbelievable.

It was a cheap, all-purpose chef's knife. J'aime didn't even know they owned this? She never saw her mom chop anything.

She stood up, spreading the holiday towel out on the kitchen counter then gingerly placing the big knife on it. Now that she'd struck knife gold, J'aime was determined to find that half-quart saucepan. What if there was a cutting board in here? J'aime dug through restaurant magnets, old fish food from her only pet, and more fast-food toys. Half shoved under the bottom flap of the junk box, a long black handle peeked out. She pried her fingers under it, revealing a slotted cooking spoon, the yin to her broken spatula's yang. Not bad, but still no saucepan.

Through the living room doorway, her mother's three boxes were scattered around the recliner. Being the only boxes left in the duplex, the toppled shrine tempted her with the possibility. J'aime picked up the chef's knife and walked into the living room. She kneeled down by one of the forbidden boxes. The blade pierced the packing tape. J'aime pulled open a box flap. Her heart raced. What part of her Mom's life would she see first? Earrings? Those beat-up romance novels she used to read. That fuzzy robe with the snowflakes on it?

The cardboard edges screeched. When the box opened, J'aime half expected to smell coconuts. Knife in hand, she froze. At first she thought maybe she had the wrong box. These boxes were strictly for her mother's personal belongings, but this one was filled with paper. J'aime reached in and pulled out a sealed white envelope. It was from the hospital. She grabbed another one. This one was from a collection agency. The stamp was dated three years ago. A different bill was postdated last month. J'aime stared into the box. There had to be hundreds of bills packed inside.

Frantically, J'aime opened the other two boxes. She gasped. They were both filled with mostly unopened mail, envelopes containing bills, threats, and warnings that were years past due.

Digging through the third box, she realized the truth. These boxes weren't a way to remember her mother, or even a crazy filing system. They were a hiding system. Her dad had never paid any of her mom's hospital bills—not a single one.

•

J'aime sat on the clammy front stoop, rubbing her finger. A paper cut from one of the medical bills throbbed. It wasn't the only wound causing her pain.

Why did Dad lie to me?

For all these years he pretended like her mom's things were in those boxes. But that wasn't the worst of it. J'aime believed that her dad had paid off her mom's medical bills. From the looks of it, her dad hadn't paid anything. She didn't really understand how banking interest worked, but she knew it existed. Some of the opened bills were for hundreds and thousands of dollars. How much money did they still owe?

Her phone faintly buzzed against her hip. J'aime froze. The collection agencies. She'd followed her dad's rules and never talked to them or listened to their messages. Her phone buzzed again. Slowly, J'aime took it out of her pocket and stared at the area code. Chicago.

Every once in a while, her dad ranted about how debt collectors shouldn't be hounding kids about owing milk money. A chill tingled through J'aime. *What if all this time they weren't calling about my lunch debt?*

Her phone buzzed once more. Anger boiled up inside of her. Her thumb hovered over the button. All J'aime wanted to do was find a saucepan. That's why she opened those stupid boxes, so she could cook at home again, test her new skills, and take leftovers to school.

A desperate urge to run, to get away from the duplex, pushed J'aime to her feet. At that same moment, Sarah's head bobbed into view. Of course—it was Saturday. Sarah crested the hill coming from the direction of downtown.

"Hey," J'aime yelled, jogging down the driveway in her new running shoes.

Sarah waved back and slowed her pace.

J'aime tried to sound calm, but her voice came out a little panicked. "Can I join you?" she asked.

Sara stopped in her tracks. "Sure," she said, catching her breath. She eyed J'aime. "You okay?"

J'aime took a deep breath herself. "I just need to get out of the house."

Sarah smiled. "Let's walk for a bit. You should warm up."

Making their way down Fourth Street, they kept to the right side of the road in case any trucks came flying by. Suddenly J'aime remembered what she forgot to do in the cafeteria.

"I'm J'aime, by the way," she introduced herself. "J'aime McWilliams."

Sarah kept her focus on the road. "I know."

"Did Robert tell you my name?"

Sarah scoffed. "Why would he talk to me?"

J'aime shrugged. Maybe this wasn't a good idea after all. Every second with this girl reminded her that friendships were not either one of their specialties.

Sarah pointed at J'aime's feet. "Glad the sneakers fit okay."

The gray tennis shoes clipped along next to Sarah's green ones. "Thanks again," J'aime said.

She couldn't keep thanking this girl. They needed something else to talk about besides gratitude for footwear. She searched the sidewalk for an idea, but Sarah beat her to it. "Are you and Robert going out?"

Now it was J'aime's turn to be defensive. "No. Why would you think that?"

Sarah grabbed her blonde ponytail, split it in two then pulled to tighten it back up. "I don't know. You eat lunch together every day. Isn't that what couples do?"

"He's teaching me to cook," J'aime answered. "We're cooking friends, I guess. That's what we do together." She tried to change the subject and found only one thing to mention. "Robert told me about your mom's family."

"Of course he told you about my mom," Sarah said sarcastically. "That's what people love to talk about around here."

"They love to talk about Hannaville town founders?" J'aime asked.

Sarah shot her a relieved smile. "Pioneers are all the rage," she joked. "I heard you lived in Chicago?"

"I do. I mean, I did. How did you know that?"

"I read your new student bio in the school paper," Sarah answered.

The loud rattle of a truck made the girls walk closer to the weedy shoulder. An old powder-blue Ford with rust lacing its fenders drove slowly past them. In the back of the truck was a plastic rocking horse with faded paint. It bounced on the metal springs, keeping it in mid-air as the truck headed back to town.

"Mom's going to be mad she didn't get that for the store," Sarah said as the horse bobbed past.

"Where's that stuff coming from?" J'aime pointed her thumb in the opposite direction of the truck. "Is there a weekly garage sale or something?"

"Estate sales," Sarah explained. "People die, or go to retirement homes, and the family has to sell off all their things. Flea marketers like my mom can come out to the fair grounds for the auctions. They take hours because you have to wait to bid on items."

"Really?" J'aime asked. "That sounds kind of interesting."

Sarah scoffed again, her water bottles on her waist swishing a little harder. "If you don't have to go to them all the time." They reached the end of the city sidewalk and hit the crunch of country gravel road. "I started running 'cause I got bored at estate sales, but now I want to do cross country in college, so I've got to practice too."

J'aime had no idea if Hannaville High even had sports teams. Sports really weren't on her radar. The teams could be champs of all time, and she'd never know.

"We don't have a track program," Sarah continued as if reading J'aime's mind. "I run with a high school in Churchill. I'm not on the team, but they let me join their practices. Everyone at Hannaville thinks I'm weird because I go to a bigger city school to run with other runners."

"There's nothing wrong with that," J'aime said. "I get up at dawn to cook lunch. That's weirder then running with other runners. Being passionate about what you love takes you in the direction you want to go, right?"

A smile wrinkled Sarah's thin, freckled cheeks. "I hope so. Come on, let's pick up the pace. Tell me about your weird cooking."

The countryside went by at an even pace of jogging and talking. It made J'aime nervous to talk about cooking with Robert, especially since she knew he was breaking his own family rules to help her.

They walked to the top of the next hill. J'aime's knees ached a little as she looked over the county fairgrounds. She expected to see majestic stone-cut buildings and a giant white Ferris wheel, but instead there was a rickety rodeo arena filled with vacant wooden bleachers, and a herd of farm vehicles parked on a dirt lot.

They crossed the gravel road, and Sarah pointed to a large fiberglass barn. "The sales are in there."

They passed the fair gates and headed down a winding drive. Steam rose from an unattended hot dog cart parked outside the hulking metal building. Buns in bags were piled up next to squirt bottles of bright ketchup. J'aime had buffet leftovers for breakfast, but jogging down country roads made her hungry again. She tried not to think about the warm juiciness of hot dogs.

"Mom's watching a Pyrex mixing bowl set," Sarah explained, rubbing her fingers together, feeling invisible dollar bills. "It's worth the wait."

They slipped through a tractor-sized door that was cracked open. Inside, high barn windows highlighted folding tables filled with cardboard boxes.

A second chill ran down J'aime's sweaty back. "Whose boxes are these?" she asked uneasily.

"Lucille Harmon. She died last month," Sarah said. "Mom knew her. Mom pretty much knows everyone."

The auctioneer chanted dollar amounts into his earpiece microphone. Standing on a chair, he swayed side to side above the crowd, pointing at people as they flashed white cards printed with numbers. The girls stopped to watch the bidders. It was down to a farmer in overalls and an elderly man with red suspenders holding up his potbelly. A blonde woman in a pink T-shirt with the neck cut out kept poking the old man in the back, urging him to bid higher.

"See the roasting pan in that box? That's what they're bidding on." Sara explained. "Be careful not to flash your hands, or the auctioneer will think you want to buy it." She nudged her head toward two women standing on the other side of the room. "My mom's over there."

"Sold," the auctioneer shouted at the old man in the red suspenders.

As the girls walked through the maze of tables, J'aime looked in the boxes of stuff: a snow globe from Montana, a book about horses, a stained coffee mug. Without the living, breathing woman, these pieces of Lucille's life felt lost, without context. What happened to her mom's things? Did they end up at a sale with strangers bidding over them? J'aime didn't even get to say good-bye to her mom's everydayness.

"Did you hear me?" Sarah's voice asked, followed by an awkward pause. "Are you sure you're okay? You seem—"

"I'm fine," J'aime interrupted. She quickly squinted a few times and rubbed at her nose. "There's a lot of dust in here."

"Old stuff will do that to you." Sarah pointed to a spray tanned woman in her forties. "My mom's right where I left her."

The woman had blonde hair like her daughter, but much fluffier. Then there were the sparkles. Sarah's mom had on a tight, low-cut lime T-shirt dotted with colored plastic jewels. She didn't look much like the crust-trimming type.

"Hey, darling-of-mine," the woman said in a southern accent much heavier than Sarah's. "Linda's outbiddin' almost everyone on kitchen stuff. Dorothy says I've got to hang right here if I want these mixing bowls. No way am I giving up on a complete set of aqua-blue Pyrex. Last week I got screwed out of a box of stoneware jugs. That ain't happening again."

Sarah's mom's mascaraed eyelashes fluttered over to J'aime. "Now who's this?" she said, flashing a smile straight out of Dollywood.

"This is J'aime," Sarah said, pointing at J'aime's feet. "Remember? I told you about her."

"Oh, JAH-ime!" Sarah's mom said excitedly. "I'm Gina Pruitt. Come by our store, Finally Yours, for anything you need because Lord knows, we've got it."

Sarah rolled her eyes. "You don't have to hard sell her, Mom."

Gina's mouth fell open. She turned to the older lady next to her. "Dorothy, I ask you, who's the store owner here?" she said with mock dismay.

Dorothy pushed up the sleeves of her Muddy Mo Golf Tournament sweatshirt and laughed. "You're the money, Gina."

Before Sarah could say anything, the auctioneer hopped off his chair and started dragging it straight toward Gina's table.

"Oh, here comes Jimmy," Sarah's mom said absentmindedly touching her hair and then the mixing bowls. "You girls go have fun. Grab a hot dog if you want. Tell Artie to add it to my tab."

J'aime and Sarah pushed their way through the swarming bidders as Jimmy's chanting voice started up again. Outside the barn door, J'aime caught a whiff of boiled meat, and her mouth watered. Sarah walked right by the hot dog hut as if it wasn't even there.

"I guess we're not stopping," she said quietly.

"You don't want those hot dogs." Sarah handed J'aime one of the water bottles strapped to her waist. "Don't worry. I haven't drank from that one yet," she said. "Knock yourself out."

J'aime sipped from the tiny bottle. The water wasn't a steaming hot dog covered with diced onions, but it would have to do. J'aime's missing saucepan crossed her mind.

"Finally Yours has lots of cookware?" she asked. "Even cheap stuff?"

"Tons." Sarah pulled off a water bottle for herself. "Estate sales are full of kitchen things. People don't get rid of potato peelers until someone does it for them."

Or they need a box for hiding bills, J'aime thought.

Chapter 17
Fresh-Start Starter

A LOUD DOOR SLAM VIBRATED THROUGH THE duplex floors, waking J'aime. Her eyes fluttered open. Bundled in her mother's T-shirt quilt, she'd fallen asleep on the floor next to the recliner. Over her shoulder she heard her dad hooking the chain lock on the front door and the rustle of a plastic bag.

J'aime sat up in her nest of blanket as his footsteps shuffled toward the kitchen. She waited for him to notice the scattered boxes, but he didn't. The kitchen ceiling light glowed, illuminating a quilt patch near her foot, a restaurant her mom waitressed at called Aunt Becky's Waffle House. Next came the suction pull of the fridge door and the faint clink of glass. Pulling the blanket up over her Sliver Dollar uniform, she decided to stay on the floor. "How was the rest of work?" J'aime asked.

A beer cap rattled on the counter. "Damn Saturdays," her dad said, leaning in the kitchen doorway. Even in the dim kitchen light, J'aime could see the exhausted half-moon circles under his eyes. "I broke down and bought some beer at the Casey's. Got you a liter of soda."

"You spent money on beer?" J'aime asked in disbelief.

"I said I got you a soda." He shook his head at her ingratitude.

J'aime wanted to say something about the hidden bills. Ask him why he lied, but she wasn't that brave, not yet.

Her dad went on talking about his day. "There were two buses of Gold Rewards members when you were at work this afternoon, right?"

J'aime nodded. Those were the hardcore gamblers who traveled the country in sponsored Silver Dollar Steamboat buses. All employees were supposed to treat them "extra golden." What J'aime had experienced so far is that Gold Rewards members were "extra annoying."

"Damn," her dad said again, shaking his head. "Sonya was carrying the last pan of T-bones to the buffet and tripped on a Gold Reward member's air canister. The ambulance had to come from Tipton and the last of our T-bones were trashed. When the late rollers walked in for steak night, and there weren't any steaks..." He took another swig of beer. "It's way past midnight. I'm going to bed. Turn off the TV, daughter, and get some decent rest."

The TV. It was still on? J'aime glanced up at the bright light of the muted screen as her dad closed the white panel door to his bedroom. She looked around at her mother's boxes. She wasn't trying to hide what she did, that was for sure. Her dad was so tired, he either didn't want to see them or couldn't.

Silently a commercial for Applebee's played on the screen. Twirling plates of $9.99 dinners landed in front of a family squeezed into a snug booth. Without even pressing the mute button, J'aime knew that the friendly announcer was telling the TV world about Applebee's Spring Sizzlers. The ad played every other commercial break on the Food Network. A happy woman and an even happier little girl were pretending to be related as they scooped forkfuls of breaded green beans from their skillet plates.

J'aime searched for the remote, finally spotting it halfway under the recliner. She fished it out as her favorite chef, Bentley, came on the screen, standing in his "Get Fresh" TV garden.

She flopped back onto the floor and curled up into a tight, sleepy ball. The British chef's mouth was moving while his hand pointed at rows of vegetables. A breeze ruffled his scruffy, red curls.

J'aime figured the wind probably came from an off-camera fan and not the English countryside. His shirt was carelessly misbuttoned. She guessed he was in his late twenties and the clumsy button was a strategic fashion statement. All the other chefs on the channel were older, and Bentley was the young, hip chef. In interviews he played off his hit show like it was an accident. Even if his modesty was fake, J'aime liked him anyway.

She meant to click the off button, but instead hit mute. Bentley's English voice flooded the living room. ". . . goes to hungry people in my hometown. Now the Food Network and I want to give you a chance to make a difference in your community, just like I get to do here in the UK."

Bentley fumbled a smartphone out of his jean pocket and held it up to the camera. "Record your brilliant food idea about how your community needs a fresh food start. Then post your video to Bentley's Fresh Start on FoodNetwork.com. That's it, guys, so simple. The winner will get one hundred thousand dollars to change lives in their community. I'll even come to the winner's town to kick off their "Fresh Starter" and we'll film an episode of *Getting Fresh with Bentley* right in the US of A."

He gave a modest smile and picked up a huge basket of carrots sitting next to him on the ground. "Food can do good anywhere, so why not your hometown? Go online to learn more about how to submit your own Fresh Starter idea. Cheers."

The camera pulled back. Bentley dug for more carrots while a web address flashed on the screen. Suddenly Bentley's garden was gone, and J'aime found herself drifting into the soft butter sheen of Stella Lee's downhome kitchen. Before the Southern chef could say what she was cooking, J'aime clicked the off button.

The quilt gathered around her feet. Sometime during Bentley's speech she'd stood up, but she didn't remember doing it.

"One hundred thousand dollars to help change lives in your community." That's what he'd said. $100,000.

Alert and wide-awake, an idea swirled in J'aime's heart.

•

"Good food doing good." J'aime had written that on the back of her work schedule after snapping awake during the night. The words just came to her. It was like a motto, a tagline, or something. She'd been working out a plan in her head for the Fresh Starter contest when she'd fallen asleep and her dreaming self summoned it up for her.

Now with the late morning sun reflecting off J'aime's cracked phone, she scrolled through the endless list of Fresh Starter contest rules a second time. She'd jumped out of bed, worrying that maybe she'd made up the whole Bentley thing, but a quick check of the Food Network website confirmed it was real. The $100,000 dollars was real too. That kind of cash could help solve a lot of problems.

She scrolled through the Fresh Starter contest page again. A bunch of people had already submitted video ideas. Apparently, the contest had been going on for a while, and there was only a week left. How had she missed the ads? *Maybe they weren't pushing it too much because of the big bucks*, she thought. The rules were overwhelming, but she squinted her eyes and kept reading.

"J'aime?" her dad's muffled voice called from outside her bedroom door. "You up?"

"Uh-huh," she said, scanning another line. "No employees of the Food Network or their relatives may enter. All entries can be used for Food Network advertising purposes to promote Bentley's Fresh Start and other contests and programming."

"Do you want breakfast?" her dad asked through the wood paneling. There was a pause and then, "Can I please talk to your face instead of this door?"

Please? He wasn't going to go away. He was also being suspiciously polite.

"Sure," J'aime answered, laying her phone down on the bed.

The door handle turned, and her dad's head peeked in the room. What was left of his hair was standing up on one side.

"I brought some strawberry tarts home from work. I thought we could have breakfast and talk."

"I'm not really hungry," she said. It wasn't true, but the way he added "talk" in there didn't sound good.

Her dad's eyes slid over her room, a casual inspection. "What's up with you? You never used to pass up freebies from the buffet. You're letting food sit around in the fridge. I had to eat all that fried cheesecake by myself."

J'aime looked down at her cloud bed sheets. Of course he brought up the deep-fried cheesecake. She sighed. "I told you, I'm trying to cook more things myself."

"Come on out and have a tart."

"I'll eat later. I promise," she said, trying to remain calm.

"It's that Rios guy from work," her father said decisively. "He has a lot of nerve to send gifts for my daughter through me." J'aime rolled her eyes.

She'd already heard this speech, but her dad kept delivering it. "I'm the one who puts food on this family's table."

With her fingers, she twisted the cotton sky into a storm. "Dad, it was soup," was all she managed without totally getting upset.

"I was a guy," he interrupted. "Hell, I am a guy. I know how we think."

J'aime couldn't take it anymore. Her dad was spinning into idiot territory.

"Don't say stuff like that. Robert's just my friend." She picked up her phone and opened up the screen. "Can you please leave me alone? The duplex Wi-Fi is working right now and I've got stuff to do."

Her screen lit back up. Without even glancing at the doorway, J'aime felt her father stand up a little taller.

"I saw what you did," her dad said.

His accusation hung heavy in the six feet that separated them. If she looked up, she thought she might be able to see each word suspended in midair like stars fading in and out on a screensaver.

"You're not supposed to touch those boxes," he said. "You know that."

"I was looking for—"

"I don't care." His voice rose. "Those boxes are off limits. They're my personal property."

"More like your personal problems," J'aime snapped. "What did you do with mom's stuff?"

"I do what I have to do to keep us safe," he snapped back. "And you do what I say."

She bolted upright. "Or you'll what? Ground me from work?"

"Hey," he shouted, "without our jobs, we'd be living in that Suburban. Is that what you want? No bed to sleep in?" His hand tightened on the door handle, ready to yank it shut.

She turned away, throwing herself back down into her cotton cloud sheets. He knew what would scare her, but she knew what would scare him too.

"I saw the bills," J'aime said to the wall. "We can't hide from them forever."

On cue, her bedroom door slammed.

From the hallway, her dad's feet stomped off toward the bathroom.

And she knew he'd be going into work early.

Chapter 18
Garden Fajitas

"GARDEN FAJITAS THIS MORNING." ROBERT grinned as he pulled ingredients out of his lunch bag and set them on the classroom counter.

J'aime tied on her apron, eyeing a giant, heavy head of broccoli. "You grew that thing?"

"Our broccoli and cauliflower are amazing this year. Must be where we planted them. It's a shadier part of the garden, not as hot." Robert proudly smiled at the tight bunch of green trees all sharing the same root. "If the farmers market was still around, we could get ten bucks easy for this, easy."

J'aime watched him beam at his broccoli. "You really love ingredients, don't you?"

He handed her the vegetable. "I love the whole cooking process, from recipe to plate."

A whiff of sizzling beef drifted into the room. A gritty, sweet scent followed, reminding J'aime of coffee cake. They both stopped to smell the air for a second.

"Can you guess what it is?" an older woman's voice asked from the doorway.

J'aime and Robert spun around to see a lunch lady carrying a bucket-sized can of tomatoes. At first the paid cooks had kept to themselves, ignoring the cooking refugees, but when tasty aromas began to drift out of the old home ec room, the whole staff started dropping by.

"Spaghetti sauce and cinnamon rolls?" J'aime guessed.

"She's good," the lunch lady said. "What are you cooking up?"

Robert held up a pepper. "Veggie fajitas. Want us to save you some, Odie?"

The lunch lady waved off his suggestion with her free hand. "Nah, I'll steal off Lyn's plate. You have fun cooking, now." Odie disappeared with her can of tomatoes.

"She's the food scout this morning." Robert pulled out the cutting boards. "Once you've cleaned the broccoli, start cutting off the stalks. Leave some stem on, so it's not just the heads."

J'aime turned on the faucet and washed her hands before rinsing off the veg. Her Fresh Starter idea had percolated all Sunday to the point that now she was almost too nervous to bring it up. What if he didn't like it, or wanted to do it without her? She picked up the broccoli and searched for something else to say.

"You missed some excitement at the casino this weekend," J'aime said.

"Did someone win the Mississippi Millions?" That was the Silver Dollar's grand sweepstake prize. J'aime wondered if it was even real. It seemed suspiciously like it was a sign the casino printed to lure people in.

"Not that exciting," she said, washing in between the tight green broccoli heads. "The Gold Rewards members were there."

Robert groaned in sympathy. "They're the worst. I'd say I was glad I missed it, but Rios Rancheros was crazy busy too. We had three shifts of college professors come in. They were in town for a psychology conference, and I swear they tried to use mind games to move up on the waiting list. Then we ran out of lettuce. I was stuck making everyone feel good about their naked tacos."

J'aime cut into the bunch of broccoli. The heads were so dense she forcefully poked, then stabbed, until finally a single stem sliced free. The prep work felt good and freed up her courage too. "I saw something cool on TV," she said, prying off another piece.

Robert's hands busily peeled a carrot under a steady stream of cold running water. "What?"

She picked up the single broccoli stem and held it like a miniature microphone. Maybe making him laugh was the way to go with this. "Tired of working at your mom's restaurant?" she said in her best sappy announcer voice. "Chef Bentley wants to give you one hundred thousand dollars to make your chef dreams come true."

Robert stared at her like she'd lost her mind then started peeling again.

J'aime lowered her vegetable microphone. "That was supposed to be hilarious," she joked. "But for real. I think we should enter this contest. It's called Fresh Starter and all you have to do is—"

"I've seen the Fresh Starter ad," he said stoically, flipping the faucet off and resting the carrot on his cutting board.

"You've seen it already?" She forgot about her broccoli prep. "I saw it for the first time Saturday night."

"It's on a lot." He cut the carrot in half, and then quickly sliced the halves again. "Don't you watch Bentley?"

"Do you watch Bentley?"

"Of course. He's the best chef on the Food Network."

J'aime stopped, suddenly puzzled. They'd never really talked about food TV. Which was weird. "We totally should talk about chefs," she said. It was tempting to ask his opinion on Angel Kim's new show, *Grill It Girl*, but that was way off topic.

"Fresh Starter. Come on, Robert, let's do it. Let's enter the contest."

"What would be the point? We're high school students cooking in a forgotten home ec room." He glanced at the barely chopped vegetable in her hands. "We're never going to sauté that thing if you don't hurry up."

"You make us sound so pathetic." J'aime picked up her knife, and forcefully cut off a broccoli head. "It's not that far-fetched. Your food truck idea got me thinking. We could do that with the prize money. Travel around to different small towns without a grocery store or a restaurant. I even thought of a name, *Food Carma*. Spell it with a *C* instead of *K* because of the whole vehicle thing."

Robert sliced a section of the carrot into long thin strips. The side of the blade made a soft crunch before making a dull thud of the cutting board. "But why karma in the first place?" he asked. "I don't get it."

"Because we'd give back to the local food pantries too." J'aime was talking fast, her excitement pouring into every word. "You know how some companies say, 'you buy this item and we'll donate something to a cause'? I was thinking we could sell fresh fruit and vegetables, like a farmers market on wheels. We could donate leftover fresh produce or even give a cut of the sales to the food pantry. Lots of businesses do that kind of thing."

Robert shook his head. "My idea didn't involve donating anything. Doesn't sound like we'll make a lot of money if we did it your way."

"But we'll make money eventually, right?" Nervously, J'aime twisted off a broccoli head with her fingers instead of the knife. "And we'll be giving back. St. Lawrence's practically feeds this whole town. You said there were lots of Hannavilles out there without grocery stores. We could help them out by giving people some place to shop and donating to the pantries at the same time. Plus, we'd get to cook and earn money doing what we love. I think in the business world that's called a win-win?"

Robert stopped slicing and moved on to the next ingredient. "When did you get all *Shark Tank*? Why don't you go to business school instead of me?"

"Come on," she pleaded. "We should totally enter. We only have to send in the idea. I even have a slogan. *Good food doing good.*"

Thin slices of onion followed the blade of Robert's knife. "Now you're the one who's crazy."

"Why? What if we won? We'd get a food truck. We'd get to be the chefs and cook all the time." J'aime kept going, "Think about it. Bentley would film in Hannaville. The Food Network would be right here. Can you imagine it?"

The water was running again. Robert dropped a handful of round green peas into a strainer and stuck them under the stream. They bobbed around in the flood of tap water oblivious to everything except their colander spa. She tried to guess what was keeping him quiet.

"The video part won't be that hard," she added.

"Video?" he said. "Great. It gets worse."

"Quit being such a wuss," J'aime half-teased. "Sarah told me that she makes videos of the Churchill track team running. She could help us," she paused. "I don't get it. Why aren't you into this? I thought you wanted your own food truck?"

"Dude," Robert said, turning the peas with his free hand, "There isn't going to be a food truck."

"Did you call me 'dude'?"

"Yeah, because you won't back off." Robert flipped the faucet. The water suddenly stopped. "My mom would freak out. I can't be making videos and entering a contest so you can meet a celebrity chef."

J'aime slammed her knife down on the counter harder than she meant too. The loud metal on metal sound shocked them both. "I don't care about meeting a celebrity chef," she snapped. "Sure, it would be cool, but not as cool as being real chefs in our own kitchen. Why don't you just tell your mom what you really want?"

"That would be perfect," he almost shouted. "'Hey, Mom, I know you want me to get a degree so I won't screw up everything for the rest of the family; but listen, instead of going to college, I want to waste a bunch of your money on a food truck.'"

"It's not your mom's money," J'aime said. "It's Bentley's money. God, are you a chef, or not?"

Robert muttered something to himself, then said, "Even if I win, any money we make on a food truck is still my family's money. We work for each other. That's what families do." He shut off the faucet and dumped the poor peas recklessly into a bowl. "You're free to do whatever you want because you don't have a family."

J'aime went numb. She watched the tiny green peas chaotically roll and tumble over each other. An awkward silence filled the room. *He's right*, was all she could think. *In so many ways my family died with my mom.* It took all her willpower to find her voice again.

She took a shaky breath. "There are a lot of things I don't have," J'aime said quietly.

Robert's hands kept moving, chopping, cooking. He sliced, making the onions smaller and smaller and smaller. The dull chopping sound filled the space where Robert should have said something. He was blocking her out, ignoring her feelings. She wanted him to understand and that meant taking a risk.

"I brought up Bentley because I wanted to pay you back for helping me. Every time we cook, you give me a way to make my life better, and that's a big deal. I'm tired of not knowing where my next meal is going to come from. If I don't look out for myself, no one else will. Robert, we can change our lives. I know we can win this contest."

Robert finally stopped chopping. "I'm sorry about your situation," he said to the cutting board and not to J'aime's face. "There's no real way we can run our own business. I mean, you're a junior. I'm a senior. It might not seem obvious, but my family has problems too. You've still got another year to figure yourself out. I don't have that anymore. I don't have a choice. They need me."

J'aime's anger flared again. His choices were about whether or not to go to college. Her choices were about whether she'd go to bed hungry or eat the rest of a customer's half-finished dinner. J'aime threw the rest of the huge broccoli into the sink. It landed with a hollow steel thud. "If you want to give up on your dreams, then fine, but I won't give up on mine."

Picking up her Whole Foods bag. "They're all I've got, " she said and stormed out of room 4B.

Chapter 19
Strawberry Tarts

J'AIME WALKED HALFWAY UP CLIFF DRIVE
before she called in sick for work.

"Captain's Steamboat Buffet, how can I help you?" her dad
asked in his manager voice.

An RV bus with coyotes painted on the side drove by, and
J'aime waited for it to pass before saying anything. "Dad, it's me."

"Hey," he said awkwardly. "Where are you?"

J'aime could hear the clank of hotel pans in the background
and knew he was in the kitchen. "Dad, I'm not feeling well. I can't
come in tonight."

Frogs croaked by the river. Could he hear that? Did he know
she was practically in the parking lot?

"You okay?" he asked.

No, she thought. *I totally went berserk on Robert. He's working
tonight and I can't pass out clean plates while he ignores me. There's
going to be this weird barrier between us, like personal sneeze guards,
and I can't face that or him. Of course, Manager Dad wouldn't understand that. Regular Dad definitely wouldn't get it either.*

She went for the safest, no-further-questions excuse. "It's girl
stuff, Dad," she said.

A quick, "Whatever," came from her phone. "Trish can cover
you," her dad explained. "Half my staff called in today. One more
won't matter."

"Sorry," she said as kitchen sounds clicked off, and her dad vanished back into a world of steam kettles and convection ovens.

When she got home, she dumped herself on her mom's recliner with the remote and the box of expired strawberry tarts. Her dad had eaten three. That left three for her. All she wanted to do was shove this food into her face and forget everything she'd said in the home ec kitchen.

Her fingers pried up soggy crust from the Styrofoam container. Fruit juice ran down her hand and right onto a restaurant logo for The Sizzlin' Sirloin and Bar-Bar. She wiped at it with her elbow then decided the red blended in with the rare hunk of meat.

Sprinkled sugar dusted her lips as she took a bite. Crust crumbled down her white V-neck T-shirt and into her bra. She shoved the rest of the tart in her mouth. The too big bite smeared icing and jam on her chin.

That boy has reduced me to inhaling mushy pastries, J'aime thought.

She picked up the next tart, knowing it wasn't that simple. Yelling at Robert threw the whole friendship enchilada out the window, along with the cooking lessons and the extra food. Pushing people away was the easy part. Coping with the consequences made her feel desperate.

Resting the takeout container on her lap, her sticky fingers turned on the TV.

The Food Network blinked to life as she stuffed down her second tart. Soon the sugar would hit her and for a while she'd feel content, full. A close-up of chef hands vigorously shaking a Mason jar blurred the screen. The sound was muted and J'aime tried to recognize the apron while licking strawberry goo from the pastry paper in the box.

The chef stopped shaking the jar. A pinky ring with a British flag waved as the rest of the chef's digits unscrewed the jar lid. When the camera pulled back to get a shot of the salad, Bentley was standing behind the bowl.

J'aime wanted to hurl her third dessert right at his English face. Stupid Bentley. Unaware of his possible tart doom, Bentley poured salad dressing over baby spring greens and carrot shavings. The last tart hung in midair. She wasn't really going to throw it at the landlord's TV, only because she had no idea of what damage it might do to the screen. The last thing she needed was to owe someone else more money.

Her teeth clamped down through the crust and took another sickly sweet bite. Red goo dripped out the ends of the pastry and plopped onto her work pants. She forced the rest of the tart down and tossed the empty to-go box onto the floor.

With the nubby push of a remote button, the TV sound came on.

"Brilliant!" Chef Bentley exclaimed. "Blowing your guests away with fresh salad dressing is the best way to show off greens from your garden."

Tarts gorged, she pulled the edges of her mother's quilt around her, cocooning herself into the recliner. The desserts weren't working their soothing magic. The sugar rush coursing through her body wasn't making a dent in her heartache. She glanced at her phone sitting next to the TV. The sunlight from Bentley's kitchen reflected in the small rectangular black screen. Inside that tiny glass box, her alarm setting waited. What time would she set for her morning wake-up? She'd have to make that choice before going to bed.

Dawn was a guarantee. Robert picking her up in the morning wasn't. Sitting in the dark, waiting for him not to show seemed like a bad idea. Cooking lessons with him were over. Somehow, she'd have to find a way to keep cooking even without Robert.

She changed her alarm to a more humane wake-up time.

"First rule of secret cooking school, don't yell at the chef," she mumbled. "Even if he was being a completely stubborn a-hole." Asking him whether he was a chef or not meant she basically called him out as a chicken. "Nice," she muttered.

J'aime removed her phone's protective case. A folded photo slid off the back of the phone and fell onto the quilt. Bentley flashed a knife on the screen, and the light in the living room flickered. Smoothing out the creases on her knee, the picture flattened then tried to fold in on itself again. A young woman with long dark hair gazed back at J'aime.

In the photo, a teenaged version of her mother stood in her backyard, her shy hands clasped behind her back. Her face was calm with a nervous smile that the camera almost missed. In front of lush summer bushes, her cheeks had a healthy glow. It was hard to believe that this person would one day be her mom.

J'aime had found the photograph underneath the recliner seat cushion. How the photo had gotten in the chair, she couldn't guess, but she'd rescued her teenage mom from an eternity of crumbs and the darkness of suffocating velour. Her thumbs pinched the edges of the captured memory. She held it close so she could see her mom's young face in the screen glare.

"Do you think he's ever going to talk to me again?" J'aime whispered to the girl in the long-ago twilight. "Mom, what if I never find the kitchen of my heart?"

Chapter 20
Black Bean Tacos

"COME ON, ST. LAWRENCE. PLEASE, HAVE TACO shells," J'aime prayed as she dug through rows of Hamburger Helper.

The Tuesday night crowd buzzed around her with their boxes and plastic bags. The line had been less intense than Saturday's and so far, J'aime had scored almost everything she needed for black bean tacos, plus her groceries for the rest of the week.

Last night it took thirty minutes to get the tart goo stain out of her work pants. Scrubbing at the sink, she'd decided that expired dessert bingeing hadn't worked any coping magic. The last thing she wanted to do was moan about her chef dreams covered in a layer of crumbs. If she was going to have a full-fridge life, then she was going to have to cook it up without Robert. Luckily, the pantry had Tuesday-night hours, and she had that night off.

There was only one more row of boxed dinners left. If taco shells didn't magically appear, then she'd have to think of a new recipe. Maybe she could make the filling and serve it on top of lettuce as a hot beans-and-greens-type dish? The hot part was the trick. Until she could get a few cheap saucepans from Finally Yours, her only plan was to walk to school in the predawn darkness and cook in the home ec kitchen by herself. Hannaville's dark winding side-walks and ramshackle houses crept through her mind.

I can see the news story now, J'aime thought. *Girl disappears. All authorities found was a backpack full of black beans.* She laughed to herself. *I'm sure the Bean Council of America would send a search party.*

"Hi," a familiar voice said behind her.

J'aime spun around with a box of BOLD Firehouse Chili in her hand. Like a cooking mirage, Robert was standing there in his bright-yellow casino chef's uniform.

"What are you doing here?" she asked.

He shrugged. "I'm on break at the casino. Mom asked me to drop off some baked goods."

J'aime shifted her pride and her bag of donations. If Robert came over here to watch her shop the pantry for food then he might as well help. "I'm looking for taco shells," she said awkwardly. "It seems like they're out."

He reached into the way back and pulled out a green box. "Cheesy Mediterranean Tuna Helper won't work?" He waved it at her, making the white-gloved character dance.

She smiled. "Not exactly."

He put the box back on the shelf. Now that she was happy, his emotions flipped to serious. "I thought about what you said." He paused. "I am a chef."

J'aime's natural instinct was to look his outfit up and down, tease him, and say, "No kidding?" But she didn't. His expression was chopping-onions focused. He was wearing his casino chef's outfit in a place his mom frequented, in front of ladies who liked to gossip.

She set the box of chili back on the shelf. "Okay," she said. "Why are you really here?"

"Because I'm in."

"Why did you change your mind? You were so mad yesterday." She looked away. "Plus, I said stuff too."

"No, you were right. We need to enter the contest. I'll talk to my mom," he said, then added, "I can handle her."

Robert held his yellow chef beanie in his hands. His hair was smushed from the tight hat. There was sincerity with a hint of worry in his voice.

J'aime believed him. But at the same time, she couldn't shake an uneasy feeling.

"What will your mom do when you tell her about the contest and the food truck?"

Robert chuckled. "Banish me." He touched her arm. "I'm kidding. Don't worry about it. I'm like the family golden child. It'll be fine. Mom will get mad, but I've got to tell her how I feel at some point."

She eyed him cautiously. Something wasn't right. How could he change his mind so quickly? Yesterday, it was like his life was on the line if his mom found out what he wanted was different than their plans for him.

"Come on," he said, grabbing the handle of her pantry bag. "My break's almost up, and you've got to sign out."

She let him carry her goods to the table. The elderly lady working the sheet smiled big. "Hi, Robert," she exclaimed.

"Hi, Mrs. Stevens," he said while J'aime signed.

"Thank your mom for the conchie desserts," Mrs. Stevens said.

"I will and they're conchas," Robert corrected.

"Oh. They sure are yummy," Mrs. Stevens said, then took the pen back from J'aime. "Robert, it's nice of you to help someone less fortunate like . . ." She tried to read J'aime's name upside-down. "Jamie."

Less fortunate, J'aime thought. *This lady basically called me needy in front of Robert.* Before he could say anything, she swiped her bag of groceries from Robert's arms.

"I can carry my own bag," she said quickly and walked toward the exit.

Behind her, she heard Robert mumble, "See you, Mrs. Stevens."

She flew down the steps, pushing herself out into the parking lot, further away from a question that she didn't want to ask him.

"Wait," Robert yelled. The slap of running feet on pavement followed her. "Stop." His hand caught her shoulder. "Mrs. Stevens is like ninety," he explained, his dark eyes round with apology. "She didn't mean anything by it."

Her question spilled out. "Are you only helping because you feel sorry for me?"

Standing under the harsh flicker of parking-lot lights, Robert's chef's jacket shined like golden metal. He looked down at his black sneakers, stained with splashes of salad dressing.

She was making him say it. "We don't talk about it, but you make comments all the time like I'm your personal volunteer project."

"Okay. Fine," he answered reluctantly. "Maybe at first a little. I knew you couldn't afford groceries, and I wanted to help."

That was all she needed to hear. She turned on her heel and stomped away. She didn't want to be a charity case to him. She swore she couldn't be that to herself anymore.

Robert grabbed her arm. For a second time that night she spun around. "That's not why I said yes to helping you," he said. "Not really."

She blinked hard. "Then why?"

Without asking, Robert took her grocery bag from her and held it up like it was Exhibit A. "Who shows up at a pantry with a reusable Whole Foods bag?"

"Anyone can," she said defensively. "The bag was a freebie."

"Nope." Robert shook his head. "Not anyone. That first time I saw you, you stood in the pantry with your gourmet shopping bag and a grocery list. I could tell you were substituting ingredients like they do on *Top Chef* when they go to a store and it doesn't have what they need." He shifted the bag, cradling it in both of his arms. "After you left, I looked up where the noodles in ramen originally came from. When I saw you were right, I hoped you were as serious about food as I am . . . I thought you might, you know, get me."

J'aime slipped her foot in and out of her flip-flop nervously. "Then why did you question me so hard in the cafeteria?"

Robert smirked. "I told you. There's a big freaking difference between a foodie and a chef. I don't have time for foodies. I wanted to see how you'd react to that, to make sure we're on the same recipe, you know."

J'aime blindsided him with a playful, shoulder slap. "You're such a food snob."

Robert hammed up an injury, making her laugh. Relieved, she grabbed her grocery bag back.

"You do realize," she added, "that the deadline for the contest is this Saturday at midnight."

Robert straightened his chef's jacket. "Not sweatin' it."

She rolled her eyes. "Now you're an insane food snob. We only have four days to figure out a whole video. What are we going to film?"

He shrugged. "I don't know yet, but it's got to be Food Network-worthy."

J'aime grinned. "No pressure there at all."

Chapter 21
Hard-Boiled Eggs

WEDNESDAY EVENING AT THE SILVER DOLLAR
Casino, J'aime and Robert brainstormed by the dessert bar.

"Our video entry should show how much Hannaville needs
Food Carma," Robert said. Wrapping his hands around a gallon
jug of chocolate sauce, he used the buffet edge to help pour the
thick syrup into a smeared bin.

J'aime straightened a stack of already-straight plates. "How do
we show it?"

"We need a big crowd of hungry customers." Robert kept pouring
and thinking aloud. "There's this private parking lot on Main Street,
in front of an empty general store. We could set up there and do sort
of a fake food truck with free food. That'll really bring people out.
I know the owners of the parking lot. I'm sure they'll let us use it."

J'aime liked the free food part. For once she'd be the one helping others. The chocolate gurgled out in a ribbon of dark sugar.
She wanted to stick her finger into the running stream. "How do
you fake a food truck?"

Robert sighed. "Cooking for people out in the open on Main
Street will get a lot of attention. It'll feel like a food truck even
though we won't have one."

"Do you think people will eat food from random cooks in a
parking lot?"

Robert yanked the chocolate jug upright, spilling brown liquid on the edge of the bar. "That's what a food truck is. What are

we going to film if we don't cook?" he asked. "This is the Food Network. Chef up, J'aime." He nudged her with his elbow then started pouring again.

J'aime pulled on one of the stretchy tips of her plastic gloves. "I know. I'm just nervous. What if I burn the food and ruin the whole thing?"

Robert tipped the jug completely upside-down to drain out the last of the chocolate. "You won't because *A*, you can cook, and *B*, we won't have a stove in the middle of the parking lot. There's nothing to burn. Here's what I'm thinking. We've got Friday off from school for a teacher workday. So we'll hang 'Free Food' signs up all over town. Saturday, we'll set up a few tables in the parking lot like a pop-up restaurant. All the food will be precooked and prepped, so no worries there. If Sarah will film the thing, then we don't have to worry about that either."

J'aime pictured the attention-getting long pantry line streaming from their fake food truck. "Are you really okay with all this?

The last of the chocolate syrup trickled out. Robert gave it a hard shake. "I told you. Don't worry about my mom. I'm handling her. Plus, the fake food truck will be up and down in less than an hour. As long as we get a few minutes of filming, it'll all be good."

The early-bird dinner crowd finished their main courses and started lining up at the dessert bar. Soon retirees with strawberry shortcake on their brains would stampede them. J'aime bit her lip. A streaming, worldwide outing of the Mess Magnifico might push his mom over the edge.

"Yeah, but," she said.

Robert cut her off. "You talked me into this. Now are you trying to talk me out of it?"

J'aime moved out of the way of a woman balancing a plate full of butterscotch pudding and coffee cake.

Was she trying to talk Robert out of this? Something wasn't right about this whole situation. She couldn't shake this weird feeling that Robert's sudden change of heart was because he wanted to get into trouble. No. That was a crazy thought.

"Okay," J'aime said, letting go of her doubt. "What do we pre-cook for our pop-up food truck?"

"Free On-the-Go Huevos Rancheros," Robert said, nodding to the pudding lady. "It's easy to prep, and it's portable. There's only a few parts to plate. I'm thinking we cook it all tomorrow morning. We'll need a bunch of eggs."

"How many eggs are we talking?"

He screwed the cap on the empty gallon as they both walked toward the kitchen swing door. "At least fifty, with a few extras for backups. Plus tortillas, salsa ingredients, and stuff like paper plates."

A cold-hard-cash reality settled on J'aime. "We need money."

A long drip of chocolate squeezed down from the rim. Robert tried to catch the sweet trail with his gloved finger, but it hit the floor. "I can borrow some supplies from home and the restaurant, but not everything. Honestly, I don't have that kind of money right now. I just had to pay for repairs on my truck."

J'aime wiped his mess up with a sanitation rag. "How much do you think you need?"

"To do it right on a tight budget?" Robert looked up at the ceiling to calculate. "Maybe a hundred?"

J'aime knew where she could get that money. She scanned the restaurant for one face in particular. Her dad must be in the kitchen. Asking him for the cash was pointless. If he wouldn't give her ten dollars, then he wouldn't give her a hundred.

If her dad never paid off their debt, then why should she put her extra money in the jar? It wasn't really helping them. The casino had paid her twice so far. Even if her dad took half of her paychecks to cover utilities then there was at least a hundred dollars of her pay left.

"I might be able to come up with it," she said. "Can we drive to Churchill and get supplies tonight?"

Robert gave her a surprised look. "Sure. I'm covering a split shift right now. I'm outta here at six o'clock."

J'aime took a deep breath. "I'm off at six too. We'll need to swing by my house first."

•

For someone who believed in conspiracy theories, her dad wasn't very good at hiding their only savings. She sat on the closet floor, counting the cash through the pickle jar glass. In Robert's truck, she'd done some quick math. Two weeks work, twenty hours at minimum wage, minus taxes, half for bills—that left her $105.

On a piece of paper she wrote, *I owe our bank account $105. I will pay it back.*

Robert was waiting with the engine running. The note was written. All she had to do was unscrew the lid and take her portion of the cash, but she couldn't do it. J'aime couldn't stop thinking about her dad's face when he finally saw that white piece of paper mixed in with the remaining green.

Maybe I shouldn't even leave the note? she thought. *He hadn't brought up the fact I didn't give him the five-dollar tip. Maybe he forgot. Maybe he isn't counting the cash as much as he used to?*

A car passed by outside and J'aime jumped. Her heart raced. The bottom line was, her dad still counted the cash. He would find out. Opening the boxes pissed him off. Taking this amount of cash would top that. She almost wished Robert would honk his horn so she'd have to do it, but that wasn't his style and this was her decision.

"Sorry, Dad," J'aime said as she unscrewed the metal lid. "I'm not going to waste this money. I promise. I'm going to do something great for us."

•

Thursday morning J'aime and Robert loaded their fridge with bags of groceries and fired up every burner in the home ec kitchen. For an hour, they gently simmered eggs in thirteen-minute batches. Eventually, the delicate, hot shells were lowered into ice baths. Water and ice-cube-filled silver mixing bowls covered the classroom kitchen counters. Swimming hard-boiled eggs huddled at the bottom like sleeping manatees. J'aime stared at them. It wasn't because she was hungry, but because they were paid for by her big gamble. Last night when she slid into the passenger seat of his truck, the money stuffed in her Whole Foods bag, the only question Robert had asked her was, "Are you sure?" Once J'aime nodded, he didn't ask her about the cash again.

"The eggs need to chill. We'll peel them after we make the salsa," Robert instructed. He arranged supplies on the counter like it was any other cooking lesson. "This is Abbi's recipe for pico de gallo, so it's guaranteed. Everyone will like it,"

"Sure," J'aime said back. Curiosity pricked her lips. She stopped herself from asking, *Why doesn't your salsa-making-girlfriend ever join us?*

Robert's answer might be, "Great idea! She wants to meet you."

Yeah, no—Abbi cooking with us was the last thing I want. The thought rattled J'aime. She didn't want to admit how much she liked keeping Robert to herself and pretending that this invisible girlfriend didn't exist.

Two bundles of cilantro plopped in front of her. "You wash and mince these, and I'll start chopping onions," Robert said. "We're making four batches. I've written the recipe out so we can focus."

A piece of notebook paper sat in between them with Robert's blocky handwriting on it. J'aime was used to thinking in single teaspoons for two people; this was mega measuring for fifty.

"How'd you figure out these measurements?" J'aime asked, rinsing off the spindly springs of cilantro.

"Restaurant math. Everything is in large quantities. It's funny. Chefs get used to cooking for big groups. It's hard for them to come down in size and cook for a couple."

Their knives tapped and sliced away. J'aime held the end of the long cilantro stems in her left hand, slowly chopping the leaves until she ran out of leaves to chop. Setting the stems aside, she tried her best to cut the pile of sliced leaves even smaller. Clingy cilantro bits stuck to her fingers.

"Why does anyone mince anything?" she complained.

"You've got to take things small sometimes for better flavor." He pointed at the notebook paper and tapped it. "Read the directions."

"You're such a recipe follower," she teased, then flung her hands in his general direction.

"Stop waving your cilantro fingers around." He pointed his knife at the herb. "Mince."

A different question lingered on J'aime's knife like a dead weight. She knew she had to ask it. Her blade slowed down to a crawl. "What made you change your mind about the contest?"

Robert moved on to chopping tomatoes. "You called me out about being a chef," he laughed and sliced off the tomato's stem end. "And I guess Abbi," he said more seriously. "I talked to her about the contest and stuff. I don't know, it sounds cheesy, but she has a way of seeing into my heart. She's always been like that."

J'aime stopped working. The scent of cilantro potpourri burned the back of her throat. *That's love*, she thought. If this Abbi chick could see into hearts, she'd know J'aime's was minced into a million tiny pieces.

Robert's knife chopped away at the tomato.

J'aime willed her voice not to crack. "She sounds pretty great."

He scraped juicy chopped pieces into the communal mixing bowl. "Abbi wants to meet you. She keeps bugging me about it."

J'aime cut into the cilantro again. Was he really this predictable? Her knife left a trail of spilled cilantro bits led straight to their shared mixing bowl. Every piece of green pointed to the facts—this was Abbi's recipe. This was Abbi's boy.

Chapter 22
Chilled Water

THE CLEAR PACKING TAPE LET OUT A SQUEAL AS J'aime tugged it from the red dispenser wheel. She stretched the tape across the top of a free food flyer, smoothing it onto the brick wall, then added a second tape strip to the bottom.

FREE FOOD
SATURDAY MAY 18TH NOON
AT THE CORNER OF MAIN AND CHESTNUT.
$$DONATIONS TO ST. LAWRENCE PANTRY APPRECIATED!

Sarah had made twenty copies of the flyer on her mom's fancy copier. Between her, J'aime, and Robert, the flyers were all over downtown.

The only other people on Main Street were the occasional gamblers cruising by. It was so empty that J'aime could hear Robert and Sarah talking as they walked down the sidewalk toward her.

"They never put cocaine in Coke." Sarah said. "That's a myth,"

"Yes, they did," Robert answered. "I saw it on the History Channel."

Sarah laughed. "I saw *Ancient Aliens* on the History Channel, sooo ..."

Robert rolled his eyes at Sarah and handed two flyers to J'aime. "We've got some spares. We ran out of tape."

"Let's leave them by the register at Mom's store," Sarah said.

In the shade of old storefront awnings, J'aime trailed behind Robert and Sarah. Today was her first time walking through downtown, and she couldn't stop peering into the dark windows of the empty stores. Dust-covered glass, cobweb curtains, and years of grime coated her view. Occasionally she could make out amazing details like the flourish of a sculpted ceiling, the glow of stained glass, and the glitter of a chandelier.

"Hannaville was fancy once, wasn't it?" she asked, catching up with the others.

"It was a river town," Sarah said. She stopped at what looked like a department store on the corner of High Street and Main. "It still is, obviously, since there's still a river. But being a river town doesn't mean anything anymore."

Sarah pulled on the store's glass door. A cowbell clattered loudly, as J'aime and Robert followed her into a dim carpeted hallway and then into the lighted store space.

J'aime gasped. The open room was filled with aisles of stuff, tons of it. Three huge glass chandeliers sparkled above the shelves of estate sale goods. All the forgotten beauty she saw in the passing buildings was alive and gleaming in Gina's store.

Sarah's mom leaned on a glossy wooden counter with carved vines growing up the sides. J'aime thought it looked like it belonged in a Victorian hotel where people carried parasols.

Flipping a page in her magazine, Gina's pink T-shirt gems caught the light and glittered like the chandelier above her.

"Hey, Mom," Sarah said. She dropped the spare flyers by the register and walked behind the elegant checkout.

"Hey there, Hon," Gina said without looking up from what she was reading. "Garrett Ryan and Sage Whittney broke up. Can you believe it? *Slant* says it's because he cheated with that singer Soule, but I think it's because they both have double *T*'s in their name. They're full of nothing but 'trashy tantrums' if you know what I mean?"

"I have no idea what you mean." Sarah bent, disappearing below the counter. J'aime heard the sound of a mini-fridge opening.

"Don't drink my Bolt. I'm gonna need that later." Gina flipped the page and the rest of the group finally caught her eye. "Look who's here," she squealed at J'aime and Robert. "Here I am going on about celebrities, and I have two future ones standing right here in my store."

"Uh, thanks," Robert said.

Sarah stood back up. "She saw the flyer," she explained, handing them both cold bottles of water. "Mom, did you pay Dub for that armoire? The payment's due today."

"Sure, sure, I did," Gina replied, looking back down at her magazine.

Sarah's brow furrowed. She scanned the top of the messy counter, lifted an empty yogurt cup, and flipped through a pile of bills. "Right. I'll forward him money from the store account later."

"Oh, honey. Stop it," Gina said, shooing off her daughter. "Why don't you show your friends around? Give them the usual friend discount on anything they want!"

Sarah came out from behind the checkout. "This way, please," she said sarcastically, and started down the first aisle.

"You all have a good time!" Gina called after them. J'aime turned to wave, but Sarah's mom was lost in her magazine again.

Down the aisle, on either side of J'aime, were cases of statues, knickknacks, holiday decorations, teapots, records, books, vases, lamps, bookends, hats, shoes, even a box full of glass doorknobs. Robert stopped and picked up a twelve-inch-tall ceramic hobo with stars for eyes, a crazy grin, and a handful of deflated balloons.

"Where does your mom get this stuff?" he asked.

Sarah turned to see what caught his eye. "At estate sales mostly, sometimes online or garage sales. That's an antique whiskey decanter."

"A whiskey what?" Robert asked, turning the hobo over and looking at his feet.

She took the figurine from him and with a soft pop, pulled off the breakable head. "See, he's got a cork for a neck. You pour your whiskey inside his body and then put his head back on."

Robert closed one eye and looked inside the bottle. "Why would you want to do that?"

Sarah pushed the head back on. "I don't know, but people collect it, so we sell it," she flipped the hobo over and checked his price tag, "for thirty dollars."

Sarah sat the whisky decanter down on the glass shelf, and J'aime noticed a big round white pot. It had a thin metal bucket handle with a wooden grip in the center. It looked like the perfect thing for the cowboys to boil beans in.

J'aime touched the cool metal. "Is this a pioneer saucepan?"

Sarah smiled. "It's a chamber pot."

J'aime quickly pulled her finger back and wiped it on her shorts.

"Don't worry," Sarah reassured her, "it probably hasn't been used in decades."

They skipped the first floor and weaved their way to the second-floor stairs. Upstairs, there was a whole wall of amateur art: black velvet cacti, watercolors of English moors, spattered canvases trying to pass for modern art and several celebrity portraits.

Robert gazed up at a cluster of Elvises. A few were in pencil, some were in paint, and one was even in seashells. "I like the stitched one," Robert said. "How much is it?"

Sarah looked dumbfounded. "You like a big hand-embroidered portrait of Elvis?"

"Who wouldn't?" Robert answered.

"You keep getting weirder," Sarah said as she climbed up a nearby ladder to check the price. "Hundred bucks with the discount."

"How can that be worth a hundred dollars?" Robert said.

"Have you ever threaded a needle? It's hard," Sarah said. "It's not as expensive as the seashell one, though. That's crazy money. Now, the small five-by-seven cross-stitched Angelina Jolie might fit your price range better."

Robert waved her off as if she had lost her mind, and they went up to the third floor.

"This is Mom's sorting area. Most people don't come up here," Sarah explained. Out of nowhere she opened a door that blended in perfectly with the wall. "Come on, let's go out the fireman's way," she said excitedly.

J'aime pictured a fireman's pole and Chef Darius sliding chunks of lamb down silver skewers on *Meat Made Easy*. She didn't think she'd be as graceful as a cube of meat.

"Uh," she started to protest, then spotted over Robert's shoulder the black iron stairs of a rickety fire escape. She sighed a little. "We had one of these escapes in Chicago, when I was ten."

"How many apartments ago was that?" Robert asked as he carefully went down the creaking stairs.

J'aime had to think. "Five," she answered, "that was when Dad worked at an Eastern European buffet."

The fire escape dumped them out in the small parking lot behind the building. Sarah walked them toward the tent under the tall shade of a maple tree.

A breeze with a dash of late-afternoon heat blew through the maple's leaves. Tiny propeller seeds waltzed down through the air. J'aime caught one of the gracefully awkward helicopter-shaped seeds.

Sarah lifted the edge of the tarp and a pile of seedpods slid off the side. Shiny silver flashed. "It's a trailer," she said, knocking on the aluminum side. A hollow thud echoed on the inside.

J'aime stepped closer to help Sarah hold up the cover. "Is it an Airstream?"

"That's the brand. The model is called a Land Yacht," Sarah said, making her voice all fancy. "At least that's what the plaque says." She pointed to a yellowing piece of factory plastic under the window.

Robert pulled the handle and the door popped open. "You should lock this," he said.

"There's no need," Sarah answered, pushing them in.

"Whoa," J'aime exclaimed. She'd seen pictures of Airstream trailers with built-in everything: couches, tables, beds, showers. People liked to trick them out like mini-loft apartments on wheels. This one had built-in nothing.

"They gutted it," Sarah said, walking to one end of the hollow tin can room. "I think it was someone's retirement project that they abandoned, that's how Mom got it super cheap."

Robert nudged a round hole in the floor with his shoe. "Not too comfortable for camping. You'd be better off in a tent."

"We don't camp. Mom says she's going to resell it or remodel it herself."

J'aime looked up at the curved ceiling and imagined it covered with Gina's bejeweled sparkles.

Sarah continued, "I doubt she'll get to it. She's not into fixing big things." She nodded at J'aime, "There used to be a kitchen right where you're standing."

J'aime automatically took a step back and looked at the stained crepe-thin cream carpet. "Really?"

"The pipes are in place. All it needs is a new sink and stuff."

Robert took a closer look at the hole in the floor. "How can you tell?"

"I looked at the floor plan on online." She showed them the outline the counter had left from years of standing in the same place.

"It would be fun to cook in a tin can," J'aime said.

"And hot," Robert added.

The ring of an old-fashioned bicycle bell filled the gutted trailer. Robert pulled his phone out of his pocket and swiped the screen. "That's my first alarm for work. I gotta go soon."

The three of them headed back into the shop through the back door, where Robert dashed back upstairs. "I forgot something," he called out. "I'll catch up with you."

J'aime and Sarah finished their downstairs tour.

"I was saving the best until last," Sarah said. "This is our kitchen area."

J'aime gasped. Half the downstairs was filled with shelves of kitchen everything. A full assortment of cookware, glassware, and bakeware gleamed in the rays of chandelier light.

"We've got cast iron skillets, old-fashioned coffee percolators, collectable cartoon drinking glasses, and every kind of gadget or small appliance from the last fifty years. People love buying kitchen stuff."

A brown handle reached out to J'aime from behind a white Crockpot.

She carefully pulled the vintage saucepan with a matching lid from the shelf. A tiny tag marked $5 in blue ink dangled from the pot handle. The pumpkin-orange paint had a few scratches, but the dancing brown flowers were in good shape. She lifted the lid. The smooth black non-stick coating looked brand new.

"A fresh start," she said quietly.

Sara clattered a stack of aluminum Jell-O molds. "Did you say something?"

"Yeah," J'aime said. "How much is that friend discount?"

"How much do you want it to be?"

J'aime held up the last of her tip money. "I've got four bucks."

"For that old saucepan, let's take 50 percent off. You owe Finally Yours two dollars and fifty cents."

J'aime laughed. "That's not how bargaining works. I'm supposed to ask for the lower price."

"Remember the shoes? You'll give me all your cash if I ask you for it." Sarah smiled. "Think of it as the super friend discount, okay?"

J'aime beamed proudly. "I'll take it."

"Hey," Robert said, jogging toward them. He held up an eight-by-ten pencil portrait of young Elvis. "How much is the friend discount?"

Chapter 23
Rios Grab and Go

AT 12:01 P.M. SATURDAY, J'AIME AND ROBERT stood behind a foldout table in an empty parking lot. On the ground between them was a Kozy Kooler filled with forty-seven peeled hard-boiled eggs. Only three hadn't survived peeling. Food storage bags, puffed up like pillows, kept the delicate eggs extra protected on a nest of ice.

The glare from the parking lot hurt J'aime's eyes. Behind her, Sarah sat on top of a doublewide Igloo cooler filled with pico de gallo salsa and pepper jack cheese slices. A cartoon deer on her T-shirt said, RUN YOUR TAIL OFF! AT THE BUCKHORN *5K/10K*. Sarah scrolled through her phone, looking like she was ready for a nap instead of a run. Robert popped open a casserole-sized plastic container and checked the tortillas a second time. J'aime watched his lips silently counting them.

Yep. Eighty tortillas . . . again.

The rest of the parking lot wasn't completely empty. Parked between washed-out yellow lines were two more of the Rioses' folding tables and some camp chairs. All morning long, Robert hadn't mentioned anything about talking to his mom. J'aime was dying to know what she said. The talk must have gone okay because a Rios Rancheros sign that said, *Rios Grab and Go*, was tied to the front of their prep table.

"It's four minutes past noon," Sarah called out from the big cooler.

"Where's Lyn?" J'aime asked. "I was hoping for one guaranteed customer.

Robert unwrapped another set of paper plates and stacked them up. "No worries, she'll be here." A warm breeze kicked up and sent a paper plate flying.

"I got it," J'aime said, chasing the plate UFO across the parking lot.

The plate drifted until it hit a curb. She bent down and pinched the crinkled edge between her fingers. The singsong flow of a distant conversation drifted down the sidewalk. Looking to her left, she spotted a small crowd less than a block away.

J'aime spun on her flip-flops and yelled to Robert and Sarah, "People! They're coming."

"Hurry," Sarah shouted back. She handed J'aime a squirt bottle of antibacterial hand cleanser, then Robert snapped on some plastic gloves as J'aime tugged on hers.

"Remember the plan," Sarah said, moving around to the front of the table. "Once you get a few orders, I'll start filming. We'll do your interviews after."

The people turned into the parking lot. J'aime removed the towel covering her cutting board, exposing it to the blue sky overhead. A commercial-sized bag of cheese slices and a container of homemade salsa landed on the table next to the tortillas.

Robert smiled at J'aime. "We're open for free-ness."

She plopped an empty spaghetti sauce jar at the front of the table. "And donations."

"Wait!" Sarah said, taping a piece of paper to the jar that read, *$T. LAWRENCE PANTRY DONATIONS WELCOME*. She dropped in a dollar.

"A dollar sign for a saint? Really?" Robert asked.

Sarah waved him off and glanced at the crowd. "I want to get a good opening shot. Be back in a minute."

As she dashed across Main Street, a familiar voice shouted at J'aime and Robert. "Hey, where can I get some food around here?"

It was Lyn. She was leading a pack of customers straight to their prep table.

J'aime realized that Lyn in her regular clothes was a lot like Lyn in her lunch lady uniform: a flowered vintage sundress, and a bandana wrapped around her head. The red cowboy boots were the only true difference.

"Chef Robert, Chef J'aime," Lyn said, "this is my cousin, Lisa. She's a reporter for the local newspaper."

A taller, slightly older woman with blonde hair that frizzed more than it flowed waved at them. "Nice to meet you all. I brought the whole office with me."

"Awesome," Robert said. "Are you ready to eat?"

"Bring it on," Lyn answered. "Where's Sarah?"

Lisa looked surprised. "Sarah's here?"

"Yes," Lyn explained. "She's filming this pop-up."

J'aime was a little surprised herself. "You know Sarah?" she asked the blonde woman.

"All her life." Lisa grinned. "We're cousins."

"But," J'aime said, turning to Lyn. "That means that you and Sarah are cousins too."

The lunch lady winked. "All her life. I'll help get these starving yokels in line."

Small towns, J'aime thought. She let the tangled family tree go and grabbed a tortilla. Out in the parking lot were two men in yellow coveralls, several out-of-apron lunch ladies, and even a few farmie guys from school. They had gone from zero to twenty customers in a matter of seconds.

"This is actually happening," J'aime said. Her stomach flipped nervously. "I'm gonna chef for real people."

Robert handed Lisa her huevos rancheros. "Enjoy it," he said. Lyn's cousin dropped five bucks into the jar. As the reporter walked away, he calmly folded his second tortilla. "Get cooking, Chef J'aime. I can't do this all by myself."

The crowd continued to grow. Lyn made her way back to the prep table. She dug around in a canvas bag with a leafy lettuce-y design and a slogan, *Eat, Drink, and Bok Choy*, on the side. "Thought you might want these," she said, unfurling their aprons from school.

J'aime slipped her usual cooking clothes over her head. The rub of apron on the back of her neck sent a wave of confidence down her spine. Funny how putting on the right clothes could make her feel more like her true self.

Lyn tied J'aime's string in the back and asked, "How else can I help?"

Robert grabbed his own apron. "Do you mind passing out the food if we get backed up?"

The lunch lady reached over to the Germ Shield pump and squirted a glob of antibacterial goop all over her hands. "Passing out food is my calling."

After fumbling through the first four customers, J'aime and Robert slipped into an easy cooking rhythm. Robert chatted more than she did, but she made sure to say hello before lowering her head to focus on her work. They served up orders to the clank of quarters tumbling into the glass donation jar.

Slicing through the tender shake of the egg white, J'aime's knife always paused when it hit the firm, yellow yolk in the middle. The textures were so different. They pushed her knife around, making her slices thin on one end and thick on the other. Her pieces were more consistent than the first time she tried to slice eggs in the cafeteria. As her fingers pressed into the spongy white, for a moment, she couldn't believe how freaked out she had been about touching hard-boiled eggs.

J'aime handed a plate to a man with a wiry gray mustache.

"This sure is a treat," he said, though his mustache did most of the talking. He waved money at her like a flag. "I got a two-dollar bill for you."

J'aime looked down at her cutting board. "Thanks."

"Everyone should be thanking you," Lisa chirped. She was at the prep table again, but this time there was a guy with a professional camera, and Sarah with her iPhone too. "I mean, check out that line."

J'aime hadn't looked further than the person in front of her in a while. The line curved around the parking lot and wrapped around the sidewalk on to Chestnut Street.

Her mouth dropped open.

"It'll be okay," Robert said calmly. "We've got eighty tortillas, remember?"

Lisa pulled her phone out of her pocket. "This could be a nice human-interest piece for the paper. Can I interview you two? I want to know how you met, how you got the idea, everything."

Sarah gave them an exaggerated silent nod.

Robert folded a tortilla and handed it to a customer. "Why not?"

Because if this gets in the paper, then all of Hannaville will know that we met at St. Lawrence's. It'll be public knowledge that J'aime didn't have enough food in her life. Did she care? Kind of. Did it really matter? Probably not. It seemed like most of the town shopped the pantry shelves anyway. "I guess so," she finally answered.

"Great," Lisa beamed. "I'll ask you questions while you cook, and we'll get some photos later."

It was hard for J'aime to cook and talk at the same time, but Robert had no problem. His answers were as steady as his slicing, and they kept coming. Eventually, she gave up and let him spill their brief history to the reporter.

J'aime focused on spreading salsa across egg and cheese. Chunks of tomato tumbled onto the tortilla as Lisa asked her a wrap-up question.

"If you win and Bentley comes here to Hannaville to film an episode, what would you do on the show?" Lisa asked.

Robert tucked the edges of a tortilla over and under. "We'd show the Food Network that Food Carma represents good food doing good. I guess we'd probably set up like this again and bring the community together."

"Sign me up. You two will look cute on TV," Lisa said. "Thank you both for the interview. We've got to get back to the office. No promises about the paper, but I have a feeling with this kind of crowd, the story will run."

As she walked away, Sarah gave them a thumbs-up. "Leave it to Lisa to ask every question we were going to put in the video. I filmed the whole thing."

Robert grabbed a fresh plate. "You think the interview is usable for the entry?"

"Heck, ya. It's perfect." Sarah looked into the crowd. "I'll catch her and make sure she's cool with it."

Except for the "cute" comment, J'aime thought as Sarah disappeared into the crowd. That might not fly with a certain someone.

J'aime folded her tortilla. "Is Abbi coming today?"

She imagined Abbi cheering, waving an immaculately hand-quilted *I LOVE ROBERT!* sign from the back of the parking lot. J'aime handed a finished plate to a young woman then slid another plate from the stack to start the next order. A tortilla flew onto her plate, barely sticking its landing.

"Are you throwing food at me now?" she asked, scooching it back.

Robert smirked. "Abbi couldn't make it. Family stuff." He spread some salsa on his eggs and pointed his spoon out at the crowd. "I think we're going to run out before everyone gets their order."

J'aime compared the waiting hungry customers in line to the dwindling eggs. He was right. There was no way they could feed all these people.

"Like they say on *Extreme Take-Out*," she said, "First-served are—"

"Robert Rios," a scalding voice shouted from the back of the customers.

Robert laid down his knife as the crowd parted. All the hungry chatting ceased. A woman with long coal-black hair stepped to the front of the line. Her face creased with fury. J'aime recognized her. It was the bread lady from the pantry.

"Calm down, Mom," Robert said quietly. He handed a full plate to the next person in line.

"You told me you were at art club." Robert's mother stared at the Rios Rancheros sign attached to the folding table. She grabbed the plastic banner and lifted it up in disbelief. "This is our sign," she fumed. "Why are you treating our business like a lemonade stand?"

J'aime dropped her knife. The crowd looked as stunned as she felt.

"It's just the old taco cart sign," Robert said. "We needed to borrow it because—"

"How did you get a permit to street vend?" she yelled. His mom pointed a finger in J'aime's direction. "And who's this? She's not my employee. I didn't hire her."

"Mama. Please, stop," Robert said. He reached out a gloved hand and gently pushed her finger down. "I can explain."

She lightly slapped his hand away. The donation jar toppled. J'aime caught it before it hit the unforgiving parking lot.

"You better," his mother snapped. She walked away from waiting customers and Robert trailed behind her. They crossed the edge of the parking lot to the sidewalk.

"Are you coming back?" J'aime asked anxiously, but Robert and his mom had already disappeared around the corner of the building.

He's not the golden child anymore, J'aime thought. She stood alone at the prep table, her hands hanging limp at her sides. The crowd shuffled and murmured. A hard-boiled egg slice stared up at her from the open-faced tortilla. She was the only chef left in the kitchen. In the hot parking lot sun, a chill crept up her back. It followed her apron strings, vaporizing her confidence. She had to feed all these people by herself.

Doubt whispered in her ear. *What do you think you're doing?*

A thud snapped her out of her cold sweat. Lyn's bok choy bag had hit the ground right by J'aime's feet. The lunch lady dug deep into the tote. In a flourish, she whipped out another apron.

"I always carry one. You never know when someone might need help in the kitchen," Lyn winked.

J'aime stared at her in disbelief.

Lyn shrugged. "It happens more often than you think." The lunch lady's eyes flicked down to J'aime's hands. "You better put that jar on the table. You're still in business."

J'aime's were gripping the donation jar so hard her knuckles were white. How long had she been holding it like that? Quickly, she sat it back on the table.

"How many tortillas are left?" Lyn asked.

J'aime peeked into the tortilla box. "Twenty, but there's only ten eggs."

From behind the prep table, Lyn yelled at the crowd. "Did you hear that? Ten eggs left. That's the way the tomato dices, folks. But I know Robert and J'aime appreciated you coming out today. Let's get the last hungry people up here. Donations for the pantry are welcome no matter what."

J'aime watched Lyn grab a paper plate and start cooking. A lunch lady was saving her bacon. Any other time, this would've distracted J'aime from everything else, but not today. All she could think about was Robert. Was he okay? Where did he go?

Lyn pushed the pico de gallo container toward J'aime. "Worry about the boy later," the lunch lady instructed. "We've got cookin' to do."

Robotically, J'aime spread salsa over yellow egg yolk. Robert hadn't told his mom about the contest. "I'll handle it," he'd promised. But he didn't.

She carefully folded the tortilla. It ripped anyway. Red tomato juice oozed out onto the paper plate.

He lied to me too.

Chapter 24
A Second Helping

THE FIRST THING J'AIME NOTICED WHEN LYN pulled her SUV into the McWilliamses' driveway was that the front door to the duplex was open. Her dad was home when he should have been at work.

Being crammed into the backseat with Robert's tables hadn't been exactly the most comfortable ride, but at least it was a ride.

"See you guys," J'aime said climbing out of the vehicle.

"Good job today, girl," Lyn said from her open window.

After the last tortilla was served, they had headed over to Sarah's house to edit the video entry for a couple of hours. J'aime felt uncomfortable making decisions without her co-chef there, but at least now they had an entry ready to upload.

She shut the car door. In the passenger seat, Sarah leaned across her cousin to talk to J'aime. "Let me know when you show the video to Robert, okay? It looks like Food Network gold to me."

"Sure," J'aime said, distracted by movement on the other side of the screen door.

"Get Chef Robert to admit its Food Network worthy," Sarah insisted. "Then enter that thing ASAP."

Truth was, J'aime could only concentrate on one thing right now: Her dad absolutely shouldn't be home. *Trouble loves a second helping.*

Lyn's arm rested casually outside the driver's window. "The fight wasn't that bad," she said, seeing J'aime frown. "Robert will be fine."

J'aime gave her a half smile. The way his mom had pointed her finger right at her, made everything feel like it was all her fault. Maybe it kind of was? But she wasn't the one lying about the Hannaville Art Anarchists or whatever Robert called his pretend art club.

Standing in the driveway, J'aime watched Lyn's SUV slowly back away. The last thing she wanted to do was find out what other problem was waiting for her inside the duplex. *This has to be about the money*, she thought.

Behind her, she heard the screen door creak open. "Hey," her dad said, faking friendliness.

J'aime turned around slowly. "Hey," she said, doing some pretending herself. "Are you on break?"

He pulled the screen door shut. "We need to talk."

Her dad was a lot calmer then he should be. *Play dumb for as long as you can*, J'aime thought, as she climbed the stairs and sat her bag down inside the living room.

"Robert's mom came looking for him at the casino," her dad said. There was an edge to the way he said, *casino*. Whatever happened there, her visit must have been as pleasant as her drop by at the parking lot.

J'aime threw her fed-up body onto the sofa. Her dad could have scooted her legs and sat down with her. Instead, he stood next to the recliner.

"His mom was pissed," he explained. "She didn't even know her son was working at the casino until this morning. She threw a hissy fit right in front of the staff. Of all the days I work a double."

He started pacing the frayed living room rug. J'aime watched his black sneakers do their frustrated dance. There were white sauce splatters all over the toes. Must be Alfredo on the buffet today.

Her dad kept on talking. "Then Mark told us that you two were selling food on Main Street. That sent the Rios lady through the roof. A busload of Gold Rewards members saw the whole thing go down." He paused. "Look at me when I'm talking to you."

J'aime chose to focus on his shoulder. It looked relatively less agitated compared to the rest of him.

"What I don't get," he asked, adding a dramatic parental pause, "is why you didn't tell me you were going to sell food in the middle of town?"

She wanted to scream, *Why didn't you tell me you never paid Mom's bills?* But J'aime took a calming breath instead. Sara was right. J'aime needed to talk to Robert. The sooner her dad went back to work, the closer she was to posting that video.

"We like to cook, okay?" she answered. "We weren't breaking any laws."

"Yeah, you were. You need a permit to sell food in public," her dad said firmly. "There are health codes, legal papers that have to happen."

"We weren't selling anything. Why do you guys keep saying that?" She winced at her high-pitched shrillness. "We were shooting a video for a Food Network contest."

Her father stopped fidgeting. His fists squeezed into tight balls like raw pizza dough. "That's why you stole $105 from me? To enter a TV contest?"

J'aime kept silent and watched his hands. They looked awfully angry.

"You know," he said, his flushed cheeks were spreading to his bald spot, "when you didn't give me that five-dollar tip I was going to make you hand it over, but then I thought, let it slide. Things have been tough lately. Hell, really tough. If I'd have known that five dollars was going to lead to almost every penny I own being stolen, that my own daughter was a thief, I would of, I would of..."

Her dad was so mad he couldn't get the right words out. "That Rios woman yelled at me right in front of the general manager," he yelled. "The general manager. I'm so screwed."

He stomped over to the front door. J'aime waited for him to shove open the rickety screen, but she heard a hard thud instead of a metal creak. He punched the wall, his fist hitting the space next to the doorframe. Even though she was several feet away, J'aime jumped, pushing her body back into the sofa. His hand recoiled back as if to punch again, but he stopped. The drywall was still intact, no hole, no expensive damage done. There was blood on his knuckles.

J'aime froze, waiting for whatever would happen next.

"Damn it," her dad shouted. "That laptop you use, I'm selling it the first chance I get," he said bitterly. "You owe me that money."

"The laptop isn't mine," J'aime protested. "It belongs to the school. You can't sell it, and I didn't take almost all your money. Part of it's my money too."

"That jar keeps us safe," her dad yelled then tried to collect himself. "Stay away from that Rios kid." her dad grumbled. "I have to get back to work. There's a managers meeting."

Her dad's injured hand grasped the screen-door handle. J'aime was sick of parents yelling at her. The words flew out of her mouth before she could stop them. "A managers meeting?" she blurted. "You can barely manage anything."

Her dad stopped. For a second he stood there and J'aime wondered if he'd punch the wall again. Instead, he walked over to the recliner. Her heart pounded. His eyes blazed, but he didn't move closer, keeping the chair in between them.

"Shut up," he yelled. "I put in twelve-hour shifts to keep us off the streets." Her dad's favorite lecture kicked into gear. "I work my butt off because of you. Who keeps a roof over your head? Who puts food in this fridge?"

"Me," she yelled back. "I'm the one who goes to the pantry. Not you."

J'aime was breathing hard. It felt good to finally say the truth, no matter how much trouble it brought with it.

Another angry finger pointed directly at J'aime. "Two mouths are harder to feed than—" her dad stopped himself from saying the rest of it.

J'aime finished his sentence for him. "One."

The words bounced off her dad like a feather. No impact. Nothing, because they were true. The sad fact was they used to split food three ways. After her mom died, it sickened J'aime to notice how her portions had gotten bigger. If she weren't around, her dad's life would be less complicated and fuller.

Anger drained out of her voice, leaving it ragged. "You haven't even asked why I'm entering the contest," she said. "Have you ever thought that *maybe* I'm trying to make things better too?"

Her dad rubbed his forehead hard. He didn't deny anything. He glanced at his watch. "I'm going back to work."

With a creak and a brutal slam, he made it out the screen door this time.

Quiet twilight settled in the living room, hushing away the emotional static arguments leave behind. J'aime heard the Suburban's engine snarl and drive off down the street.

He must've gotten gas. The everyday thought drifted through her mind like the fight hadn't just happened. To her own surprise, she let loose a pathetic laugh. *He has no problem spending his tips.* J'aime sank onto the hardwood floor, curling up into a ball.

Once upon a time, when she was little, her dad read sci-fi books to her the way most parents read their kids picture books. He'd act out all the parts until she burst into giggles. Where did that dad go?

Chapter 25

Food Carma

IT WAS OFFICIALLY DARK OUTSIDE. J'AIME pulled herself together. Walking into her bedroom, she didn't bother flipping on a light. The only thing she turned on was her loaner school laptop. Slipping a pink USB drive into the port, she watched their Food Carma video.

Earlier in the day, J'aime debated what to cut, but now, the entry film looked seamless. Sarah did a great job trimming and making the chaos seem organized. Luckily, she'd stopped filming right before Robert's mom stormed in. The event still had that happy blue-sky feel to it. Robert made them sound like chefs who could truly make a difference. She paused the image on his face. He was talking about teaching her to chop onions. His eyes were so wide and bright. Even on a bad day like today a pulse of hope still found its way to her skin.

During the thirteenth viewing, she decided the video entry was Food Network-worthy and texted Robert. If he wanted to approve it, he'd have to come over. J'aime double-checked every word of her text. This wasn't the time for autocorrect to turn *the video is good*, to *the video is gouda*.

If Robert came over then they could talk about what happened, and of course, the lying, which after the fight with her dad seemed like a minor offense. She sent her text and leaned back against the side of her bed. The faded coil rug that covered part of her bedroom floor pressed into her legs. Since her dad slammed the front door and roared off down the street, J'aime felt the urge to only sit on the floor.

Thief, she thought, remembering her dad's word. *From now on, he'll always wonder if I'm stealing from him.*

No matter how uncomfortable or dusty the floor was, she needed to ground herself. J'aime's phone chimed in her hands. That was fast. Her nerves buzzed with the device. Robert must have been looking at his phone when she'd texted. The screen, however, dashed that idea. A non-Robert phone number appeared. It wasn't her dad or Sarah. It was her old pal, 1-773-555-8502. A debt collection agency.

J'aime laid her buzzing, chiming phone face down on the coil rug. Turning her ringer off wasn't an option. If Robert wrote back, when Robert wrote back, she didn't want to miss it. The phone chimed two more times then stopped. It was 7:00 p.m., five hours until the contest deadline.

While uploading the video entry to her desktop, loaded questions simmered in her mind. Why didn't Robert tell her that he hadn't talked to his parents about the contest? They spent hours together almost every day. Weren't they close enough to tell each other this kind of stuff? Why did he keep it from her?

Robert doesn't need to tell me everything, J'aime thought. *He's got Abbi to spill his guts to.*

Then again, she never directly told Robert that their grocery-shopping spree was paid for with secretly borrowed money. The phone screen lit up again. The device chimed, buzzing like a swarm of bees as the debt collectors gave the number a second try.

She ran her fingers over her laptop keyboard and pulled up the Fresh Starter website. J'aime scrolled through six pages of hopeful people with food dreams. Her throat tightened. Five hours until the deadline meant there was still time for even more people to enter. She looked at the black phone screen. *Come on, Robert.*

Being a chef mattered too much to both of them. Winning the contest meant everything—especially now.

She texted him. I'M ENTERING US.

Before she could change her mind, she clicked on the entry form, filled out a few short lines, then clicked on the fateful upload button.

As the upload percent grew larger, their Food Carma video was almost on its way to Bentley. J'aime checked the Wi-Fi bars assuming she'd lose her internet or the site would glitch, but the digital universe was on her side. For better or worse, she was making life happen.

A message popped up on her computer screen. *Thank you for your entry. Stay tuned for more Fresh Starter information. Cheers!*

"No going back now," she said.

Her phone rang for a third time. J'aime picked up her mom's old phone and stared at the collection agency's number. For years, her dad let her think these calls were about her lunch debt. In her new open-box-reality, there was a 90 percent chance the creditors were calling about all those unpaid hospital bills.

They'd moved their old debts from apartment to apartment for so long. J'aime was tired of running and leaving a trail of fear behind them. If she won that contest she could be the one to stop the debt scavengers from circling. The idea of it was such a relief. They could stop moving all the time. They'd finally have enough and a real place to call home.

She had to win this thing.

But first she needed to know how much trouble they were really in, down to the last penny.

The phone rang a fourth time; J'aime's finger hovered over the screen. A little voice in the back of her mind whispered, *Don't answer it.*

J'aime pushed the fear away, tapped her phone, and said, "Hello?"

Chapter 26
Banana Split

THE NEXT MORNING, J'AIME TIPTOED OUT OF the kitchen with a banana. Sunday brunch plate dealing was on the schedule. In the sunlight, a trail of her dad's clothes led from the front door to his bedroom. Quietly, J'aime reached to unlock the front door, but it was already open a crack. Pulling the front door open further, she found her dad's keys dangling from the other side of the keyhole. For part of the night, their door was an open invitation to robbers, or worse. Safety definitely wasn't on her dad's mind when he got home. Judging by the way he shed his manager's uniform, and the lock situation, the casino must have given the closing kitchen staff free drinks last night.

J'aime pulled his keys from the door and tossed them on his abandoned black pants. He wasn't managing brunch today. If she went to work, they'd run into each other during passing shifts. That would be way better than a run-in in the living room.

Dread. She dreaded running into him. J'aime was already in trouble, and then she stirred the pot further with the debt collectors. Odds were good that he didn't know she'd answered their call, not yet. With a "Hello," and simply saying her dad wasn't home, she confirmed and located the McWilliamses for them. But that wasn't all J'aime said. She actually talked to the vultures. She found out exactly what they owed for her mother's medical treatments. The insane dollar amount blared through her brain like a tornado siren.

J'aime took her own keys out of her pocket. Locking the front door seemed ridiculous after her key discovery, but she did it anyway.

She found Sarah sitting on the front porch steps. Sweat marks dotted the back of her purple tank top. Sarah turned around. "Hi," she said.

"Hey," J'aime said surprised. "What are you doing here?"

"I was running by and remembered you said you were working brunch this morning, I thought I'd walk with you."

Just like an opening fridge door, a little light clicked on inside J'aime's heart. She smiled. "Thanks. You want half my banana?"

Sarah stood up. "I'll have breakfast later. We better hit the side-walks if you want to get to work on time."

As they made their way down to the crumbling cement path, Sarah asked, "Did Robert like the video?"

"I don't know." J'aime pulled up the straps of her canvas shop-ping bag. "I didn't show it to him."

Disappointment sunk Sarah's bare shoulders. "You didn't enter it."

J'aime stopped to crease the banana peel with her fingernail, breaking the skin.

"I did," she answered.

Sarah's mouth hung open. "Without Robert seeing it?"

"He never texted me back," J'aime explained. And it was still true. So far this morning there was nothing but cellphone silence from him. "What was I supposed to do? Not enter?" She peeled her breakfast and thought about the mostly empty jar. "I didn't really have a choice."

"Wow," Sarah said a little shocked, "balls."

"Balls?" J'aime mumbled with a mouth full of banana.

"Heck ya," Sarah grinned. "You've got 'em."

"Uh, no," J'aime pinched off a bite of banana and handed it to Sarah. "That's such a sporty thing to say."

Despite her breakfast refusal, Sarah tossed the banana chunk into her mouth. It bulged, giving her a one-sided chipmunk cheek. She pointed at her T-shirt.

The phrase *EVERY DAMN DAY*, covered her whole torso.

"Balls, it is." J'aime laughed.

By the time they reached the turn off for Cliff Drive, the banana was long gone.

J'aime peered up the road's sharp incline. She sighed. "I hate this street."

"Cliff Drive?" Sarah asked, peering up at the cement peak. "How could you hate a street?"

They started to climb. J'aime said, "I can't walk up this thing without stopping to catch my breath at least three times."

"Three isn't that bad," Sarah said. She gazed up the incline. "I love Cliff Drive."

"Why?" J'aime asked, as a few cars cruised by, making their way to the casino parking lot.

"When you get to the top, if you walk twenty more feet there's a city limit sign," Sarah said wistfully. "I run up Cliff Drive every week and stand on the other side of that pole."

"You just stand there?" J'aime puffed.

"I think about leaving town," Sarah said.

J'aime stopped walking. "I need an air pit stop." She bent over, breathing deeply. "Leaving town isn't hard," she gasped. "You go to Churchill all the time, right?"

Sarah jogged in place. "Churchill is practically Hannaville. I've been going there all my life. I'm talking about *leaving town* for good. The big *L*."

Sweat beaded on J'aime's forehead, and she stood up again. "I've left a lot of places. It doesn't mean they leave you."

Without a warning, Sarah started to climb again. J'aime tried to catch up.

"I can't stay here," Sarah said, her feet moving as fast as her words. "Only two people in my whole family have left Hannaville and never moved back. This town is all my family knows. Even Lyn came home." Sarah's pace picked up even faster. "In a big city, you're mostly invisible, aren't you?"

Hustling behind her, J'aime could only nod. Spending air on words wasn't going to get her up this hill, not with Sarah.

"Can you imagine every person in Chicago knowing your whole life history? My mom only makes things worse. She loves the attention. Do you know she loses the bank deposit at least once a month? It's almost like she's begging for more drama, and I'm the one who holds her together."

Taking a couple of more breaths, J'aime dug around in her bag for her water bottle. They were almost at the top. She took a sip. "I know what you mean."

Sarah put her hands on her hips. "Really?" she asked.

"The McWilliamses might not be good at actual running." J'aime took another gulp of water. "But we're good at running from our problems. The bad part is, the problems follow us around anyway."

•

The first thing J'aime did when she walked into work was check the schedule.

"Robert Rios" wasn't listed. She swore he was coming in for the brunch shift, but with all the prep for the video, did she get confused? Or maybe Robert's mom forced him to quit?

J'aime tried not to think about that as she passed out plates to a Lutheran early morning choir on a post-performance high. If he had been at work, she wasn't sure what she would have done anyway. Robert's mom was beyond mad. Her dad was furious with the added bonus of being hungover, and Bentley might be viewing their video entry right this very second.

Her nerves couldn't handle it. "I'm so stressed out," she accidentally said to a blue-haired choir member as she handed her a fresh plate.

"Honey, aren't we all?" the little old lady said back, then dipped up some chocolate pudding.

After work, she walked home alone with only a buffet to-go box for company. She missed Sarah speeding along in front of her. When J'aime finally reached her block, she spotted Robert's truck parked outside her house under the shade of an oak tree. As she got closer, she noticed the vehicle was empty. Was he on the porch? She took a hard right and started up the yard to her front steps.

"Hey," said a tired, gravelly voice.

J'aime faced the truck. The passenger window was open. Robert was suddenly sitting there, straightening his shirt like he'd been sleeping. He must have been lying flat in the front seat.

"I texted you," J'aime said, making her way down the sidewalk.

Robert scooted over a little closer to the window but didn't get out of the truck. "I saw it."

That's when J'aime noticed he looked awful. His clothes were beyond wrinkled and his gelled pompadour was dented.

"You okay?"

Robert looked out the front windshield as if willing the road to take him anywhere else.

"Mom wouldn't listen to me," he said. "Last night, we kept fighting. It was stupid."

J'aime put two and two together. "Did your mom kick you out?"

"Basically," Robert said. "She told me I needed some tough love, that I don't appreciate what we have and that our pop-up made her hard work look like a joke."

J'aime remembered Robert's story about his cousin. "So are you banished now?"

"I don't even know." He let out a heavy sigh. "Mom and I need a break from each other. I can't go back there right now."

J'aime hesitated. She needed to ask him something, but at the same time she didn't want to make things worse. A voice whispered in her head. *He lied to you. You deserve to know why.*

"I'm sorry," she said, "I need to ask you—"

"No," Robert said quickly. He hung his head. "I'm sorry. I should've told you I didn't tell mom about the contest."

J'aime held her tote bag a little tighter. "It's okay," she said softly.

"No, it's not," Robert said. He gazed out the dusty windshield. "I thought I could handle her when she found out, but I was wrong. There's no handling her."

The tree rustled overhead, making shadows flutter across his face. J'aime glanced at her duplex then back at Robert. It was empty. Her dad wouldn't be home for hours. "You want to come in?"

He shook his head.

"Where did you sleep last night?"

Robert looked down like he was messing around with his phone, but she knew he wasn't.

"You slept in your truck?" she guessed.

"It was late. I parked in a driveway of one of those boarded-up houses near the casino." He paused. "I didn't sleep much."

J'aime shuddered. She couldn't imagine sleeping outside one of those dilapidated homes. Her chest tightened at the thought of being homeless. If she'd never suggested the Food Network contest, Robert would be safe in his own bed, or at least in a building with sturdy walls. "How about your sisters," she suggested. "They don't live at home, do they? Could you stay with one of them?"

"My mom hates me right now, and everyone knows," Robert answered. "None of my family will let me stay with them. I told you. She's their boss. They depend on her." He shook his head again in disbelief. "They won't help me until she isn't mad at me anymore. I'm going to crash with Mateo. My cousin's not the most reliable person, but he'll let me stay there."

Robert took a deep breath. "Listen, I'm still glad you entered us in the contest."

The sun found its way through the leaves and warmed J'aime's face. She squinted from the glare. "I don't know why. All I did was get you kicked out."

He poked a thumb back at himself. "I got me kicked out. You just had a good idea."

J'aime wasn't so sure. *Dad punched a wall.* She swallowed her anxiety.

"I was thinking," Robert said. "If we win the Fresh Starter, this'll be our rock-bottom moment. Those always happen right before your dreams come true, right?"

Now she was the one who wouldn't look him in the face. Homelessness was actually happening to him. She needed more than dreams to make everything okay again. "Are you sure you don't want to stay here?"

Robert raised his eyebrows at her. "I don't think your dad would like that much."

He was right. Robert sleeping on their sofa wouldn't fly. Her dad was looking for more reasons to fire Robert. "Here," she said, stepping forward and sticking her to-go box through the car window. "Take it. It's what's left of my employee lunch. It's salad bar stuff, but it's pretty good."

Robert eagerly glanced at the food but pretended like it was nothing.

J'aime knew that look. "I've got more leftovers in the fridge," she lied. "Take it."

She felt the Styrofoam container slip from her hands into his lap.

"Thanks," he mumbled, scooting back over to the driver's seat. "I've gotta go. Mateo lives in the next county. I'll see you around."

"Wait," she said as he started the truck. The engine hummed happily. "Are you going to school tomorrow?"

"School?" Robert repeated like it was a concept he'd never heard of. He grasped the steering wheel hard and stared straight ahead, as if he was trying to see what the next day would bring. He let out a sad chuckle. "I can't even think about that right now."

Before J'aime could question him more, he drove off.

That's one way to end a conversation you don't want to have.

Chapter 27

Heirloom Veg

ONE WEEK LATER, J'AIME, AND ROBERT WERE sprawled out on the McWilliamses' front steps. A spring breeze made the dandelions in the overgrown yard dance.

"My dad is never going to mow this yard," J'aime said.

Sitting on the top step, Robert stretched out his legs into full recline mode. "It's hard to take care of a yard when you work twelve-hour shifts," he answered, a white fuzzy weed between his fingers.

She leaned back on the step with him, her legs almost meeting his. Her dad was officially not talking to her. Ever since their Saturday fight, he only communicated through texts and avoided being conscious when they were home together. Sleep was an excellent way to ignore her presence.

J'aime scrolled on her phone. Her dad's messages were all about working late or going in early. None of the texts mentioned debt collectors. She was waiting for the timer to go off on that bomb. Even the collection agencies had stopped contacting her. No more missed calls on her phone with Chicago area codes. Her whole point of answering the phone was so they could finally clean up their money messes and move on. Weirdly enough, the silent phone and blank screen weren't as reassuring as she hoped they would be.

Worries crowded in on her peaceful afternoon. Finding the Fresh Starter website, she double-checked the announcement

time again. J'aime scrolled. Nope. Everything was still the same—
Fresher Starter winner tomorrow at 9:00 a.m. sharp.

"What time are you showing up at Sarah's house tomorrow?"
she asked.

"Eight," Robert answered.

"An hour early?"

"I promised to help Sarah set up and stuff. She offered to let me
stay on the sofa, but I don't know."

Robert's truck was parked in front of her house again, except
this time it wasn't just a truck. The Toyota was his everything: bed,
living room, and kitchen. Staying at Mateo's hadn't worked out.
Robert wouldn't say exactly why. J'aime got the vibe that his cousin's problems maybe ran deeper than bossing the boss around.

"Where did you park last night?" she asked, not sure she really
wanted to know.

"On Water Street. After the last flood, no one lives there anymore."

He acted like camping out in his truck was nothing, but the real-
ness of Robert's situation completely rattled J'aime. Sleeping rough
can get dangerous fast. It made her sad that his reliable family life
was suddenly as crazy as hers. She *did* ask him to enter the contest,
but it wasn't totally her fault that he was sleeping in his truck. Yet
she couldn't shake the feeling that she definitely triggered the situation. J'aime glanced back at the duplex, grateful for her safe, secure
bedroom. The idea of spending the night in an abandoned neighborhood next to the dark swirl of the Missouri River was too much.

"You really should stay with Sarah," she said. "Couch surfing is
a lot better than sleeping in vacant lots."

Robert avoided answering by focusing on the dandelions.

"Stay somewhere safe," she tried again, "before something bad
happens. I don't think your mom really wants—"

"I'm tired of doing what my mom wants," he snipped.

"I know," J'aime said, keeping her tone calm. "But if she kicked
you out, aren't you doing exactly what she wants by not going home?"

"I'm pissed at my mom, and she's pissed at me, okay?" Robert said. "I'm not going back until I'm ready to deal with her."

He sat up and rested his arms on his knees. Robert was usually ultra clean. He was almost polished. Now his jeans had that constant look of worn clothes, dirty around the cuffs and permanent wrinkles. "Stop worrying. I can keep myself safe."

J'aime bit her lip, trying not to ask about Abbi. Aren't girl-friends supposed to shelter boyfriends in times of trouble?

Her willpower on low, she gave in. "What about Abbi?"

Robert lifted his head, peaking an eye up at her.

"What does she think about you sleeping in your truck and stuff?"

"Abbi worries too much," Robert gave her a forced half smile. "Like someone else I know."

He stood up and stretched. Robert's arms reached up toward the sky. A thin line of stomach peeked out from underneath his white T-shirt. She remembered the way her finger had touched the seam of his shirt the first day she talked to him in the school cafeteria. J'aime slowly reached toward the glimpse of skin. Her finger was about to make contact when he suddenly jumped off the steps.

"I've got something for you," he said, changing the subject.

Quickly, she drew her hand back. Did he know she was about to touch him? "What?" she asked.

He ran to the truck. Leaning over the edge, he dug around in the bed. Now the skin on his back flashed her, but she ignored it. Robert stood up with a Styrofoam to-go box in each hand.

"Are those from Rios Rancheros?" she asked.

"You really don't listen to me." He walked back up the sidewalk. "I can't step foot in that place right now."

J'aime knew he couldn't go to the restaurant. She was just hoping for some good food. Without ingredients from his home fridge, their morning cooking lessons had stopped, and so had her extra meals. Robert was even planning on shopping the pantry with her next week and storing some of his food in her fridge.

Our lives are upside-down, she thought.

Both of the containers were torn in half, and their lids filled with dirt. She eyed them skeptically. "Is this a new organic cleanse or something?"

Robert sat the makeshift flowerpots on the steps. "You think you're so funny." He patted down the dirt with his fingers then grabbed J'aime's water bottle and sprinkled the soil. "I stopped by my dad's seed shed last night. It's way out in the pasture. No one saw me."

Never once had she said anything about starting a garden. "Are these for me?" she asked.

"Yes, you, Farmer Fish Head. You want to cook with fresh ingredients, right?"

She picked up a container. On the bottom, little holes were poked into the Styrofoam for drainage.

"The silt soil on Water Street is really rich because of the flooding," he explained, emptying her water bottle. "It's been flooding there for centuries. At home, our gardens are in the flood plain. Man, that veg grows and grows there . . ." Robert trailed off, stirring the soil with his finger.

He loves this town, his home, so much. She cradled the container in her lap.

"You know, I miss Chicago every day," she said. "Not a specific apartment or anything. We never lived in one place long enough to care about it, but I miss the sound of the city. When we moved to Hannaville it's kind of like the soundtrack of my life stopped."

Robert put his hands in his pockets. Not knowing what to say, he nodded toward the to-go container sitting on the step. "This box has heirloom tomato seeds planted in it," he explained. "I wrote a *T* on it, so you won't get them mixed up."

Spinning the Styrofoam container around in her lap, J'aime spotted the letter *C*. "Coconuts?" she asked.

Robert laughed. A black curl of hair bounced on his forehead. "Cilantro for the Cilantro Queen. Once the plants get stronger and some height to them, I'll help you transplant them into the yard." He pointed to a sunny patch of grass. "You can grow a good garden right there."

She thought about the tiny seeds nestled in Hannaville dirt. Under the soil surface, they were already growing and changing. Sprouting heirloom shells inside to-go sized homes. J'aime sat the tomato container back on the steps.

"I can't really plant these," she said, pulling her knees closer. "You know that right?"

Robert dismissed her. "Your landlord won't care."

"It's not that," she said quietly. "Who will take care of them when I leave Hannaville?"

It was his turn to be surprised. "You're moving?"

"I'm always moving."

Robert bent down and picked up both to-go containers. Determinedly, he marched over to the sunny patch and sat the Styrofoam boxes down on the tall, green grass.

"Water them once a day, but not too much, or you'll lose some of your soil," he instructed, straightening the hopeful plants into a neat row. "This is good dirt to grow roots in."

Chapter 28
Mango Breakfast Pizza

AT 8:25 THE NEXT MORNING, J'AIME CREAKED open the passenger door to their maroon Suburban. Her dad waited in the driver's seat. The text he sent her at midnight had said, I'M GOING WITH YOU.

She didn't have to ask where.

"Let's get this contest over with," he said, annoyance peppering his voice. "I told Sam I'd be at work by ten."

"Sarah's house is downtown. It'll take like two minutes to get to the casino," J'aime answered. Why did he insist on coming? When she won, she'd do more than pay him back. She'd fix their lives. She promised herself that. He was her last living relative. She didn't want him to think she was a thief for the rest of her life.

"Tell that to the Saturday Pancake Slam."

Her dad put the car in reverse before J'aime had time to buckle in. "Last weekend we had a hundred people go through the pancake line in an hour. Broke our record in Saturday sales. No one hands you success in the restaurant business, you know. You've got to put sweat into it."

J'aime clicked her seatbelt. He'd been talking like this all morning. He hadn't spoken to her for days, and now he was a fondue fountain of un-motivational advice.

"Pulling that off with your Food Caravan will be a rude awakening," he said, spinning the steering wheel to the left.

"Food Carma," J'aime corrected. "The truck's called Food Carma."

J'aime was trying to keep her sanity in check. They were on the tipping point of a fight. That was the last thing she needed. She was anxious enough without adding a shouting match to it. What she wanted was some air. Rolling down her window, she leaned her head out a little. The brisk morning breeze calmed her as downtown Hannaville trickled by.

"You know how many people entered this thing?" he asked, not waiting for an answer. "two hundred forty-four."

J'aime rested her head as close to the window as possible. That was the last entry number on the website. She'd seen it this morning. The call of the prize cash must've made him check out all the stats on the competition. No shock there.

"You've gotta figure." He took a drag off his cigarette. "With that many people entering, your chances are slim."

She pulled her full attention back into the car. "Thanks, Dad. That's super supportive."

"I'm being realistic," he said. "Even if you win, I wouldn't partner up with that Rios kid."

"Why would you say that?" J'aime asked.

Her dad braked for a speed bump. "He got you to steal my money, and he lied about working at the casino. You can't trust a guy like that."

Robert didn't convince her to do anything. If anyone wore the convincing pants in their relationship, it was J'aime. "He didn't have anything to do with the money. That was all me. I'll pay us back."

"Sure you will," her dad's lip curled into a sour smile before taking another smoke. "You're just sorry you got caught."

She steadied herself. Since she found out the exact amount of her mom's medical debt, she felt even guiltier about stealing from their savings. "Stop talking, okay. No more talking until we get to Sarah's."

Her dad went quiet, agreeing to the forced silence. When they pulled on to High Street five minutes later, cars lined the curb. The closer they got to Sarah's house, the more packed the road got. Their Suburban was deep into the next block when they finally found an open parking space.

"Why are there so many people at this thing?" he asked, pulling in next to a vacant curb.

"According to you, they're here to watch me lose," J'aime answered.

Truth was Sarah warned her that after the newspaper article, J'aime was now a small-town celebrity. Any kind of excitement, no matter how minor, brought people out.

They walked down the crumbling sidewalk to the Pruitts' Victorian house. As they climbed the elaborate porch stairs, the low tones of mingling drifted through the front-porch screen door.

"This house looks like it was built during the Civil War," her dad said, despite himself. "Runner chick must be rolling in old dough."

Anxiety knotted up J'aime's stomach. She wanted this all to be done. To be post-announcement so her dad would shut up, and she'd drive off with Robert in their new food truck reality. Before she could knock on the wooden screen door, Gina hollered at her.

"It's unlocked!" Through the mesh, J'aime watched a flicker of sparkles coming toward them. A bejeweled sleeve pushed open the door to reveal Gina Pruitt's big smile and bright blonde hair. "J'aime, get your butt in here." Her eyes rested on J'aime's dad. Gina's glow seemed to double. "Hello there. Now who's this tagging along with you?

"Stephen," her dad stretched out his hand. "Stephen McWilliams."

Gina shook hands, but didn't let go. "It sure is a pleasure to meet you, Stephen." Then she giggled. "It's not too often tall, handsome, big city folk move to town."

J'aime's jaw dropped.

Out of sight, she heard Sarah sigh. "Mom, just let them in."

"All right, all right. Is it against the law to be nice around here?" Sarah's mom released her lingering handshake. "I better check the breakfast pizza. Robert's already messed it up with mangos," she said, disappearing from the doorway.

J'aime expected Sarah to make a quiet exit, needing to keep track of her mom, but her friend stayed right next to her. An unfamiliar crowd was scattered around the living room. Total strangers were here to celebrate her big win. Suddenly Lyn's kerchiefed head flashed into view.

"Hey there, J'aime," Lyn said. In the lunch lady's hands was the donation jar. Sarah's scribbled sign was still taped to the front. Instead of being full of cash, the spaghetti sauce jar bloomed with yellow daisies.

Out of the corner of her eye, J'aime saw the sleeve of her dad's casino-issued polo. With the mood he was in, the less people he met from her daily life, the better. Sadly, her dad was sticking right by her side too.

"Hi, Lyn," she said cautiously.

"Father Eric wanted to thank you for the generous donation." She held out the daisies. "He had Mass this morning and couldn't make it."

J'aime reached out to take the jar, but her dad stopped her.

"Donation?" he asked. "What donation?"

The flowers retreated. Lyn studied him for a second. "I'm guessing you're J'aime's dad," she said. "I'm Lyn Pruitt. I work at Hannaville High."

"Are you a teacher?" he asked.

Lyn smiled. "Lunch lady. I helped J'aime and Robert serve up their food on Main Street the other day."

Her dad frowned. "You know they didn't have a permit, right? You could've been arrested."

Every muscle in J'aime's body tightened. This conversation was going in the worst possible direction.

Lyn's eyes sparked a bit. "Arrested? I doubt it. The police chief's my uncle. If he put me in jail, he'd have to answer to my grandma and no one wants to do that."

She placed the jar of flowers firmly in J'aime's hands. "The money you raised will go a long way to helping lots of people. Father Eric says, 'Thanks' and that he'll see you at the pantry next week."

She patted J'aime on the shoulder and walked back over to the crowd. J'aime leaned down to sniff a daisy petal.

"This whole town knows we get charity food. That's going to make my employees respect me even more," her dad scoffed. "I'm gonna smoke." He was out the screen door with a slam.

The mingling hushed for a second. Guests peered over to see what the noise was about, but J'aime didn't turn around to acknowledge them. She stayed focused on the screen, making sure her dad didn't linger on the porch. Hopefully, he'd take his smoke break far away by the riverbank. "Good. Go. No one's going to stop you," she muttered.

"Is he leaving?" Sarah asked.

"I hope so," J'aime said. She wanted to stick her face into the soft petals and disappear.

"It could be worse." Sarah smiled slyly. "My mom could've asked your dad out on a date."

J'aime laughed. "Don't even say that."

Sarah waved at J'aime to follow her. "C'mon. Let's put your flowers in the kitchen so no one messes with them."

They passed through the dining room. A group of people lingered near a tall antique china cabinet. In the middle of the group, was a tall, well-dressed man who was older than J'aime's father. His hair flopped to one-side in a dashing way that reminded her of an actor. He gave Sarah a nod, but she kept walking, not even giving him a glance.

"Who's that guy?" J'aime whispered when he turned back to his entourage.

"That's the mayor and some city council members."

"The mayor?" J'aime asked then promptly shut her mouth. Small town rumors in the flesh. J'aime fumbled her words, trying not to embarrass Sarah. "I've, uh, never been in the same room with a mayor before. It's kind of a big deal."

Sarah glanced over her shoulder at J'aime. "Trust me. He's not."

With a shove, she pushed the swinging kitchen door open. Gina and Robert stood around a kitchen island, staring down at trays of English muffin pizzas.

"I don't know about this," Gina was saying.

Robert reassured her. "It's okay. Mangoes and cheddar taste good together."

"Something about that fruit reminds me of Starbursts," Gina leaned against the counter, cautiously eyeing the food. "Man, that candy makes me pucker. Maybe you should sprinkle sugar on those mangoes? Sweeten them up some more?"

Robert threw his hands up in frustration. "If you're that worried about my recipe, why don't you serve Pop-Tarts?" That's when he noticed J'aime. "Whatever you do, don't let Sarah's mom talk you into cooking for her."

"I could've told you that," Sarah said.

J'aime set her jar of flowers on the counter. "Hi to you too."

Exasperated, Gina put her hands on her hips. "I'm not an adventurous eater. Ain't nothing wrong with that. Plus, I don't wanna gross out my guests with crickets or something."

"Bugs?" Robert defended his breakfast pizza.

"Mom, come on," Sarah protested. "It's fruit."

"I'm only saying mangoes aren't normal. They're not as weird as eatin' bugs. This guy on YouTube eats bugs on everything. I saw him eat scorpions in a sriracha omelet. He said it would kick-start your day. No thank you. I'll stick to my diet of—"

Shouts from the living room interrupted her. "We need Aunt Gina!" Lyn's voice yelled. "Something's wrong with the computer."

"That damn internet connection," Gina swore. "Sarah, you better come too. I might press the wrong thing."

"Sorry," Sarah mumbled to Robert and dashed after her mom.

With a swing, the kitchen door shushed the entire kitchen. Robert's knife crunched through toasted bread.

"That lady is crazy," Robert said as his knife sliced through an English muffin. Melted cheese trailed after the blade. "Someone gave her those mangoes as a gift. They were sitting right here on the counter. Showed up in the mail from Florida. She didn't know what they were and was about to toss them out. Freaking ripe, fresh mangoes. Then she told me she forgot to buy sausage for the pizza. I suggested we use the fruit. She was like, 'whatever you say, Chef.'" He flung the cut breakfast food onto a platter. "It's not whatever I say, that's for sure."

J'aime picked up a knife with the intent of cutting more breakfast pizza, but then didn't move a muscle. "It's five minutes until the announcement," she said. "I'm so nervous. I shouldn't be handling sharp objects."

As he arranged the tiny pizza slices on the platter, he scooted one her way. "Wanna be my taste tester?" he asked.

Holding the small slice up to her nose, J'aime took in the savory scent of melted cheese and eggs.

"Real mangos, huh?" she asked.

Robert pointed his knife at J'aime. "After all the trouble they've caused, they better put McDonald's mango smoothies to shame."

That wasn't going to be a problem. The second the flavors hit her mouth, J'aime didn't want to stop chewing. The fruit nectar mixed with the salty eggs reminded her of the pineapple salsa they made during their first cooking lesson. The combination was so good she was dying to lick her fingers.

He watched her eat. "Well?"

The breakfast pizza was quite possibly the best thing she'd eaten in her entire life.

"It's all right," she said, playing it off like it was nothing. She stole another slice from the platter.

"Licking your fingers? Swiping more pizza. Yeah, sure it's only *all right*."

"I swear you have super chef powers," J'aime said.

Robert stopped plating and smiled at her. "It's good to be in a kitchen again."

J'aime grinned back as the kitchen door swung open. Sarah's head peeked in. "We're back on. Murphy walked on the keyboard and jacked everything up. I fixed it."

"A person walked on the computer?" J'aime asked.

"Cat," Sarah answered. "You better get in here, though. The webcast is about to start."

Robert and J'aime dropped their food and followed Sarah out of the kitchen. In the living room, the party guests grouped together in a tight knot, completely blocking the view of the computer. She didn't see her dad anywhere. He must still be smoking outside. That was fine. He could stay out there.

Politely, she squeezed her way through the crowd. Robert gently nudged her forward. He was right behind her. She felt a tug on the back of her shirt. His fingers held on, making sure they got to the computer together. Through her cardigan she felt his knuckles accidently brush her spine. A tingle of electricity shot through her, pushing her straight to the front.

Around the soft glow of the monitor, Lyn and Sarah sat in folding chairs, watching over the keyboard like it was mission control. A smaller black video screen waited to stream the live broadcast.

Lyn glanced over her shoulder, catching J'aime's eye. "Hi," she said.

All she could manage was a nod back. Nerves sealed her lips shut. This was really happening. In a matter of seconds, Bentley would say the winner's name on this very computer screen. She'd played out the scenario so many times in her head. When he said Food Carma, Bentley would smile a little, like the very words made him happy. He would show them their giant check and say something British about what a bloody good idea it was. Robert would reach out for her hand, pull her toward him, and then . . .

A flash of light startled everyone. J'aime jumped and Robert let go of the back of her cardigan.

"Just a camera," Lisa explained. "Photos for the paper. Act natural."

Before the joke could fully ease the tension in the room, music started playing from the streaming screen.

"We're on," Lyn yelled and the room seemed to shuffle in even closer.

The Fresh Starter theme music blared. Bentley stood in the same Food Network garden patch except this time he was holding a bright yellow envelope in his hand instead of carrots.

"Ta, everyone," he smiled. "I'm live from the UK, and I've got the Fresh Starter winner right here in my hand."

He waved around the yellow envelope containing their fate. *Be careful with that*, she thought. It could fly off and get lost in the leafy rows of cauliflower.

"There were so many brilliant entries. We wanted to pick them all, but finally we narrowed it down to two ideas. I let my staff have the final vote. Let's do this. Drumroll, please." Off camera it sounded like people were beating on upside down plastic buckets.

The crowd scrunched in closer. Robert's breath fell on the back of her neck. *At least he was still breathing, because I don't think I am.*

Bentley tore open the seal and lifted out a piece of green paper. He flashed an excited smile. "The winner is . . . I've always wanted to bloody say that, Beth Neiman and her Bravo-cado School Breakfast proposal."

"What?" Lyn yelled. "We lost to another lunch lady?"

"How do you know she's a lunch lady?" Gina asked.

Flustered, Lyn snapped. "No one else cares about school breakfast except lunch ladies."

Bentley kept on talking, but J'aime couldn't hear him. It was over. The food truck was gone. The money was gone. Robert was

. . . not gone. He was staring at the black computer screen, willing it to tell him a new answer.

Blood pulsed through her ears. Occasionally letting a nearby "sorry" or a "you were robbed" float in. *Robbed*, J'aime thought. *I'm the one who did the stealing around here.* To make her own dreams come true she had stolen Robert's home and her dad's trust.

Around them the party nibbled on slices of breakfast pizza like nothing had happened. Today was completely normal for them. The mingling people grated on J'aime. She needed to apologize to Robert. She needed to tell him she was sorry she made his life a mess, but she couldn't. If she apologized, then the disappointment slowly hijacking her heart would be real. She'd start bawling. She'd cry right here in front of the mayor and all these brunching people. No way could she let that happen.

Get it together. Talk to Robert.

Glancing over at him. "This totally sucks," she said.

Robert looked away from the blank computer, watching the crowd devour his food. His clenched jaw locked in all his emotion.

People try to be so strong, she thought, *but we're as fragile as eggshells.*

"Let's get away from here, " she said. "Let's go cook something, anything."

He crossed his arms, finally looking at her. Disappointment clouded his eyes. "I can't. Not now."

"Yes, now," she said. She lightly tugged on his shirtsleeve, pulling him toward the kitchen. "Cooking is the only thing that will make us feel better."

He shook her off. The move surprised J'aime and she took a step back. Lisa seemed to pop up out of nowhere. Giving Robert and J'aime a sheepish look, she asked, "Sorry. I hate to do this, but can I interview you two for the paper?"

Robert's frown deepened. "You're kidding, right?" he asked.

Before Lisa could answer, the screen door slammed again. The party paused and all eyes fell on J'aime's dad. He stood in the entryway, his jaw clenched as tight as Robert's had been. "J'aime," he yelled, looking right at her. "We need to go."

He didn't wait for her to answer. Storming toward them, he grabbed her arm with one hand. "Come on."

"Hey," Robert interrupted. "Let her go."

"Stay out of this, Rios," her dad growled.

J'aime pulled back, but she couldn't get away. His grip was too tight. All at once the crowd faded, watching the scene and trying to be invisible to their family drama.

"Don't," J'aime hissed at her dad. "What's wrong with you?"

"Like you don't know," he spat. That's when she noticed he was holding his phone in his other hand.

Robert's arms slowly uncrossed. He was about to do something, but J'aime knew it would only make things worse. "Stop," she yelled at them both. She pulled hard this time, breaking her dad's grasp. "I'll go," she said to him.

Sarah ran in from the kitchen, shock slowing her to a stop in the middle of the living room. Lyn was right behind her.

With a shove, J'aime's dad held open the screen door. He wouldn't leave unless J'aime was with him. She couldn't look at Robert, so instead she focused on Sarah. "I'll talk to you later," she said, her voice shaking. As she walked past her dad's barrel chest, Sarah's voice followed her out the front door.

"Bye . . . I guess?"

Chapter 29
Growl

J'AIME RESTED HER CHEEK AGAINST THE SUBUR-
ban's velour passenger seat, waiting for her time bomb of a dad to
get into the car.

"I can't believe we lost," she whispered.

The driver's door creaked open, and her dad threw himself into
his seat. He jabbed his key into the ignition. About to turn it, he
snorted hard like a cartoon bull ready to charge. "I can't believe
you'd do this to me."

Before she could answer, her dad slapped his phone onto her
thigh. The screen blinked to life against her leggings. It was on
the voicemail page. J'aime waited for the list of phone numbers
to disappear into screensaver blackness. The collection agency
she talked to must've called him. The engine roared. As they
pulled away from the curb, the historic river bluff neighborhood
flowed by.

"I was out there smoking," her dad explained. Fury accented
every word. "And my general manager called. My GM. The creditors are going to garnish my wages. Do you know what that
means?"

The Suburban made a hard turn, and his phone slide off her
lap onto the car floor mat. Why did she get into the car? She
should have walked home and let him calm down.

Her dad turned on to Main Street. A stop sign almost blurred
past, but he hit the brakes in time.

"Damn it, J'aime!" he yelled. "It means no rent. Where the hell are we going to live? We're bankrupt because of your phone call. If things go bad, they might send me to prison."

"That's not what they told me on the phone," she snapped.

"You believe those vultures?" her dad snapped back. "They lie, J'aime. That's what they're good at."

A car horn blared behind them. They'd sat too long at the stop sign. Her dad fumed and hit the gas. Her whole body tugged forward and slammed back into the seat. The agent on the phone reassured her people can't go to jail for medical bill debt, but what if the agent was just trying to get their home address? If that was the case, it totally worked. She told that agent everything. J'aime's stomach flipped nervously, and it had nothing to do with her dad's driving.

"I was trying to help us," she explained. "I thought if I won the contest, we could have a new life. To make that happen, I needed to know how much we owed them."

"That's none of your business. I've got a plan for those bills," her dad shouted. "Why won't you leave it alone?"

"'Cause you won't tell me what's really going on. You told me you'd paid off Mom's medical bills forever ago, and clearly that didn't happen. For all I know, your plan is to gamble all our money at the Silver Dollar."

Her dad didn't respond. J'aime studied his face. Suddenly she knew. "Oh my God," she said in disbelief. "That is your plan. You're throwing our checks away on slot machines!"

"You threw our money away on a stupid contest," her dad spat back. The angrier he got, the faster he drove. "At least I win sometimes. If I keep playing, I'll figure out the Silver Dollar's blackjack system. I know I will."

J'aime barely heard him talking. $217, 251 blared in her head. That's what they owed the credit agencies. Her lunch debt was a tiny drop in their giant sea of medical debt. Hannaville blurred by outside her window. J'aime had to end all of this chaos.

The speedometer clicked up faster and faster. Soon the Suburban was going fifty in a twenty-five. "Dad, slow down," she shouted.

The vehicle swerved across traffic to the curb on the wrong side of the street. He hit the brakes so hard, her seatbelt tightened, cutting into her neck. "You're on the wrong side of the road!" she shouted. "We're going to get hit."

"Shut up," her dad yelled as he slammed the car into park. "Get out."

Glaring out the front windshield, her dad looked like he was driving a hundred miles an hour even though their tires were holding perfectly still.

"Why did you tell them where we live?" he demanded.

Her dad let go of the steering wheel. His hands clenched into fists again. She inched closer to her passenger door, but his fists stayed in his lap.

"I don't have time to save money again, J'aime," her dad explained. "They're going to sue me. I can't afford a lawyer. You think you're hungry now. You have no idea what's coming." He rubbed his forehead and took a ragged breath. "I can't believe my own daughter did this to me."

Enough, J'aime thought.

She clicked her seatbelt button. "You let me think the debt collectors were calling about my lunches," she shouted, as the vinyl strap set her free. "Do you know how scared I was of those stupid calls? How could you do that to me?"

"You shouldn't have picked up the damn phone," her dad shouted. "Get out! Just get out!"

Opening the Suburban's passenger door, J'aime stepped onto the street. The wind from a passing car in the opposite lane blew her hair into her face. She wasn't standing on the safe sidewalk, but on the centerline dividing the street. Broken yellow rectangles painted paths that ran forwards and backwards at the same time.

J'aime glared at her dad through the open passenger door. "I picked up the phone because I can't pretend like everything is normal when everything is out of control." J'aime took a shaky breath. "Dad, I can't lie to myself anymore. Our lives are not okay. We have to change things."

Her dad hit the gas. The metal door handle slipped from J'aime's fingers as he sped off. Driving erratically down the wrong side of the street, the Suburban raced up the rest of the hill. She waited for honking, crashing, or at least the squeal of another car, but nothing came.

Alone in the middle road, J'aime watched his taillights crest the hill then disappear.

•

At 11:00 p.m. J'aime opened her refrigerator door. When her dad left her standing in the street hours ago, he'd driven off with her Whole Foods bag. She had no phone and no food. Instead of going to the pantry, she'd gone to Sarah's for the watch party. The hollow fridge stared back at her, and J'aime's stomach growled in disappointment.

She shut the Frigidaire. A sharp rush of icy air tingled her skin. Empty fridges were so much colder than full ones. Most people don't know that. Most people just open it up and eat whatever they want. *But not me.*

Standing in the kitchen doorway, J'aime stared at the shadow on the living room floor. The recliner's hulking silhouette was like a black hole waiting to suck her in. If they had an ancient land-line, she'd call her dad. Tell him to bring her bag back, but that's all she would say. The thought of saying, "I'm sorry," made her chest ache. She'd bankrupted him and possibly worse. Normal daughters don't do things like that.

No matter how crappy he was at being a dad, she should've tried to talk to him about the contest and their debt.

Get out! echoed through her head. J'aime looked at the kitchen walls. She'd never noticed how tall they were. They looked so strong. For months, the faded strawberries on the wallpaper kept her safe from the outside world, but not anymore. The printed fruit was already in the past. That time she almost lived in a house. She swallowed hard. The thin strands of their father-daughter relationship were left in the middle of Main Street. This wasn't tough love. He really wanted her to leave.

The feeling that her dad didn't want her around had been growing ever since her mom died. It was hard to explain, but J'aime felt the truth of it in her bones. What just happened was way more than a fight. It was a finale.

Now Robert and his mom—*that* was a fight. No matter what Robert believed, his mother could never truly banish him forever. Deep down, they all knew it. They were just mad at each other. His family might not be perfect, but like their love, the Rioses' roots ran deep, holding them together.

The McWilliamses, she thought, *are nothing but drifters. If I leave, Dad won't even care. He'll be happier.*

Her hand shaking, J'aime pulled open the cabinet door. She took out her new saucepan, held it tight for a second then closed the kitchen cabinet. With the saucepan clutched to her chest, she headed into the living room. The edge of the quilt dangled over the recliner's headrest. Even after J'aime left, her dad would keep dragging that stupid recliner around. Forever broken and worn thin, this chair represented the homes that could never be homes. The recliner was a lost cause, but J'aime's memories weren't.

In one swift motion, she swiped her mother's quilt from its resting place. Waves of cheap coconut wafted up from the cushions.

Creaking open the screen door, J'aime turned her back on the duplex. Quilt wrapped around her and saucepan under her arm, she left everything else behind. Her flip-flops shuffled over the broken sidewalk. If she could get to Sarah's house, maybe Gina would take her in, at least for the night. She barely noticed the headlights coming up the road. The vehicle screeched to a halt, but she kept walking.

"J'aime," Robert shouted. He bolted out of the driver's seat. Suddenly, he was blocking her way, standing in a pool of street-light. "Are you all right?"

J'aime felt the presence of the recliner and boxes of bills lingering behind her. "I'm leaving."

Robert's eyes flicked to the saucepan. "What happened?"

"I can't live there anymore," J'aime answered.

Robert nodded. He guided her over to his idling truck and opened the passenger door. The soft dashboard lights seemed almost cozy. He didn't have to tell her to get in. She was ready to go. She slid onto the taped vinyl seat and cradled the cooking pot in her lap. Robert shut her safely inside. J'aime closed her eyes, listening for the squeak of his driver-side door.

Chapter 30
Cheesy Potato Skins

J'AIME DIDN'T HAVE TO ASK ROBERT WHERE THEY were going. She could see the Missouri River getting closer. Soon they'd be in an abandoned neighborhood washed out by flood. The gaping doors of rundown empty houses waited to welcome her home.

"After the contest," he continued. "I had to pull a double at the casino. Your dad didn't show up for his shift. Things didn't seem right. He was scary angry at Sarah's house. When I clocked out, I came straight to your place." In the dim streetlight, Robert looked over at her. "You sure he didn't hurt you?"

They drove past Sarah's street. J'aime should have told him to go down it, drop her off at her friend's Victorian doorstep, but she didn't.

"We did a good job of hurting each other," she answered.

Robert stared at her for a second longer then focused on crossing the narrow steel bridge. In the dark night, the wide river flowed beneath the truck's tires. The cool riverbank air was thick with frogs and the grit of washed rocks. J'aime's whole reality was suspended, like a spoon in limbo between bowl and bite.

The old highway curved and cruised by. Soon the only lights on the road were his headlights and the full moon. Fields of soybean sprouts filled the landscape. The truck slowed, turned left, lumbering onto a dirt road that cut through the flat growing farmland.

"Where are we going?" she finally asked.

"To my new place," he answered with a smile.

A towering shadow grew closer as they drove deeper into the fields. "What's that?" J'aime wondered.

"An old grain silo. It's mostly caved in. No one uses it anymore." He pulled up next to the crumbling building. "This land isn't far from my family's place."

The moon was so bright, J'aime could make out a faded logo painted on the side of the silo. Bricks lay scattered on the ground. They'd either tumbled off the wide hole in the roof or were blown down by hard winds.

"This land's been for sale for like ten years," Robert explained. "The real estate agent pays my dad to keep the weeds down."

"It doesn't look safe to sleep in," she said. *And it belongs in a slasher movie.*

Robert's answer was to pull off the dirt road, heading straight out into the field. With the silo way behind them, the only things J'aime could see were the roll of distant hills and the massive starry sky.

"We're here." He parked the truck and killed the engine. "This is my new place."

"You sleep in the middle of a field?"

"For now. It has a fantastic view, plus it's rent free. What more could I want?" Robert opened his car door. "C'mon. I've got food in the back."

J'aime made her way around to the back of the truck. The field would've been pitch-black if it weren't for the endless country stars and spotlight full moon. Robert lowered the truck-bed door, and they piled in back. He spread out rumpled blankets and a sleeping bag. Opening a cooler, Robert pulled out a white to-go box. "The Silver Dollar had cheesy potato skins on the buffet tonight." He cracked open the lid.

"Don't worry. I improved them. They're cold, but they'll do." Digging around in a bag he pulled out one utensil. "I didn't know I'd be having company, so we're going to have to share."

Sharing a spork with Robert at midnight was not how she thought this day would end. "Sure," she said, and scooted a little closer.

"You can do the honors." He handed her the plastic utensil. "I added barbequed smoked pork and topped the potatoes with roasted peppers."

Besides her slice of mango pizza at the watch party, this was J'aime's only real meal of the day. Stress kept her stomach preoccupied. She took a bite. Cheesy, potato smokiness hit her mouth. She ate another huge bite.

"Save some for me," Robert joked.

Reluctantly she handed him the spork. "You're such a freaking good cook," she said in enchilada awe. "Even with prepped food, you're a master."

Robert chewed. "It's not bad."

She watched the way his lips lingered on the bright-white utensil. He set a water bottle in between them. His Silver Dollar nametag flashed on his open chef's jacket.

J'aime reached over and touched his badge. "Thanks for coming to get me right after work."

He automatically reached up and felt the top of his head. "I took my beanie off, right?"

"No beanie," she reassured. He tried to hand her the utensil again, but she pushed it away. "I'm sorry about the contest," she said. "It was my idea. I kind of ruined everything."

He pushed the pile of peppers around with the spork. "You didn't ruin everything," he said.

"You're sleeping in seriously creepy places."

Robert looked back at the silo. "I know, but it's a relief to get to do my own thing. I can cook and not worry about hiding it all the time. Things are weirdly better for me."

"We lost the contest," J'aime said. "Remember?"

A night breeze blew across the field. She shivered, realizing she'd left the quilt in the truck cab. Robert slipped off his chef's jacket and handed it to her.

"That part's not better," he said as she put on the coat, "But I don't need Bentley to give me a hundred thousand dollars to prove I'm a chef. I already am one." He paused, watching J'aime button the lapel. "You look good in that, Chef. You'll be in the casino kitchen with me in no time."

"My days at the casino are over. My dad will not want to be my boss."

"Doesn't he get fired a lot? How many jobs has your dad had?"

J'aime tried to picture the collection of nametags her dad kept in a shoebox. She hadn't counted them in a long time. Next to the different restaurant logos, her dad's name was spelled multiple ways. Mostly there was STEVEN, which was wrong, several correct STEPHENs, the occasional STEVE, and the extremely rare STEVIE. He was fussy when it was spelled wrong, but he never asked them to correct it.

"Dad's never told me a number. My mom and him had restaurant jobs before I was born. I've never seen those nametags. Maybe fortyish," she guessed.

Robert looked down and asked quietly, "What happened to your mom?"

It was J'aime's turn to push the last of the peppers around. "She had a lot of health problems, diabetes, heart disease. I can't remember a time when she wasn't sick."

"Sorry. That must've been hard a way to live," Robert said, leaning back against the truck. "And not fair for you."

"Nothing about families are fair," she answered. Tears stung her eyes, and the white sides of the truck blurred.

Robert sat up. He reached across their empty to-go container and wiped her cheek with his hand. Before she knew it, his fingers pulled her face closer and he was kissing her. The faint scent of chili spice seasoned the night air around them. She held on to him, as the whole starry sky started to melt like caramel. Her fears disappeared into Robert's flavors. Everything about him tasted warm and sweet, better than anything on the dessert bar.

J'aime didn't want to pull away, but she had to. "What about Abbi?" she whispered, her lips still brushing his.

"Abbi?" Robert said. Distracted, he sat back a little, still holding her hand. "Why are you always asking about my grandmother?"

Crickets filled the silence. "Grandmother?" J'aime asked.

"Yeah," he answered, sliding the empty food container away. "*Mi abuela*. We've always called her Abbi."

"I thought," she stammered, "that she was, you know, your—"

Robert laughed, practically howling at the moon. "You thought my grandma was my girlfriend?" He made a grossed-out face then cracked himself up.

Embarrassed, J'aime tried to stand up. She had no idea where she would go, but she needed to hide somewhere and fast. All this time she swore he was seeing someone, that he never really liked her back.

Robert gently pulled her down on to the sleeping bag. She found herself nestled in the truck bed.

Robert composed himself, but he couldn't wipe the grin off his face. "I care about Abbi," he said, then brushed J'aime's hair out of her face. "But it's definitely NOT the same way I care about you."

They both laughed. He kissed her again, and this time, J'aime let the melted caramel flavors of his touch completely surround her.

Chapter 31
Sunday Family Dinner

HER ALARM WAS GOING OFF. J'AIME COULD hear it buzzing. She flopped her hand out to where her nightstand should be and hit something soft—Robert's face.

"Ouch," he said. "Hey."

J'aime's eyes popped open. She saw the empty buffet to-go container, her mother's rumpled quilt, and a wide stubbly green field over the edge of the truck bed. The buzzing stopped. She sat up, feeling her pockets for her phone and noticed she was still wearing his chef's jacket.

"It's me. It's my phone," Robert said. He was lying on his back under their shared blanket, listening to voice mail. J'aime tried to read his face, but she couldn't. "It's your dad," he mouthed. "He's looking for you."

"You're kidding?" J'aime asked.

Robert put the phone on speaker so she could hear the message. Her dad sounded more worried than professional. "Robert, this is Stephen McWilliams. This isn't a work call. I'm looking for J'aime. Call me back."

J'aime stared at the voice message screen. Her dad was actually making an effort to find her. *Why?* She wanted to know the answer and wanted to delete the message at the same time.

"How'd he get your phone number?" J'aime asked.

"I'm an employee. He has everyone's number." From the truck bed, Robert held up his phone to show her a text. "I got this too."

All the text said was, COME HOME. "It's from Abbi's cell. Mom bought it for her, but Abbi hates phones. She only uses it as a kitchen timer."

"Sounds like a Mom trap," J'aime said.

"Probably," He sighed and sat up. "But if Mom roped Abbi in, I should show her I'm okay."

If Robert was going home, then where would she go? Going home for her meant facing her dad. Was their duplex even her home anymore? Last night her answer would've been a hard no. But now that her dad was looking for her, everything felt up in the air. Their lives were trying to normalize, trying to go back to the way they were before. It made J'aime nervous.

She twisted the edge of the blanket. "Can I come with you?" she asked.

He leaned in and kissed her. "You can go anywhere with me."

•

An hour later, Robert's truck crunched down a different gravel road leading them into different river bottom farmlands.

An old, but well-kept white farmhouse came into view. "That's our home," he said. "It's been in my dad's family for years."

Through the windshield, J'aime inspected weeping willow trees standing on either side of the two-story flat-faced house. The trees long leaf tendrils draped to the ground in a mop of foliage. A screened porch bumped out into the side yard. On the grass next to it was a traffic jam of cars parked at different angles, as if the drivers had pulled in, jumped out, and barely closed the car door.

"Why are there so many people here?" she asked.

"It's our Sunday family dinner," he answered.

"At 10:00 a.m.?"

Robert shrugged, and pulled the truck into a free grassy spot. "Everyone works different shifts. They drop by when they can.

Abbi always has something ready. We usually spend most of the day cooking until everyone is stuffed."

"Sunday grazing instead of Sunday grace," she said.

He smiled. "I've never thought about it like that."

They both watched the farmhouse for a second, waiting for something to happen. J'aime nervously patted her hair. Her gas station bathroom look was definitely not going to make a great second impression with his mom. The last time she saw Robert's mom, she was yelling and pointing at her.

"If that text is a trap, what does your mom want?" J'aime asked.

Robert didn't take his eyes off the front door. "Bottom line? To talk me into managing at Rancheros," he said. "But I've got to stick to my chef plan."

J'aime reached over to the steering wheel and squeezed his hand. The swish-slam of a screen door made her break her nervous connection to him.

A gaggle of little kids burst from the porch. Squealing past parked cars, they disappeared into the rustle of a cascading willow tree.

"The welcoming committee." Robert smiled. "You gotta watch out, they bite."

"Note to self," J'aime laughed, but then went silent.

Robert's mom was standing on the front porch. She must've walked out behind the kids. Her black curly hair was piled up on her head. She was wearing a green flowered apron with her arms tightly crossed around the middle, and she glared in the general direction.

"Mom won't come to us," he said. "We've got to go to her."

If Robert hadn't gotten out of the truck, J'aime would've stayed right where she was. Reluctantly, she followed him up to the porch. Robert's mom uncrossed her arms and planted her hands firmly on her hips.

"Mama," he said. "I—"

But that's all he got to say.

"I told you to cool off, not disappear," she snapped.

"You kicked me out," Robert snapped back.

His mom stepped closer to him. J'aime waited for a slap, a jabbing finger, something physical, but all Mrs. Rios did was fume.

"You put our family business in jeopardy," his mom argued. She clamped her mouth shut. She held up her hands as if to stop words from flying between them. "We are not having this argument again."

Before Robert could respond, his mom hugged him tight. "You should've called me back," she said, pressing her cheek into his griddle grease stained T-shirt.

J'aime couldn't believe what she was seeing. She hadn't mentally prepared for mother and son make-up hugs.

Not letting go, Mrs. Rios looked up at her son. "You get one text from Abbi, and like magic, you're here. What does that say about me?"

Robert hugged his mom back. "Sorry. I wasn't ready to talk, okay?"

His mother let go and looked him straight in the eye. "It's not okay. I'm your mother. Always call me back. Even when you're mad at me."

Robert gave her a reluctant nod then asked, "Where's Dad?"

His mother wiped her eye and straightened her apron. "Helping the Andersons repair that old tractor."

There was a moment of awkward silence. J'aime shifted nervously in her flip-flops. *Say something. Anything*, she thought.

"Uh, hi," she said. J'aime extended a hand to Robert's mom. But all she could think to say was the absolutely wrong thing. "You might not remember me. I was at the pop-up on Main Street. I'm J'aime. J'aime McWilliams."

"Doing food prep," Robert's mom said. She shook J'aime's hand. Her grip was crazy firm. "I remember you," she said. "I'm

Violeta Rios. I'm glad you came. We all have something to discuss." She let go of J'aime's hand and stepped off the porch. "Follow me."

J'aime and Robert followed his mom through the yard. As they rounded the corner of the house, what caught her eye first was a weathered gray barn. It had a giant white square with a red-and-blue star painted near the roof.

They walked past a rusted laundry pole and toward a cluster of busted restaurant booths. Hummingbird feeders hanging from poles pierced the ground, forming a circle around the red benches. The brightly colored plastic tubes caught the morning light and the sugar water glowed.

Bird party lanterns, J'aime thought. She wanted to ask Robert about the booths being in the yard, but she felt like she wasn't supposed to talk. As the house grew more distant behind them, the more serious his expression became. They passed a few beat-up trailer homes parked in the huge backyard. Around the mobile homes, children's toys dotted the grass like mushrooms.

The yard was vanishing. They were wandering into a weedy no man's land separating mowed lawn from farm fields. As she walked up an incline, J'aime wanted to hold on to the back of Robert's T-shirt, but she didn't. When they reached the top of the hill, J'aime gasped.

"Sarah's trailer," she said.

The Airstream was right there next to a cornfield.

"For you, Robert," his mom said, opening the rusty, silver door.

Robert didn't move an inch. "What? Why are you giving this to me?"

His mother stuck her hands in her apron pockets. "I bought it days ago for Tomas, but he wants to live above the new bakery instead. I saw in the paper that you lost your Food Network contest. I thought you might want it."

She held out the keys to her son. "Clearly you need a little more freedom."

Robert's fiery "Live Free, or Die" skull swung through J'aime's mind. She couldn't believe what she was hearing. Was his mom honestly going to give them a food truck?

"You always say nothing is for free," Robert said carefully. "What's the deal?"

Violeta smiled and threw her hands together in a triumphant clap. "You're the only one who actually listens to my business lessons." She excitedly straightened her apron. "After your parking lot pop-up, Hannaville people kept coming to Rios Rancheros and ordering your huevos to go. I had to put the dish on the menu."

"Really?" Robert and J'aime said in unison.

"It made me think your Rios Rancheros food truck idea wasn't a bad idea after all. We've been looking for a better way to sell to the college bar crowd in Churchill. Here's my plan. You can come back to the restaurant. Keep working front of the house until your dad fixes up the trailer. When it's ready to roll. You can manage it. You can even decide the menu." She nodded toward J'aime. "You can do food prep. I'll hire you."

J'aime's heart jumped in her throat. Robert's mom gave her a kitchen job like it was nothing.

Robert took J'aime's hand and squeezed it tight. Shocked, J'aime and his mom both stared at the way their fingers fit together.

"No, Mama," he said.

"No?" his mother's eyes narrowed. "I thought you wanted a food truck?"

"Yes, but I want to be my own chef too. Let me buy it from you."

She dismissed him. "You don't have that kind of cash."

"I get a buffet paycheck. It'll take a while, but I can pay you for it."

His mother shook her head. "I need a food truck for the fall semester." She chewed on her lip for a second. "How about this? I'll trade you renovation work for payment. When we open in the fall, I'll advertise the trailer as a Rios Rancheros food truck. I'll pay food costs. You can chef and manage it. After a year working for me, you'll own it. Rename the food truck. Sell crepes for all I care. But if you're sick of working in a tin can by then, Rios Rancheros will buy your half of the trailer."

A long pause followed. *Crepes? Robert's never mentioned French food ever.* J'aime let the thought go and focused on her heart. It was racing. Robert's mom was making him the kind of offer he wanted and wanted to avoid.

"I want to keep my job at the casino while I'm fixing it up," he said.

"Work two jobs, renovate the trailer, and go to school?" She blew him off. "Not possible."

"One job, Mom," he said. "I'll stay at the buffet. I'm not working Rios Rancheros front of house anymore. I don't want to let the family down, but I can't let myself down either."

She looked him over, appraising how far she could push him. "You've grown up, Robert."

"Thanks," Robert said. "And I'd like a contract, please."

"That's my son," his mother said proudly. She walked over and kissed him on the cheek. "Take a look inside the trailer. I'll type up a contract." She hurried toward the house, and Robert sank down into the grass.

"Are you okay?" J'aime asked.

His head was in his hands. "She loves to negotiate. It's her hobby."

J'aime sat down next to him. The Airstream trailer and their soon-to-be food truck was right in front of them. "This is a good thing, right?"

Robert looked up. "We both win. She gets Rios Rancheros name out there to the bar crowd, and I get to chef." He gave her an exhausted grin.

"And then you can sell crepes," J'aime teased.

Holding back a grin, he flopped back on the grass. "I like to make crepes. What's wrong with that?"

"I thought she was joking!" J'aime yelled. She laughed and gave him a gentle shove. "You can make crepes, and you didn't tell me?"

Robert blushed. "I don't know. French cooking doesn't seem very cool."

"Don't be stupid," J'aime said. She flopped back on the grass with him. "Plus everything you cook is very cool."

Then he did it. Robert smiled that smile. The one she loved. A few of his front curls had sprung free and formed a little Superman swirl on his forehead. She reached up and pulled the curl, making it bounce.

"J'aime," her dad's voice said. He was standing behind them, holding her Whole Foods bag. "What are you doing here?"

Chapter 32
Heritage Buffet

BOTH J'AIME AND ROBERT STOOD UP QUICKLY. J'aime's dad was standing in the Rioses' yard in his casino uniform.

"Dad," she said.

He took two steps forward, and J'aime felt Robert move closer to her.

"I came home last night," her dad explained. "But you never did." Her dad glared at Robert. "And this jerk never called me back."

"A reoccuring theme today," Robert muttered.

"What?" her dad snapped.

They both looked capable of flashing fangs at each other. J'aime stepped between them. "Dad, don't."

"Can we talk somewhere alone?" her dad asked, thoroughly annoyed at Robert's presence.

J'aime felt Robert touch her arm. "We'll go over here to the booths," she said, resisting the comforting pull of his hands. "I'll be back in a minute."

Robert unlocked the trailer door as J'aime led her dad over to the circle of rainbow hummingbird feeders and red booth benches. Nervously, she reached for her bag. Her dad tightened his grip on the handles, not wanting to let it go, then the canvas bag dropped into her hands.

Instead of sitting on his own bench, he decided to sit with her. She couldn't remember a time in her life when they'd both sat on the same side of the booth.

"When you didn't come home this morning," her father said. "I remembered that rich runner girl. She told me to look at my casino paperwork to find Robert's number and address. I felt dumb that I didn't think of that."

Sarah, J'aime thought, *She was probably worried about me too.*

"When I left you in the road yesterday, I kept driving and driving," he explained. He gazed out at the whimsical bird feeders. "I was so mad, then all of sudden I couldn't stop thinking about the day you were born."

This comment made J'aime look straight at him. "Why?"

Her dad bent over and picked a piece of grass. "You know you were born in Indiana, right?" he asked, smoothing the blade between his fingers.

J'aime nodded. The hummingbird feeders swayed in the breeze. She felt Robert watching them from the trailer.

"Your mom and I were both working at Heritage," her dad explained, "this all you can eat, home-cooking buffet. By nine months, your mom was so big, she couldn't stand long enough to scoop macaroni and cheese. Jessica sat in a booth," he patted the bench next to him, "kind of like this one and rolled silverware for hours to get some pay. That's what she was doing when her water broke. I was back in the kitchen, basting the turkey breasts—"

"You were a cook?" J'aime asked in disbelief.

"I started out in the kitchen, a dishwasher then a cook. I was good at it. Can't remember why I started waiting tables in the first place." He pondered the blank spot in his memory while twisting the piece of grass. "Anyway, I dropped the baster and ran out to Jess. It was around 3:00 p.m., so no one was in the restaurant, and that's how it happened. Luckily, this doctor walked in to pick up a pie for a party—"

She interrupted. "Wait. Are you telling me I was born at a buffet?"

Her dad smiled, his cheeks rough with stubble. "Right by the dessert bar. I'm not going to lie. You might have been conceived there too. Your mom and I used to close up the place quite a bit."

"Nope," she shuddered. "Did not need to know that."

"After you were born," her dad continued, "we were riding to the hospital in the ambulance. Your mom said you were a dessert baby because you were so sweet. She picked that Frenchy name for you. 'Love' because she loved you that much and there was chocolate crème brûlée on the buffet that day." He chuckled. "She craved that brûlée like no one's business, but I wouldn't let her name you Brulée."

He let the blade of grass drift from his fingers to the ground and looked at J'aime. "It's hard, but I kind of get why you called the debt collectors. I did try to pay some of the bills. Nothing I paid ever made a real dent in what we owed. It didn't matter how much I worked." Her dad let out a tired sigh.

"Still, I know this situation, our situation, hasn't been good for a long time. Selling your mom's stuff was one of the toughest things I've ever had to do, but we needed the money, and I didn't want to put you through that."

The wide country sky shrank around J'aime, almost taking her breath away. She wasn't going to pass out from shock, but then again, she might.

Our situation hasn't been good for a long time.

How long had she wanted him to say something like that? This was really happening, and her heart could barely believe it.

J'aime tried not to choke up. She thought of Robert's mom holding him so tight. She glanced at her dad. He sat there like a boulder. Hugging wasn't his thing.

"I'm sorry, Dad," she said. "I never wanted you to go to jail."

"Damn allergies." He lifted the short sleeve of his polo shirt to wipe his eye, though J'aime doubted the surrounding fields had anything to do with his tears.

"We'll deal with the law if they come," he said. "You had a good point. I should suck it up and at least talk to the creditors to find out what my options are. Right now, I need you to come back home."

"You mean that?" J'aime hesitated. "You want me around?"

He paused. She could tell he was choosing his words carefully. "Your mom would've wanted us to stay together, and I want that too."

With a mix of relief and worry, J'aime picked her own blade of grass to twist. She looked over at the Airstream trailer. Robert watched her through the window. J'aime decided it was time to take another risk. "Robert's going to open a food truck. I want to invest in it," she said. "We should stay and try to put down roots in Hannaville."

"Invest?" Her dad shook his head. "Do you know how many restaurants fail in their first year? Nine out of ten. It's a real fact." He gave the trailer a new weary look. "We can't give him money, J'aime. We've got our own problems."

"It doesn't have to be money," she argued. "I can cook extra hours there. Invest my time."

He crossed his arms tighter. "It's better if you stay at the casino. It's a steady paycheck. You can't flip food for free."

"I didn't say it would be for free. He'll pay me. His mom said—"

"You know how many times I've heard 'I'll pay you' from new restaurant owners?" Her dad shook his head. "More times than they've followed through, that's for sure."

J'aime's skin prickled. The family memories and inklings of trust evaporated. "You need me around because of my paycheck," she said, her voice flaring like a hot burner. "Don't you care that I want a steady life? A real home?"

"Of course, I do," he said, trying to be calm. "Listen, you're not a chef. You're a kid who barely cooks at home. A commercial kitchen's a tough place. I'm trying to save you from making mistakes."

An old-fashioned hand bell clanged, jerking their attentions away.

Robert tentatively appeared in the trailer doorway. "We better go back," he called to them. "That's Abbi's dinner bell."

•

The first thing J'aime saw when she stepped into the Rioses farmhouse was a tall garden statue of the Virgin Mary. The saint wasn't the only person in the front room, but she might have been the only one who noticed their arrival. Friends and family of various ages squeezed themselves into the narrow warm living room, lounging wherever they could fit. A plastic picnic table filled the floor, and every part of it served as a chair for someone to sit. Conversations flowed loudly from one language to the next as people sipped drinks. The wooden screen door slammed behind Robert.

"Hey, everyone!" he shouted, "Say hi to my guests."

The conversation paused, and there was a smattering of *holas*, heys, and waves from the family standing closest to J'aime and her dad, then the chorus started back up again.

A squiggly line cut through the crowd as Robert's mom wove her way past bent arms holding bottles. "You're her father?" she asked, when she spotted J'aime's dad in his casino polo.

"Yes," he answered, with a hint of apprehension. Violeta Rios had made a powerful impression. He didn't want to face that hurricane again. "Your party looks nice, but I have to get to work."

"Stay for a bite," she insisted. "Abbi's cooked up all of Robert's favorites."

J'aime's dad inched toward the door. "Sorry. I'm late already."

"Take it to-go then?" Robert's mom said. "I will grab you something." She disappeared into the crowd of people.

"Mom won't give up trying to feed you," Robert explained. "That's why she owns a restaurant."

"If she catches me by the time I get to my car then I'll take it," her dad said. "Whatever's cooking does smell amazing." They all sniffed the air.

"Tortilla soup," Robert confirmed. "And like ten other dishes."

J'aime's dad gave her a tentative smile. "I expect to see you at the duplex tonight," he said.

She'd have to go home. If she stayed with Robert, her dad might fire him. Managers do things like that to employees they hold personal grudges against. Even if she stayed with Sarah, her dad might still fire Robert just because she didn't come home.

As if he could read her mind, her dad turned toward Robert. "You better pick up the phone next time I call, or it's your ass at work."

Robert held up his hands in peace. "Got it, Mr. McWilliams."

For an awkward second, her dad hesitated. Instead of waving, he patted J'aime awkwardly on the shoulder then made his getaway out the front door. J'aime was so glad to see him leave. So much had happened this morning, and so much was still the same. All she wanted to do was focus on the intoxicating smell of home cooked food.

"You need to meet Abbi," Robert whispered.

Twenty-four hours ago, she would have dreaded this official meeting. This time she grabbed his hand first. "I can't wait," she said.

There were so many people in the living room that they had to push their way toward the kitchen. Suddenly, her feet were shuffling from wooden floors onto the square bumpy surface of linoleum tiles. Her nose told her it was the kitchen before she even looked up. A sweet-and-sour smell with a hint of tomatoes, lime, and the bite of chilies drifted to the back of J'aime's throat.

Hanging baskets of fruit and dried peppers dangled around the room as if they were edible chandeliers. Above a sink piled with greasy frying pans and wooden spoons, a jungle of potted plants lined the kitchen windowsill. The delicate herb branches pressed against the yellow haze of pollen-coated glass. In a blaze of 100-watt glory, the ceiling light glared off huge aluminum pans wrapped in foil. The covered food filled every last inch of counter space.

Standing in the swirl of hot food and dirty dishes was the tiniest, oldest woman J'aime had ever seen. The room wasn't very big. The only person in the kitchen was this round, elderly Latina woman with white braids circling her head. She had on a pink jogging suit with a blue apron tied around her waist and hamburger-shaped oven mitts on her hands.

Robert's mom was wrapping up some food for J'aime's dad. "Mama," Violeta said, "*aquí están la amiga de* Robert. J'aime."

The elderly woman smiled at them. Her cheeks crinkled like yellow onionskins. Robert let go of J'aime's hand and wrapped his arm around his grandmother's hunched shoulders. She patted Robert on the stomach with a burger-shaped oven mitt and gave him a side hug.

"Abbi," he said. "Meet J'aime."

J'aime couldn't stop staring at her. Yep. It was true. Robert's amazing girlfriend Abbi was his grandma. J'aime gestured to the army of tin-foil wrapped pans. "Did you cook all this food?"

"*Con un poco de ayuda,*" Abbi said in a raspy voice.

"Abbi's being modest," Robert's mom said over her shoulder as she hurried from the kitchen. "She cooked all night so we can eat all day."

The old woman smiled at J'aime again, pointing a padded burger in the direction of the stove.

"*Tienes que probar la sopa,*" she said. Her words rattled and danced like a hoarse butterfly.

"Sorry." J'aime fretted. "I don't understand." Her two years of French was not helping her.

"Robert," Abbi scolded lightly, "*ensenale a hablar espanol a tu amiguita.*"

He kissed his grandma on the cheek then quickly blew a soft strawberry on the same spot. The sputtering farting nose made J'aime jump and the mischievous kiss made Abbi laugh. Still chuckling, Abbi waved an oven mitt at J'aime to follow her.

"She wants you to have some soup," Robert said, nudging his head in the direction of the stove.

All three of them walked in the direction of a huge aluminum pot. There was a burner under there somewhere, but the pot was at least three times the size of its heat source. All of her dad's restaurant kitchens had professional cookware like this, but she'd never seen it in someone's house before.

Abbi dipped a long silver ladle through the steam. The sweet, spicy smell that greeted her in the doorway flowed around her, pulling J'aime closer to the stovetop. The ladle reemerged half filled with a clear, dark-red liquid. Without spilling a drop, Abbi quickly poured the soup into a coffee cup. A printed rooster strutted on the mug. Abbi gingerly blew on the soup then proudly handed it to J'aime.

"*Dile que no le queme la lengua*," Abbi said.

"She's worried you won't like it," Robert translated.

Abbi swatted him with her hamburger mitt. She gave J'aime an exasperated smile. "Silly boy," she said with a heavy accent. Abbi playfully glared at Robert before turning to a cutting board in between the sink and the stove.

"We better help her with the pico de gallo, or she won't forgive me," Robert said. "Plus, the soup needs to cool. It'll burn your tongue."

"Okay," J'aime said tentatively, setting the hot mug down next to the stove. She had no idea what happened between them, but it seemed like Robert wasn't being a good interpreter for his grandma.

Abbi started dicing tomatoes. The tip of her dripping chef's knife beckoned J'aime over to the cutting board. A freshly washed tomato and an extra knife lay near the plastic surface.

The ingredients waited for her in a familiar way. She glanced over at Robert. He was on one side of his grandmother, chopping. He sliced the onion while Abbi chopped through the luscious, juicy skin of a tomato. Instinctively, they swayed, moving with the same cooking rhythm.

J'aime thought that Robert had learned to cook from TV and from cooks at the family restaurant, but it wasn't true. She slid in next to Abbi and picked up the spare knife. The woman's eyes glowed with approval. Crammed around the same cutting board, happiness wrapped around them like a warm tortilla. The feeling was as comforting as the cooling soup in her mug. With cilantro plants dangling overhead, chipped clean plates on the counter, steaming pots on the stove and dried peppers hanging on the walls, every inch of their kitchen was covered in food love. J'aime's knife sliced through the tomato. She heard the tap of her blade hit the cutting board, and she fell into the calm, nourishing flow of the Rioses' kitchen.

This room is their heart, and I belong here.

Chapter 33
J'aime's Blue Bowl Special

WITH HER WHOLE FOODS TOTE ON HER SHOULDER and her mother's quilt draped over her arm, J'aime watched Robert's truck taillights disappear down her street. Her lips were warm from his kiss.

J'aime's pocket buzzed. Taking her phone out, Sarah's text flashed at her.

YOU OK? SORRY I TALKED TO YOUR DAD.

J'aime texted back: No worries. I'm home. Want to come over?

Sarah texted back instantly, YES!

A canvas tote strap slid off J'aime's shoulder. She felt the weight of the bag pull her in a new direction. Unlocking the patched front door, she went into the duplex. Dusk light hushed the rooms. She hesitated in the kitchen doorway.

"Hello chocolate chip cookie," she said, flipping on the light.

The kitchen was still Kraft Mac & Cheese all the way. J'aime was the one who was different. *Cooks make the kitchen, right?* Sitting her Whole Foods bag on the floor, she dug around until her hands hit Tupperware. She pulled out a container of delicate farm eggs and inspected their shells through the plastic.

"No cracks," she said.

Before leaving the Rioses' house, Robert filled her grocery bag with fresh food and a few leftovers. She lined the counter with crazy good ingredients: tortillas, chopped mangos, diced onions, black bean salsa, cheddar cheese, green peppers, limes, butter, and a whole avocado. The dark green fruit wobbled across the countertop until it hit the stove.

When a panicked line cook at the Tudor Table Buffet had asked her, a busgirl in a serf costume, to help plate a hundred sides of guacamole, that one hour in the kitchen changed J'aime forever. That was when her chef dreams officially began. Like a bumpy avocado, her life would never roll perfectly. She wouldn't always do the right thing. Her dad would never understand her, ever. That was the truth, and she knew it. The more she told her dad who she was and what she wanted, the less he listened.

Paychecks shouldn't have opinions, she thought.

She rolled the avocado back and forth one more time. But dads do have taste buds though. *I have to try*, she thought. *No matter how much he doesn't get me, or how many mistakes we make, he's my only family.*

Throwing open the bottom cabinet, she pulled out her mini skillet and clanked it down onto the stove. She grabbed her saucepan from the bottom of her Whole Foods tote. She was ready to prep herself and her cooking space. Minus a cutting board, she'd have to use a paper towel. She laid her knife next to the paper edge and found her black slotted spoon. The clock was ticking. If her dad didn't pull a double, he'd be home in an hour. There was a time limit on this cooking experience. That wasn't a bad thing. Robert told her that when they opened Food Carma orders would come up fast and she'd have to practice doing short-order cooking.

J'aime scanned her ingredients again and came up with a recipe. First she'd chop the vegetables then sauté them in butter. She'd crack three eggs and scramble them in the same pan with the sauté. She might as well make enough for her and Sarah too. Finally she'd add some salsa, mango, avocado, cheese, and a squeeze of lime juice. For the grand finale, she'd serve the eggs with warm tortillas. She'd have to cook those in the skillet, so the main dish would have to fit in her new saucepan.

"Here we go again," J'aime said, remembering the Cajun concrete satellite in the bushes and the broken spatula handle on her dresser.

This time will be different, she promised herself.

The chopping started. When J'aime got to the avocado, she didn't hesitate. Her hands knew exactly how to peel it. Fresh avocados were her old food friends now. She could count on them just like she counted on Robert and Sarah. A half a tablespoon of butter plunked into the saucepan. Turning the heat on medium high, J'aime smeared the butter around adding a thin coat to the bottom of the pot. When the sizzle started, she tossed in her neatly chopped veg.

Sautéing onions changed the kitchen atmosphere from hollow to cozy. J'aime cracked the mocha-colored eggshell on the side of the saucepan, carefully releasing the golden yolk. The translucent egg whites draped onto the softening chunks of green pepper. She let the food guide her, smells and textures telling her when it was time to add this and stir that. When the runny yolks started to firm, she scrambled them with a fork. Yellow clumpy clouds of egg formed in the bottom of the pan. In went all the other ingredients. Calmly, she stirred again. Serene spice flavored the air. The bubbling salsa was doing its job.

She put a lid on the pot and turned off the heat. Smearing some more butter in her skillet, she heated a fresh tortilla. Without a spatula, J'aime flipped it by pinching the tortilla edge with her fingers. Burning her skin a little was worth it this time.

Inside the cabinet above the sink, a single object sat on a dark shelf. She pulled out a large ceramic bowl. Forgotten by a past renter, it was sky blue with a crack running down the center. J'aime stuck it under the faucet to wash it, but never turned on the water.

Cradled in the center of the bowl was the package of instant noodles Robert had accidently slipped into her tote bag.

But was it an accident?

J'aime picked up the crinkly package. Nothing about Robert was an accident. She smiled. Her Ramen Noodles Guy hadn't only sparked her feelings, he'd fueled her passions. In the drama of the past few weeks, she'd totally forgotten about these noodles. J'aime tore open the package.

"Surprise ingredient time!" she said.

Her nerves tingled with inspiration. She dished up her egg mixture into the clean bowl and filled the greasy cooking pot halfway up with water. Soon, instant noodles were boiling away on her stove. J'aime set an alarm on her phone. Two minutes was all the ramen needed until they met their new Tex-Mex fusion fate.

The kitchen was hot with cooking, but it felt good. J'aime noticed that the rest of her butter stick was slowly melting on the counter. If she wanted to keep it for another recipe, the butter had to get in the fridge ASAP. She wrapped the melty stub in its paper and pulled open the door of the Frigidaire.

J'aime froze. Her fridge wasn't empty.

Sitting alone on the rusted rails was the money jar. The last of their cash was still inside. A new piece of paper was taped to the front of the jar. One word was scrawled on it in her dad's handwriting.

J'aime.

She sat the butter inside the fridge and picked up the pickle jar.

"Surprise ingredient number two," she murmured.

Random duck quacking made her jump—the ramen alarm. J'aime shut off her phone and the boiling burner. The rush of cold air pulled her back to the open fridge.

Her dad must've come home on his lunch break and written her name on it. Reaching inside, she pulled out the jar and hugged it hard. J'aime glanced around the duplex kitchen. Her seedlings in their to-go boxes were perched on the edge of the linoleum counter. Little green stems peeked up from the dirt, waiting to catch the morning light. Soon she'd have her own herbs growing on the windowsill. Every meal coming from her Hannaville kitchen would have the chance to be as good as she could make it.

The Frigidaire's cooling motor kicked on with a squeak. The sign to shut the door and eat her home-cooked meal. J'aime sat the jar back inside the fridge. It was still the best place to keep her hope and maybe her dad's too.

Using a plastic spork and the slotted spoon, J'aime scooped the ramen into the bowl with her egg recipe. She skipped the soy sauce seasoning packet and instead squeezed more lime juice onto the hot food. She gave the curly noodles a toss, coating them in salsa, mango, and a tangle of sautéed eggs and veg.

J'aime carried the steaming bowl onto the front porch. The dusky overgrown yard was settling into night. Hannaville was coming alive with the sounds of country crickets. She leaned in close to the bowl and smelled her new recipe. Hints of Tex-Mex ramen comfort and spice tickled her nose. Her stomach rumbled along with the insects.

It was beyond time to eat. Her plan was to taste test the dish then serve it up to her dad and Sarah. Even if her recipe wasn't great, maybe they could give her ideas about how to make it better.

Using the spork, she twirled up a piece of every ingredient. J'aime held the food up to her lips and whispered, "My heart is full, just like my life."

Opening her mouth wide, she closed her eyes and took a perfect first bite.

On-The-Go Huevos Rancheros

Serves 1

Cooking supplies needed:
Cutting board, chef's knife, spoon, 2 paper towels, microwave-safe plate like a ceramic, glass, or paper plate

Ingredients needed:
1 peeled, hard-boiled egg
1 flour tortilla
1 tablespoon water
1 slice pepper jack cheese
1 tablespoon salsa
1 tablespoon of black beans—drained and rinsed

Let's cook it!
Set the peeled, hard-boiled egg on the cutting board. Place the fingertips of your non-knife hand on each side of the egg. Using the knife, cut lengthwise into ½-inch-thick slices. There should be a yellow bulls-eye yolk in the center of each of your slices. Set aside.

Place one paper towel on your plate. Sprinkle it with half the water. Lay your tortilla on top of the paper towel. Set the other paper towel on top and sprinkle it with the rest of the water. Heat it in the microwave for 20 seconds. When done, take the tortilla from the microwave and remove the paper towels.

Lay the slice of pepper jack cheese in the center of the tortilla.

Spoon the salsa on top of the cheese. Spread it around so it's not one big glob.

Add the black beans.

Lay the egg slices on top of the beans and salsa. Make sure the egg slices overlap a little bit.

Fold one edge of the tortilla and wrap it over the filling. Tuck the opposite edge under that, like you're making a bed. Take the ends and fold them so they are resting on top of the burrito. Give the folds a good press with your fingers so they will stick together.

Using your hands, gently and with courage, flip the burrito over so that the folded side is resting face down on your plate.

Eat with your hands or a fork.

Acknowledgments

Thanks to . . .

My husband, John, and his endless support on this ten-year project.

My family, who taught me that cooking is love.

Emily Ghertner, for being a dear friend and constant cheerleader.

Carolina Fernandez-Mazzoni, for her sweet translations.

Allyson Lassiter, for her happy onions cover art.

Mayfly Design and Marly Cornell for their eagle eyes and book expertise.

Harvesters and Feeding America, for fighting hunger every day.

And to you, dear reader. With the purchase of this book, you are helping to fill someone's plate, fridge, and heart.

Thank you.

About the Author

STEPHANIE YOUNG grew up in a family that talked about food as if it were another family member. She likes to blend storytelling and cooking into tales about life, love, and enjoying every bite. Stephanie has a degree in creative writing and spent years recommending books as a kids/YA bookseller, children's librarian, and story time reader. Her first graphic novel, *Star Beasts*, was published in 2021. When she's not inventing new recipes and characters to go with them, she helps fight hunger at local food banks and takes professional cooking classes. Stephanie lives over the rainbow in Kansas with her sweet husband John and their handsome cat, Mr. Whiskers.

For more *Kitchen of My Heart* recipes go to kitchenofmyheart.com

www.ingramcontent.com/pod-product-compliance
Lightning Source LLC
Chambersburg PA
CBHW070012120726
47909CB00003B/902